Published by DREAMSPINNER PRESS
http://www.dreamspinnerpress.com

Published by DREAMSPINNER PRESS
http://www.dreamspinnerpress.com

Readers Love ANDREW GREY

Inside Out

"I love how Andrew Grey pulls you into his stories and creates characters that you really grow to love. I would highly recommend this story and all his works."

—Top 2 Bottom Reviews

"I promise you don't want to miss this one."

—The Novel Approach

"I adore Andrew Grey and once again he impressed me by writing a great story."

—Gay List Book Reviews

"The chemistry is off the hook and the storyline is intriguing."

—MM Good Book Reviews

"Inside Out is funny, sexy and a must have for any fan of romance!"

—Guilty Indulgence Book Reviews

"This was a fun, sexy, and very sweet story with some seriously hot scenes. Go, Andrew!"

—Rainbow Book Reviews

A Daring Ride

"All the things we've come to love from Grey are there in the print. An emotional, engrossing, and sexy ride is what's in store with this latest work from one of the best authors in the genre."

—MM Good Book Reviews

"I quickly got sucked in by the story and the characters. There really is so much substance in the plot and the people… he doesn't need a lot of extra language to pull you in."

—Mrs. Condit & Friends Read Books

Readers Love ANDREW GREY

A Heart Without Borders

"I felt like I was right there with the characters, feeling the heat, the desperation and the total devastation right along with them. There is no doubt in my mind that this book will stay with me for a long time."

—The Novel Approach

"In true Andrew Grey fashion, this book delivers not only a romance but a powerful lesson on the courage, hope and optimism of people in a country devastated by disaster and poverty."

—Hearts on Fire Reviews

Stranded

"A great story of how time passes and people allow their relationship to settle into routine and they lose their appreciation for their partner. This doesn't mean that they are no longer deeply in love, sometimes they just need a reminder."

—Gay List Book Reviews

"*Stranded* is an amazing combination between an intense thriller-like stalker story, a sizzling romance, and a character study which, through tension and drama, brings out the worst and the best in both main characters."

—Rainbow Book Reviews

The Fight Within

"I loved this book, these characters, and this story. Get it today. Read. Understand and through understanding, enjoy."

—Mrs. Condit & Friends Read Books

"This is a story that is rich in detail, delving into the Native American culture and also sharing the suffering that the Native American's still face today."

—MM Good Book Reviews

UPSIDE
ANDREW GREY
DOWN

Dreamspinner Press

Published by

DREAMSPINNER PRESS

5032 Capital Circle SW, Suite 2, PMB# 279, Tallahassee, FL 32305-7886 USA
http://www.dreamspinnerpress.com/

Upside Down
© 2014 Andrew Grey.

Cover Art
© 2014 L.C. Chase.
http://www.lcchase.com
Model: Dirk Caber
Photographer: FLYFOTO
Cover content is for illustrative purposes only and any person depicted on the cover is a model.

ISBN: 978-1-63216-033-1
Digital ISBN: 978-1-63216-034-8
Library of Congress Control Number: 2014943217
First Edition August 2014

Printed in the United States of America
∞
This paper meets the requirements of
ANSI/NISO Z39.48-1992 (Permanence of Paper).

To Dirk Caber. Thank you for the use of your image on the cover and for serving as the physical inspiration for Spook. You were wonderful to work with, and I appreciate your graciousness.

CHAPTER ONE

"I THINK I'm getting too fucking old for this," Lowell said to himself, dropping his carryall on his kitchen floor. He could barely take a single step, he was so tired. He kicked off his shoes and walked through the small apartment toward the bathroom. He passed nothing of any importance. There was truly nothing there that meant anything to him. The pictures that hung on the walls had been bought at a thrift store. The framed photographs that sat on the shelving unit in the living room were of people he didn't know—pictures he'd found years ago and had carried with him. They made good camouflage, and that was what he was an expert at. The few times he'd had people over because of a job that his cover as a reporter had demanded, his guests would have found nothing he didn't want them to find. There wasn't a single thing in this place that wasn't put here by him either to deceive or to tell a guest, invited or uninvited, absolutely nothing about him. He was a ghost, someone who wasn't supposed to exist. In fact, his real name had been uttered so few times in the last ten years, he had almost forgotten it.

His phone rang as he reached the bedroom. Lowell thought about not answering, but he knew who it was, so he reached for the damned thing. "Yeah."

"Is that any way to talk to the person who just spent half the day trying to save your ass?" There was little heat in the female voice.

"So? I doubt it's worth saving," he countered. Lowell was tired and mighty cranky. "Besides, he can be angry all he wants, but the whole mess was his fault for not doing his homework and giving me crap information. So you tell *His Highness* that either he pays up or my next contract will be my own, taken out on him. And remind him I know where his weaknesses are." He had had enough of temperamental royalty. They thought they were above everything, but they died just like anyone else. Lowell knew a million ways to kill and how to do it without leaving a trace.

"I made sure he knew," Moonstone told him. He knew her by that name and didn't care what her real one was. She was his handler and one of the few people he trusted, but even then only up to a point. His characteristic lack of trust had kept him alive for years, so he went with it, telling everyone, including her, only what he wanted them to know. "But I doubt we'll be getting any more work from him."

Lowell scoffed. "We will. He needs my services and he knows it. How else is he going to take out the enemies that lurk around every corner? At least the enemies his paranoid little mind keeps telling him are lurking. But I think it best if the next time he calls, I should be unavailable."

"Very well," Moonstone said with no emotion whatsoever.

"So did he send payment?"

"Yes. I transferred your funds through a new route to the usual account. They are available now. And I have another job for you."

"God, no. I can't do anything more right now." Lowell was too exhausted. He'd made up for the fiasco that had happened a few months earlier, when he'd been unable to convince a colleague to take a job. That had been the last time he'd been this tired, but then he'd taken the job and he'd been bested by some kid. That was not going to happen again. He knew his limits, and he'd gone against his judgment then. He wasn't going to now. "These jobs are getting harder, and I need some time to rest." He wasn't as young as he used to be, and he didn't recover as quickly anymore either.

"This is a good one and it pays very well. A Central American businessman has a rival that he desperately wants eliminated. It should be a quick in and out. I'm sending over the details." Lowell remained quiet. "This is a lucrative job, very lucrative—they're willing to pay twice the usual rate. I told them you would need some convincing."

"I'll do it for three times the usual rate… for me. Whatever you get above that, you can have. Call me back when they agree." Lowell cut off the call and tossed the phone onto the bed. Then he went to his closet and grabbed a wire coat hanger. It made a simple but effective key. Lowell dropped to his hands and knees and carefully threaded the curved end of the coat hanger into a knot in the old woodwork molding. He went through a rather complicated set of motions that had to be done just right—otherwise the user would find himself with a face full of cyanide gas and be dead within seconds. Lowell had done this multiple times and felt the mechanism open under his practiced fingers.

He pulled back the section of molding and took out a thin case that contained his secure laptop. Using it, he logged into an encryption service and then routed his connection around the globe before logging into his account. He saw the funds Moonstone had said were deposited and immediately transferred them to a different account at the same bank and then out and through a series of accounts to one only he was aware of.

As soon as he was done, he closed every connection. He'd been online for only a matter of minutes, but he wanted to leave no trail and no way for anyone to trace his movements. Then he replaced the laptop, locked everything back up, and went into the bathroom, where he turned on the water. He removed the facial alterations he'd used on this job. It pulled like hell on his skin, but part of the beauty of what he did was that few people actually saw his real face.

When all the crap was off and he'd shaved and cleaned his face so his skin could breathe, Lowell stepped under the now hot water with a sigh. These damned jobs were taking too much out of him. He'd been thinking that he was getting close to retirement for a while now, but a few more jobs to add to his bank account, or even this one job, if Moonstone could arrange it, could tip him over the edge and then he wouldn't have to do this any longer. Granted, he'd have to find something to occupy him for the rest of his life, but he could certainly do that. He put all that out of his mind and concentrated on the feel of water sluicing down his skin. It felt like weeks since he'd been truly clean and free of all the things he had to do for his job. Once he was clean, he stood still and let the water run over him, shutting off his brain for a few minutes and just letting himself... be.

Of course, that relaxed feeling only lasted until he got out of the bathroom. His phone was already ringing. He picked it up and glanced at the number before answering it.

"He agreed to our price." He knew Moonstone had added plenty for herself, but he didn't care—he was getting what he wanted, and that was enough to make up for the inconvenience.

"Good. When do I leave?"

"Tickets and information are being delivered to your door right now. You know what to do once you get them. All the details you need will be in there. Of course, you and the client are not to meet."

"Don't know who he is?"

"You are to avoid him at all costs. There can be no connection between the client and the end result. That's the one stipulation. You know the deal. Make it look like an accident or natural causes and you'll get a 50 percent bonus."

"Sounds like someone's desperate," Lowell observed, not expecting an answer.

"Let's just say they're motivated," Moonstone said in her usual unflappable tone. "Look, you're going to need to be on top of your game for this one. Even though they say this will be a quick in and out, you know there can be potential complications that could make this difficult. I don't know if there are any, but if I get wind of them, I'll let you know. I also suggest that you do your usual homework." She hung up, and Lowell dropped the towel from around his waist. He pulled on old but comfortable clothes and left the bedroom. He thought about pouring a shot of his favorite tequila, but at this point alcohol was not a good idea.

When the front door buzzer sounded, he went down to the lobby and took the sealed packet from the bicycle messenger, checked that it was unopened, and then tipped the kid before returning to his apartment. It had surprised him early on that Moonstone used messengers, but just like sometimes it was best to hide in plain sight, he knew that sometimes the simplest things were the best. Lowell dropped the envelope on the table as he walked to the kitchen. He opened the refrigerator and stared at emptiness. After closing the door, he picked up the phone, ordered Chinese delivery, and settled on the sofa to review the details of his next assignment.

"I'M GETTING way too fucking old for this." Lowell dropped his carryall on the floor of his apartment. This time he ached from head to foot. He'd accomplished his mission with remarkably few problems, and no one had been the wiser. The problems had started when he'd gotten ready to leave the country and the bastard who'd hired him had tried to renege on the deal. Apparently, the "businessman" liked to get things for free and didn't care how he went about it. It had meant a great deal of additional effort, but Lowell had gotten his money, complete with bonus, when he'd met the client in his own bedroom with a gun. Suddenly the wheels were greased and everything became an understanding. Payment had been very forthcoming at that point, and Lowell had left without a further word.

The little snafu had messed up all kinds of plans, and while he'd been able to get out of that godforsaken country, he hadn't been able to get a flight home for two days and he'd gotten tired of hotels, bad food, and… hell, he was just getting tired.

Lowell grabbed his secure phone and made his call. "I'm back, and if you ever send me on a job like that again, I'll hunt you down wherever you are and make you my next job."

Moonstone laughed. They both knew that was pretty much impossible, mainly because he had tried. It was in his nature. But there were too many safeguards in place to protect both of them. For one thing, they had never met and only communicated through prearranged methods that changed on a regular basis. "But you're home," she said.

"Yes." He already knew they'd been paid and he was about to transfer the money where he wanted it. "And I have no intention of taking another job. Not now."

"I wasn't going to ask." She was lying and Lowell knew it. "But I have plenty of work for 'Spook' whenever you're ready." He had no doubt of that. "Spook's" talents were very much in demand. They always had been. But he was simply too tired right now to take on anything else.

"Give me a few weeks and I'll be in touch." He was going to take a vacation, and as much as he hated to admit it, he needed some advice. There was only one person he knew of who he could turn to. It was too bad that guy would probably tear him to pieces as soon as he saw him. The more Lowell thought about it, the dumber he realized his idea was. There was no way he was crossing paths with him ever again. He'd made a mistake back then, and the guy had handed him his head.

He headed for the bathroom and shook his head when he saw his reflection in the mirror. He pulled at the chin and cheek extensions, wincing slightly as they came away from his skin. He hated this part, but it was necessary. Changing his features allowed him to pass undetected. They also went with the various passports and identities he'd created. Once his face was his again, he turned on the shower and stepped under it, washing out the temporary color he'd placed in his hair to darken it. His normally mousy brown hair was an asset when he traveled to certain parts of the world. It made it very easy for him to darken or lighten it when he needed to.

The water ran dark for a few minutes as he shampooed out the color. Once it was clear, he washed the rest of himself and then stepped out. He wrapped a towel around his waist, feeling a hell of a lot better. He had no jobs on the horizon and nowhere to be or anything that he had to do. Lowell got dressed and retrieved his laptop, transferred his funds, and then disconnected. After stowing the piece of equipment again, he flopped on the sofa, ordered delivery, and turned on the television. It would surprise most people to know that a guy who took care of other people's problems in the most lethal way possible vegged out in front of the television like anyone else when he had nothing better to do.

Lowell's dinner arrived a few minutes later. He went down to the lobby to get his food because he never let anyone in his apartment if he could help it, paid the guy, and climbed the stairs back up. His phone was ringing when he entered, so he placed the bag on the counter and answered it. "Yeah."

"We've got a problem," Moonstone said without preamble. "Your location has been compromised. Apparently your last client has many more connections than we figured, and he arranged through contacts for you to be followed. We don't know how close they got, but you need to get out of where you're holed up and to a safe location. Destroy and dump this phone. We'll go to emergency contact procedures." The line went dead.

Lowell took a deep breath and calmly retrieved the few items he needed from the apartment. He placed the phone in a plastic bag, then smashed it with a hammer into tiny bits. His computer and other vital tools he placed in his carryall, and then he dumped the dirty clothes in a trash bag. He heard nothing out of the ordinary, but checked outside anyway, just in case. Of course he saw nothing, but then he most likely wouldn't. For this he couldn't rely on his sense of sight.

When he had packed what little he needed, Lowell sat at the counter and opened the bag of food. He sniffed the beef with broccoli and his stomach roiled. He dabbed the sauce with his finger, then sniffed it again. His finger tingled slightly, and he wiped it with a napkin before washing his hands thoroughly at the sink. "Amateurs," he whispered. It wasn't impossible to poison a guy like him, but it was damned hard. His system had been exposed to so damn much that on some level it alerted him. Lowell's stomach was cast iron, so if it rebelled at the sight of food, then there was something definitely wrong with it.

Lowell smiled and dumped the food in the plastic bag with the pieces of his phone. That would mess up anything that anyone could try to get from it. Now he was sure they would be watching the building, so he went to his closet. After pulling off his comfortable clothes, he changed into an outfit he'd "borrowed" from his older neighbor when the man had left his clothes in the laundry room.

Soft footsteps on the stairs alerted him to someone approaching. He peered out into the hall and saw the older man whose clothes he was using enter his apartment. This was perfect. If the place was being watched, they would think the man had changed clothes and was leaving again.

Lowell picked up speed and powdered his hair with a touch of gray. Then he grabbed a jacket and his carryall and left the apartment. He made a quick stop in the trash room, where he opened the soupy plastic bag and dumped the contents down the chute. The rest of his trash followed. He didn't care about that. Nothing could be traced to him, and only the phone had anything of value and it was now gone. With just his small carryall, he slowly descended the stairs and continued down to the basement. Long ago he'd devised an escape route in case he needed one.

Just before opening the door at the bottom of the stairs, multiple footsteps that weren't as muffled as their makers had hoped sounded on the stairs overhead. They were moving fast, and Lowell knew he didn't have much time. He walked to the laundry room and closed the door. His heart raced, but he kept his thoughts clear. He pushed the last dryer aside and pulled open the small door he'd installed there when he'd first taken the apartment. He crouched down and made his way through the small space, then pulled the dryer back in place and stepped out into the alley just down from the back entrance to the building.

He looked both ways and saw the inevitable man standing beside the back door. Staying close to the building in the shadows, Lowell turned and made his way down the alley. Once he was far enough away, he picked up his pace. At a main street, he caught a taxi and told the driver to take him to the train station.

CHAPTER
TWO

JEREMY HODGSON stood in line outside Bronco's with his roommate, Tristan, and his friends Kevin and Zach. "Why are we standing in line?" he asked Zach. "You know they'll let us all in the back door."

"Bull's working out front tonight," Zach answered. The line moved forward, and soon they were at the front. Zach walked right up to Bull, his lover of almost a year. The man was intimidating as hell to look at, but he was a really nice guy once you got to know him. "Are you gonna frisk me?" Zach said, putting his arms in the air and wriggling his hips.

Jeremy put his hand in front of his face to keep from giggling as Bull's eyes bugged out of his head. Zach was wearing this short, tight shirt, and when he raised his arms, a line of skin appeared. When he moved his hips, it was something to see. "I'll frisk you later." Bull took Zach's arms and pressed them down as he kissed Zach. A chorus of "ooooohs" sounded from behind them.

"If I do that, can I get in for free?" a guy asked from behind them. Bull pulled Zach to him and growled loudly at the guy, who kept quiet after that.

"Go on inside, guys, and have fun," Bull said, turning to Zach. "But not too much fun." Bull swatted Zach on the butt, and the four of them entered the club. They found a table in one of the corners, out of the way, but where they would still be able to see the entertainment for the night.

"I'll go get drinks," Tristan offered, and Kevin went as well, leaving Jeremy and Zach alone at the table.

"What's been going on lately? You're quiet and standoffish. Is something wrong?" Zach asked, practically bouncing in the chair with his usual energy.

"Nothing anyone can help with. Tristan's been dating this guy Eddie, you have Bull, and even Kevin was seeing someone, at least until last week, when he and Phil broke up." Jeremy looked over to where their two friends were working their way up to the bar. "I haven't had a date in six months, and the last guy I saw turned out to be a real loser who was more interested in merging our comic book collections than he was in me."

"I thought Lenny was nice."

"He was. But I found out that comic books were about all we had in common. He didn't actually read anything else… at all." Jeremy sighed softly and wished they'd return with the drinks so he could start on the buzz he intended to get. Maybe he'd even get drunk so he could forget how alone he was feeling. "He loved your work."

Zach had developed a graphic novel using Bull as the model for the hero. It had started slowly at first, but his work was gaining in popularity, and he'd already finished a second and was working on the third installment. "So you'll find someone else," Zach told him.

"I sure as hell hope so." Dating his right hand was not going swimmingly. He looked around and saw Kevin and Tristan walking toward the table. They set down the drinks and then took their seats.

"Is Eddie busy tonight?" Jeremy asked Tristan before sipping from his martini glass. He wanted to gulp the thing and then get another, but Tristan had ordered the good stuff, and it was way too fine to waste like that.

"Eddie's working late. He said he'll join us a little later." Tristan grinned. Jeremy knew he should be happy. Tristan obviously was, and Eddie was a nice enough guy. But he was having trouble feeling good for anyone now. Maybe he should have stayed home and moped there instead of bringing everyone else down. He wished he knew where this case of the lonely grumps had come from. This wasn't him, and he hated being this way. He told himself to snap out of it. A few seconds later the music started.

"Come on and dance with me," he said to Tristan. They had all been friends for a while, and he'd known Tristan for years. "Eddie isn't going to mind, and I promise to watch out for your virtue." He needed something to knock this attitude out of him.

Tristan got up, and they headed to the dance floor. The exotic dancers weren't supposed to perform for another hour, and sitting around ruminating was not going to help. The beat was great, and Jeremy began to move. Tristan was a good dancer, so they had a great time. Gradually, Jeremy let go of his worries and let the music carry him.

The dance floor got crowded and guys bumped him, but he paid no attention. He was having a good time. After a few songs, Tristan signaled that he was going back to the table. Jeremy wasn't ready to stop, so he continued dancing. A guy a little taller than he was, but stocky, with dark eyes and brown hair, moved close to him. Without thinking, Jeremy synchronized his movements to the guy's, and he came closer. The song ended and another began, this one faster. The other guy moved right up to him, sliding a knee between Jeremy's legs, cradling him with one arm around his back. Now they were moving as one.

Sweat beaded on Jeremy's skin and his heart raced in the best way ever as sexual energy built between them. Jeremy's mouth went dry and he was hard as a rock in his jeans, and the excitement continued to build. He'd always thought that dancing was vertical sex, and if he was right, then sex with this guy was likely to be wild, maybe a little dangerous, and definitely a drive to the moon. The guy leaned closer, wrapping his other arm around him, and then Jeremy was drawn even closer… and finally kissed to within an inch of his life.

Jeremy's entire body tingled. The guy tasted like peppermint, and he loved that. Jeremy returned the kiss, throwing his arms around the man's neck and holding on for dear life. He loved this feeling, like he was flying, and he never wanted it to end.

Of course the song did end, and the mood changed. Jeremy came to his senses and realized he'd been making out with a complete stranger in the middle of the dance floor, in full view of all his friends. That was not a good thing. Oh, the making-out part had been great, but he was not in the habit of moving this quickly with a stranger. "My friends are at the table," he stammered. "I should go back and join them."

"Will I see you later?" the guy asked.

"Sure. I'm Jeremy," he said, forcing a smile. "And we're sitting right over there." He turned and walked back toward the table, his legs a little unsteady. He sat down with the guys and picked up his drink, looking at the table.

"So...," Tristan began. "Who was the guy you were locking lips with? Did you know him? Or were you playing tonsil hockey with a stranger? Because if you were, you have good taste. He was pretty hot."

"We just started dancing and one thing led to another." Jeremy was glad to be away and have a chance to think without his mind completely clouded by lust. He took another sip from his glass and lifted his gaze. "Where's Zach?"

"He saw Bull walking through the club, so he followed him in back," Kevin said with a knowing wink. That meant that Zach would join them in a while with a huge smile on his face and very rumpled clothes and disheveled hair. But it seemed that wasn't the order of business tonight, because Zach made his way across the club and joined them a few minutes later. He was all smiles, but without the look he got when he and Bull had been having their fun.

Zach was carrying a beer, and he sat at the table with a smile. "Bull says he has enough guys tonight to handle the crowd, so he'll join us later for a while." Zach looked around. "Okay, what's going on?"

"Jeremy was making out with some guy on the dance floor," Tristan said, like a tattletale second-grader. "It was pretty hot too." Jeremy wanted to kick him under the table, but he'd probably hit someone else.

"He's a big boy, he can make out with who he wants," Zach said, and Jeremy was relieved that at least one of his friends didn't act like his mother. "Where is this guy?"

Jeremy looked around the club and tried to spot the guy he'd been dancing with, but he couldn't see him anywhere. Granted, there were now a lot of guys, but he had a good vantage point and could see just about everything.

"He's not here," Jeremy said and turned to Zach. "I can't see him anywhere." Zach turned in his chair, and Jeremy went back to scanning the crowd. "Oh, he's over by the bar." Zach and the others turned to where Jeremy was looking.

"Yeah, that's him, standing just behind the guy in leather," Kevin said.

Zach continued looking and then turned back to the group with a wary expression. "I know—" Jeremy began. He could tell what Zach was about to say.

"Hey, you can dance with anyone you want, and I don't care how you scorch the dance floor, but you know what happens when things move too fast." Zach turned to the rest of the group. "We all do." Zach's gaze fell to him.

Jeremy nodded. He knew all too well, which was why the whole episode had him on edge. He knew there was no harm in dancing, but what scared him was how quickly his inhibitions had deserted him in the presence of such heat.

"Don't worry," Zach said, "we're all here to look out for each other." He smiled at Jeremy and then craned his head back toward the bar.

Jeremy looked around again to see if he could see the guy, but once again he seemed to have disappeared. Not that that was particularly surprising, but in his experience, after sharing a dance like that, the guy would most likely want to be seen and would issue an invitation for an encore, or maybe something more. But this guy had vanished.

"Do you see him?" Zach whispered into his ear.

"Not right now." He knew he should stop looking and just enjoy the evening out with the guys.

"I'm going for another round. Do you want one?" Tristan asked. Jeremy shook his head. He still had most of his drink left, and maybe getting buzzed wasn't such a good idea. He turned toward the bar and saw his mystery dancer walking through the crowd. The guy smiled at Jeremy and then disappeared into the crowd. Jeremy tried to follow him, but couldn't.

"What?" Tristan asked as he got up to leave the table. "You look puzzled."

"It's nothing," he answered absently. He was getting the idea that some sort of game was being played and he wasn't privy to the rules. Jeremy loved games, but this one rubbed him the wrong way. They'd shared a dance and a kiss, but nothing more. He turned back to the table and decided to put the guy out of his mind. It wasn't important anyway.

"Zach and I are going to dance. Do you want to come?" Kevin asked. Jeremy shook his head.

"I'll stay here and wait for Tristan. You two have fun." He picked up his glass and followed them across the floor with his gaze. He watched them dance and move, having a good time. A circle formed around them, the other dancers giving them space. Word had spread through the club scene after Bull and Zach had gotten together, and no one wanted to piss Bull off. First of all, they wanted to be able to get into the club, and secondly, well, all you had to do was take one look at Bull to know pissing him off would not be a good idea.

"Why aren't you dancing?" a rich but soft voice said from behind him. Jeremy turned and looked directly into the eyes of the guy he'd been dancing with.

"I was looking for you," Jeremy said, his mouth going dry, so the words were forced. The man looked at him with such intensity that Jeremy almost felt uncomfortable… almost. Instead, heat rose inside him.

"Well, you found me… or I found you," the guy purred, leaning against the wall. Jeremy shifted on his chair, but it did nothing to quell the excitement or make the tightness in his pants abate.

"I haven't seen you here before, and I know just about everyone." It was true—the club scene was kind of incestuous. Every guy you slept with had been with the other guys in town, so it always seemed you were sleeping vicariously with half the gay guys in Harrisburg every time you took a chance on someone.

"I just got into town and I was hoping to see an old friend, but he's busy, so I figured I'd dance. And there you were like a gorgeous sunrise, so I had to take the chance and bask in your heat. I only hoped I wasn't going to get burned."

"Was that a line? Because it would be a damned shame if it were." God, he wanted this guy to be for real, but he was fairly sure he was too good to be true.

"I don't need a line. If I had only been interested in sex, I could have propelled you across the floor and to a quiet place without being noticed." He placed his hand on Jeremy's and lightly made small circles with a finger. Damn, that was so danged hot. That light, gentle touch was more powerful than being pulled into the guy's arms. It showed restraint, patience, and yet forwardness all at the same time. "I could tell how much you wanted me. I wanted you just as much. But some things take time." He leaned forward and lightly kissed Jeremy. "I'll most definitely see you around."

Jeremy nodded and blinked a few times to make sure this was real. "Would you like to stay for a drink? My…." The guy was gone. Jeremy looked around, but didn't see him.

"Are those two dancing?" Tristan asked as he set down the glasses. "The bar is a madhouse tonight." He took his seat, but Jeremy hardly noticed. "Earth calling Jeremy: Are you there?"

"Sorry. The guy I was dancing with stopped by to talk. He just left, and I'm trying to figure out where he is. But he disappeared."

"You better have a mirror and some holy water with you just to make sure he isn't a vampire or something." Tristan giggled wildly.

Jeremy shook his head. "That's really funny. Ha-ha. Look, I'm serious. He's hot as hell, about an inch taller than me, but stockier, and under his clothes he was really strong. I'd only know that from the way we were dancing, though. It's like he's an illusion."

"Who's an illusion?" Bull asked as he approached the table.

"Just a guy I was dancing with. He's playing hard to get, and I'm ashamed to say it's working. We danced, and then he did this disappearing act. Then when Tris was getting drinks and the other two were dancing"—he tilted his head to where Kevin and Zach were having a good time—"he showed up at the table and talked to me, but left a few minutes ago and I can't find him again."

"Do you see him now?" Bull asked seriously.

Jeremy looked over the room again, but it was so full he couldn't find anyone. "Not really. I don't think it's anything to worry about, just a guy trying to pique my interest." And it had most definitely worked. Bull did not look convinced and motioned to Zach, who tapped Kevin on the shoulder, and the two of them made their way over.

"Stay at the table and stay together," Bull said, catching Zach's gaze, and he nodded. Jeremy had no idea what all this was about, but Bull's tone brooked no argument. Bull scanned the room and then moved away.

"What's going on?" Jeremy asked Zach, who turned to the others.

"You don't want to know," they chorused back. That had been the answer to many things since Zach and Bull had gotten together. Trouble always seemed to swirl around Bull. Jeremy knew there had been some incidents, and that Bull had a past that involved things best not spoken about. He remembered being with Zach after he'd first met Bull, and some guy had been following them. Jeremy hadn't really seen him, but Zach had. The thing was, Jeremy trusted Bull. He'd been there for all of them, and not just by letting them into the club whenever they wanted to dance. When he and Tristan had lost the lease on their place because the landlord was a dick and raised the rent, Bull had helped them move, and when the landlord had given them a hassle over the security deposit, Bull had taken care of it. He was like a huge, quiet, but growly big brother to all of them, except Zach, of course. Basically Bull was someone they had all learned to count on. And in a way Jeremy wished he'd been the one to see Bull first.

He was the kind of guy Jeremy really wanted in his life—strong, loyal, caring, and incredibly giving once you saw what was under the gruff, intimidating exterior.

"Exactly. You don't want to know," Zach said as he continued looking around. The others did the same, but no one indicated that they saw anything.

Jeremy went back to his drink, and the conversation gradually shifted to the normal stuff: comic books, games, the music, and, of course, boys, boys, and more boys. They giggled, danced, and joked with each other until Bull returned and asked Zach to come with him. Jeremy wondered what that was about and watched them make their way across the dance floor to the door that led to the office. After a few minutes, Zach returned with one of Bull's men. "Jeremy, I need you to come with me. Frank is going to stay here with you guys."

"Are you serious?" Tristan asked.

Zach looked more serious than Jeremy could remember in quite a while. "Deadly."

Zach and Frank nodded, and Jeremy wondered what in hell was going on. He got up, and Zach took his hands and began to dance. "Just follow my lead and dance. We're heading toward the office, but I don't want to make anyone who might be watching suspicious. And make no mistake, there is someone watching." Zach threw his head back and giggled in that way he had. Jeremy went with what he'd said and giggled as well, dancing with Zach as guys moved around them. Then, when they reached the other side of the room, Zach opened the office door using a card from his pocket.

Most of the sound from the club clicked off like a light switch as soon as the door closed. "Come on. We have something you need to see." Zach was instantly all business.

"What's going on?" Jeremy asked as they walked down the short hallway and into the office. Both Harry, Bull's partner in the club, and

Bull were waiting for him. "I didn't do anything…." He felt like he was being called to the principal's office.

"We know you didn't," Bull said. "We want you to watch something." Bull pointed to the television, and a surveillance tape began. There was no sound, but he saw himself dancing, and then a guy joined him.

"That's the guy I was dancing with earlier," Jeremy explained. "We were only dancing."

"We saw what you were doing," Harry said with a wry smile. "That isn't why we wanted to talk to you." The tape continued, and Jeremy watched a replay of his little makeout session.

"I don't get it," Jeremy said.

"Look at the way he uses you to block out the camera. He's dancing, and yet we never get a clear shot of his face. He knows where the camera is, and even though you two are going at it, he still never shows us his face. The same when he was talking with you earlier. He stays in the shadows." Bull switched to another video feed. "The only time we get a shot of him is when he's walking to your table, and that's because we happen to have the camera that would normally be trained on the stage covering the crowd."

"Okay. I still don't get it," Jeremy said.

"We don't either, but this guy knows what he's doing and how to move almost undetected in a room full of cameras and surveillance. Not many people can do that, and they are usually thieves or people with very special skills and training. This is the one view we have of his face." Bull turned to Zach. "Does he look familiar to you?"

Zach stepped closer to the monitor. "No. Should he?"

"Look at his eyes and the shape of his lips. Everything else can be subtly changed. Does he look familiar now?"

Zach shook his head. "I wasn't trained the way you were. So if there's something you're driving at, just say it, Bull."

"I'm not sure myself. But you're usually very observant, so I was hoping you might have some insight."

Zach shook his head. "I've never seen him before."

"Neither have I," Jeremy said. "I told him that, and he said he'd just arrived in town to meet with someone who was currently busy… or something like that." Jeremy tried to remember his exact words, but couldn't. He'd been a little preoccupied. "I figured he was from New York because of the slight accent, but I could be wrong."

"How did you know that?"

"I lived there with my dad for a few years. He worked at Lehman Brothers before they went under. After that, he was only able to get a job here, because no one in New York would hire anyone from Lehman's. It was like everyone was tainted. That's how I heard the accent. Most people probably wouldn't."

"Okay, that's a help," Bull said, looking at the image once again. "There's something I'm missing, and I can't put my finger on it."

"Is that all you needed?"

"Yes, and the fact that I want to talk to this guy," Bull said. "He seems to appear when you're alone, so we'll arrange for you to be alone, but not alone."

"Do you think this guy is dangerous?" Jeremy shivered at how easily the guy had gotten close to him.

"If he were, and if he were after you, I think you'd probably already know it," Bull said. "I'm suspicious by nature, so I don't want anything to happen to any of you. I just want to get a chance to talk to this guy. The show starts in half an hour. Once it's about to begin, Zach is going to tell the four of you that I arranged for places right down front. You say that you're going to stay at the table. All eyes will be on the show, and if my suspicions are right, your mystery man will use that opportunity to speak to you again. If he does, just talk to him. We'll be monitoring the interaction. There's nothing you need to worry about."

"Okay, if you're sure," Jeremy said. He was so out of his depth.

"Now go back to your table, and make it look like you received a good scolding, so if you're being watched, you can allay suspicion."

"Okay," Jeremy said and left the office with Zach not far behind him. "What is all this about?"

"It's one of those 'you don't want to know' things," Zach repeated. "There are many times I wish I didn't know, but it's part of loving Bull, so I deal." Zach paused at the door to the club. "I don't know everything, but there are things we are all safer not knowing, and I trust Bull to keep me safe."

"Was he CIA?"

"It's best you don't ask. Trust me." Zach turned to Jeremy and stared at him for a moment. Then he slowly nodded, and in that instant Jeremy realized that Zach had seen things that went deeper than the happy-go-lucky guy Jeremy had always thought he was. The four of them talked comic books and about the latest adventures of Bull, from Zach's graphic novels, and online games, all the stuff they always did, but he hadn't realized until now that there was a seriousness in Zach that hadn't been there before he met Bull. "Now let's go."

Zach pulled open the door, and they slunk out and made their way over to the table. Jeremy did his best to look chastised, and Zach simply appeared furious. "I'm going to kill Bull when I get home," Zach said loudly as soon as he reached the table. "If he thinks he's getting any tonight or any night soon, he has another think coming." Zach looked toward the office and made a rude gesture. Jeremy kept his head down and tried to keep from laughing. It was a performance worthy of an Academy Award, and he didn't want to ruin it.

"What did he say?"

"He was mad at Jeremy for what happened on the dance floor," Zach said, instantly moving closer to "comfort" him. "He can be such a damned bully sometimes. I wanted to punch his lights out."

"Should we go?" Tristan asked, looking at the door with disappointment.

"Hell no. We're going to make him pay. Frank—" Zach turned to the bouncer who was looking decidedly uncomfortable. "Please tell Mr. High and Mighty that we'll be moving right up close so we can get a good look at the hot boys, and be sure to tell him that if he wants to apologize, he can do so after the show. Hell, I may get up on stage and join them. Give everyone a show. I'll teach him to act like an old prude." Zach was laying it on thick, and some of the guys around them had taken notice. Soon people were talking and whispering as they danced, and Zach grew quiet and just sipped from his glass. Jeremy saw him suppressing a smile.

Jeremy emptied his glass and went to the bar for another. By the time he returned to the table, the show was about to start. According to the plan, the others made their way to the front of the crowd, the lights dimmed, and fog machines kicked on near the stage. The music shifted, and the crowd whooped as the first dancers took the stage.

Jeremy watched the hunky guys, initially dressed as firemen or police officers, strip down to next to nothing. Normally he would have really gotten into the performance, whooping it up like the other guys, but he was too nervous, and he kept reminding himself not to look around like he was looking for someone, even though he definitely was. The first set of guys had taken it off and left the stage. The announcer revved up the crowd and then called Dirk to the stage. He was dressed as a Marine, but as soon as the music started, he began to strip down to his regulation boxers, and then what Jeremy was sure was not a regulation G-string. He was really starting to get into it when someone lightly touched his shoulder.

"Why are you all alone back here?"

He turned and looked up into a smiling face. "Oh, the guys wanted to get a closer look, but I didn't think it was necessary."

"Not interested in strippers?" his mystery man asked.

Jeremy shrugged lightly. "I've seen these guys before. They're good, but it isn't like they have something I haven't seen before." Jeremy motioned toward one of the chairs and waited to see if the guy would take him up on his offer or disappear the way he had before.

"Thanks," he said and sat down, but not comfortably, more like he was ready to run at any second. Jeremy also noted that he kept his back to the camera domes in the ceiling the way Bull said he'd been doing. "So if you aren't interested in strippers, then why come?"

"My friends were going, so I came along," Jeremy answered. "Why are you here if you're going to sit back here with me instead of joining the hoopla?" He liked that he was able to turn the man's question against him.

"I saw you and figured it would be better to talk than to watch some guys who do the same routine every night, are completely untouchable, and so incredibly coiffed, brushed, and plucked, they are almost as fake as the fog in the show." He laughed, and Jeremy saw him start to relax a little.

"I guess I could say the same thing," Jeremy agreed, wondering where everyone was. If they were supposed to be watching them, they should have seen the guy sit down. Granted, Jeremy was enjoying the conversation, and the way the guy looked at him was so intense, Jeremy was sure he was interested. But all the stuff with Bull and Zach had him on edge, and Jeremy was really starting to doubt his instincts.

The guy on stage finished up, and the announcer warmed the crowd up for more. Jeremy glanced over at the stage for a second and then back to the man at his table. He opened his mouth to ask a question and then saw movement out of the corner of his eye. He saw Bull approaching, but it was Zach's voice he heard.

"What the fuck are you doing here, Spook?" Zach said, standing in front of the guy. "I believe you were told to stay away!"

The guy whirled on his chair and practically ran into Bull.

"I don't think you're going anywhere," Bull growled. The guy Jeremy had been sitting with shifted, and Bull put him in a headlock. "We're going to the back room because I don't want all the guys in the club to see me rip your fool head off." Bull pulled the guy to his feet, and Jeremy scampered out of the way. He watched as Zach and Bull made their way across the club, hustling the guy… Spook… along with them. Guys got out of the way but made no effort to interfere. Jeremy wasn't sure what to do, so he followed, figuring he'd earned an explanation as to what was going on. None of this made any sense to him whatsoever.

CHAPTER
THREE

THIS WAS not an ideal situation, by any means. He'd been careful all night to avoid the cameras. Lowell knew he shouldn't have pressed his luck, but he'd figured the club would provide good cover, combined with his altered appearance. "Okay, you don't have to break my arms. I'm not here to cause trouble," he said once the door closed, shutting out the noise from the club.

"Then why are you here?" the smaller guy asked. Lowell remembered his name was Zach. "I kicked your ass once, and I won't hesitate to do it again if I catch you around Bull or any of my friends."

"Calm down, tiger," Bull told Zach, and then he shoved Lowell into a chair.

"Aren't you going to tie me up?" Lowell asked.

"Don't tempt me," Bull said. "I haven't forgotten the last time I saw you or what I said I'd do if I saw you again. Now, I'll say this once: you move or try anything, and I'll rip your arms out of their sockets and shove them down your throat. So start talking, and talk fast."

"I know I wasn't at my best the last time I saw you, but I came because I want to get out of the business and you're the only guy I know who's done it successfully."

"Jesus, have the years you've been doing this softened your brain? Why in hell would I help you do anything? You tried to sell me up the river, and then when that didn't work, you tried to extort money from me to make up for a fee that you hadn't earned."

21

As Bull spoke, Jeremy moved backward until he ended up plastered against the wall, and then he closed his eyes. He probably only understood a tenth of what was being said, but he'd obviously heard enough to scare him half to death.

"All I came for was to talk," Lowell said calmly. If Bull was going to hurt him, he'd have done it by now. Lowell had been in the business long enough to know bluster when he heard it. Besides, he had plenty of weapons that only a very thorough search would find, and these guys hadn't even bothered.

"Then talk, but you better do it fast. Once the show is over, I'm going back to business, and you're leaving the club and town and never returning again," Bull said. "I know you have weapons, most likely a knife, maybe a small gun, and who knows what else concealed. I'm not interested in any of that. All I want is to find out why you're here and then get you on your way. I know your reputation and what you do, and you know mine."

"I already told you. I came because we have the same life, or we had the same life, and I need to get what you have. I'm tired of drug-dealer clients and working for scummy governments who don't give a damn about who they hurt." Lowell took a deep breath.

"Okay. Well, you came to the wrong place. That bridge was burned when you showed up in my kitchen months ago. You crossed a line then, and I haven't forgotten it."

"Neither have I," Zach said.

"Fine," Lowell said. He certainly wasn't going to beg. "People don't just leave our business and live to tell about it. But you did. I wanted to ask how you did it. I'm tired and I don't want to do this any longer. I want to get out, and I want to do it with my hide intact."

"Then why did you act like such an ass?" Zach said. God, he was fearless.

"It's rule number one. If anyone crosses you, teach them a lesson they won't forget. If people think they can push you around, they will, and you end up dead. It's better to be good and have the reputation to be feared than show any sort of weakness." Lowell looked at Bull, who nodded slightly. At least he understood. Lowell wasn't sure he was going to get anywhere with Zach, though. He might have been able to reason with Bull, but Zach was a little pit bull, and Lowell wasn't in any mood to tangle with him. The kid was an unknown—he remembered seeing him coming one second and lying flat on the floor the next.

"I don't know in what universe you could think either of us would help you," Zach said. "Now I think it's time for you to leave."

Bull put up his hand, and Lowell waited. He'd learned a number of skills in order to do his job well, and one of them was patience.

"I said you need to leave," Zach repeated and stepped right in front of him. "The last time I saw you, you threatened Bull, and no one does that and gets to come back and ask favors." Zach smacked him hard across the face. "No one ever threatens Bull. Not while I'm around." Zach looked over at the big man and his expression softened. "I can tell he's considering helping you for some strange reason. But if you hurt him or anyone I care about, you can put on any disguise in the world and it won't help you hide, because I'll find your ass and roast you over a spit." Zach's eyes blazed, and when Bull placed a hand on his shoulder, Zach shrugged it off.

After his last encounter with Bull and Zach, he'd supposed that Zach was a fling for Bull, but apparently they were a lot more than that. Lowell realized he should have done a lot more homework before showing up here, but he needed to get away and somehow get the hell out of this life before it took his. "I understand." His pride would not allow him to admit he'd been wrong earlier.

Zach looked at Bull and stepped back.

"I have no reason to trust or help you," Bull warned.

"I know," Lowell said. "But you were the only one I could turn to. No one messes with you. Even when I tried to recruit you back, you said no, even to the client himself. That took guts and something else. You have something on someone."

Bull stepped forward. "I don't trust you, Spook. You have a reputation for deception on all levels. You create characters and looks to get what you want. What's the angle this time? Who are you trying to play? And it better not be us."

"No one." Lowell met Bull's gaze. He was so used to lying at the drop of a hat to save his own ass and spinning a web of deceit meant to ensnare his target that it came as second nature. But this time, if he really wanted help, he knew he had to go for the plain, unvarnished truth. "My last job ended very badly. The client tried to double-cross me. It's a long story, but I got him to do the right thing, and now he isn't very happy about it. He's decided to extract his honor from my hide, even though he's the one with no honor at all."

"There's no honor among thieves, and that's who our clients are. It may seem like governments or officials hiring us to do their dirty work, but they're all thieves and murderers. When I figured that out, I knew I had to leave, so I planned and made sure I had enough ammunition and made sure everyone knew that it would all be made public if anything happened to me. And it still will." Bull smiled at Zach, who was standing next to him. "It also helps to have friends who believe in you and have your back."

Zach growled at Bull, and Lowell chuckled. "I see you've picked up a number of Bull's traits," he said to Zach.

"So what is all this about?" Jeremy asked from the far side of the room.

"It's best you don't know," Zach answered, but Jeremy stepped forward.

"I already know plenty. So what's going on?" To Lowell's surprise, he wasn't asking the others, but seemed to be addressing him.

"I used to be a gun for hire, and Spook, here, still is," Bull answered. "That's what I did before I bought the club. I got out of the business a few years ago, and it seems Spook is looking to do the same thing. But you need to know that what we did was not romantic or fighting for right and good. We worked for whoever was paying the bills, and it's my guess that Spook took a job from a client who either isn't happy with his performance or just decided not to pay."

"Bull, he's a selfish bastard and you know it," Zach said.

"Yeah, and so was I before I left the business. Being focused on the job and self-absorbed is how you stay alive."

"I didn't say he was self-absorbed, because you can be that way sometimes," Zach said. "I can deal with and understand that. I said he was selfish, and there's a difference. He crossed a line before, and I want to kick his ass again for it." The kid was like a tiger protecting its young, only this time the smaller guy was protecting guys larger than him and showing no sign of fear. Lowell had to give him a lot of credit. Zach continued glaring at him, and Lowell stared right back. He wouldn't give the kid the satisfaction of knowing he'd hit the nail on the head. Lowell *was* selfish—he took what he wanted, and when he was done he moved on. That went with the job and was the way he liked things. No entanglements, disappointments, or distractions.

"Okay," Jeremy said. "And I take it you and Zach have a history with him." Jeremy spoke to Bull, but he kept looking at him, and Lowell liked it, though he figured that wouldn't last very long. It wasn't like a normal guy like Jeremy would be able to deal with what he'd done for a living.

"The show is just about over out front," Bull told the group and then turned to Lowell. "I need to think about this. I don't know if I want you anywhere near the people I care about. And I sure as hell don't trust you, at least not completely. But I do understand what you're trying to do." Bull stepped back and took Zach's hand. "I'll think things over. That's the best I can offer right now." Bull's expression hardened. "But in the meantime, I do not want you hanging around the club or anyone else in our lives. You're good at disappearing, so I suggest you do that for the next day or so. Leave me your number, and I'll call you when I've had a chance to decide."

Lowell knew he'd gotten the best answer he was going to get. He stood up and was careful not to make any threatening moves. He took a pen and piece of scratch paper from the desk and wrote down the number of a burn phone he'd picked up. Then he stepped toward the door and pulled it open. "Thanks." He closed the door and walked down the short hallway toward the door that led back into the club.

He couldn't help stopping to look behind him to see if Jeremy might have been looking. There was no one but him in the hall. It was a shame. Jeremy had captured his attention. The kid had spunk and something that made Lowell want to talk with him, spend time with him. But it was unlikely Jeremy would want anything to do with him now. Bull was probably explaining to Jeremy exactly what kind of work he did, and that would most likely be the last time Lowell ever saw him. He was used to it. His job made for a very lonely life. Caring for someone only made them a target and showed weakness. So Lowell had stayed away from any romantic entanglements. However, now that he might have found someone he was willing to break that rule for, Jeremy wasn't likely to want him back.

The dance music pounded as he entered the club. Lowell made his way through the dancers, who jumped and pulsed everywhere. There wasn't a spare inch anywhere, and he had to half walk and half dance his way through the crowd. He finally reached the front door and left without looking back. He strode down the sidewalk to where he'd parked his rental car and headed back to the downtown hotel where he had a room.

"Good evening, Mr. Lathrop," the woman behind the desk said to him as he walked through the lobby on the way to the elevators. One thing he always had in reserve for situations like this was a fresh and new ID that was untraceable. Harold Lathrop had been sitting around for the last few years, just waiting for an emergency. He had a complete background, credit history—everything that a normal person would have, except that he didn't really exist.

"Hello," he replied and continued to the elevator and then up to his room. He'd already checked out the possible exit routes and had made plans to get out as quickly as possible should the need arise, but it would be nearly impossible for anyone to trace him here. Basically he was safe for now. Moonstone didn't know where he was, and she certainly didn't know the identity he was using. In fact, other than to call her to let her know he was alive, he had broken off all communication. Maybe it was time to take it easy and relax for a while. He should have a chance to do that, if he decided to take it.

Inside, he closed and locked the door and then checked to make sure no one had been in the room. Nothing was disturbed, and all the little tells he'd placed were still there. It was late and he'd had a long night. He had hope, as unbelievable as it seemed, that Bull would actually help him. There was also the chance, even more remote, though, that he'd get to see Jeremy again. He didn't know his last name, but Lowell had little doubt he would be able to find him. After all, he could trace him through Bull to Zach, and from there Jeremy couldn't be too hard to find. He knew he'd promised to stay away, and he would until he heard from Bull again, but after that Lowell intended to explore if there was anything at all between him and Jeremy.

His encounters in the romance department were nonexistent. His relationships were measured in hours. But he was tired of being alone and wanted something longer. That was one of the things he wanted to change about his life. It was going to be difficult, he had no doubt about that, but he intended to try. After all, he had nothing to lose as long as he was careful, and he was always careful. It was part of his nature.

Lowell got undressed and climbed into bed, but not until he'd made sure the room was secured and that there were no listening devices in the room. He also closed all the curtains. He would not be able to sleep until he felt secure. Then and only then did he turn out the light and settle under the covers. He quickly fell asleep, but spent much of the night alternating between sleep and semiwakefulness as every sound registered with his hyperaware mind.

THE FOLLOWING morning, Lowell woke with a groan and got out of bed. He checked that the room was secure and then cleaned up and dressed. He ordered room service and spent the day working. He knew he should have done a lot more homework before showing up at Bull's club, so he spent much of the day remedying that situation. The things he could find on the Internet never ceased to amaze him. He already knew where Bull and Zach lived, but through Facebook he found pictures of Zach with his friends. He learned Jeremy's last name was Hodgson, and from there he was able to find where he lived with his roommate, Tristan.

He must have spent an hour that morning looking at the myriad photographs Jeremy had posted to Facebook. Lowell couldn't help smiling at some of the antics that had been captured, including the four friends with Bull in the background, mugging for the camera on a beach. Then there was the one of Jeremy alone, grinning like the cat who'd just eaten the canary. Lowell lingered over that picture, wondering just what Jeremy had done. He continued looking at pictures and lost track of time. When he got hungry, he ordered room service again and kept digging. He wasn't looking for anything in particular. Usually when he did this kind of research, he was looking to find some piece of information or a weakness or pattern he could exploit. But this was just for fun. And he liked it. Jeremy was becoming more three-dimensional, more real to him the more he looked.

Lowell found that Jeremy had a Twitter account, but his tweets were mundane and an almost boring account of his daily activities. Lowell did find one thing in particular, though, that they had in common: Jeremy's love of comic books. When he found a picture of Jeremy's collection, he couldn't help resting back in the chair, a smile growing on his face. He remembered as a kid walking the half mile to the corner store near his home. Each Saturday when he got his allowance, he was allowed to buy one—and only one—comic book. His mother didn't think they were appropriate and that was the only concession he'd been able to get from her. He used to take his walk, get a candy bar, soda, and comic book, and then walk home and lock himself in his room with his childhood vices.

So many things had changed in the intervening time—things he had shoved into a box in the back of his mind and then thrown away the key. Lowell stared at the picture and then closed the window to kill the application. He needed something to do and some time outside this room. He was going stir-crazy with too much time on his hands and not enough movement. He grabbed the small case that sat near his desk and carried it into the bathroom. He pulled off the prosthetics that made up Harold Lathrop and carefully set them in the case. He was going to need them again. Then he cleaned his face, staring at it in the mirror, and got dressed. What he needed, he realized, was some time in his own skin. He'd spent so much of the last few years being Spook, Carl, Lyndon, José, and Muhammad that he hadn't had any time to be Lowell. It wasn't as though anyone would really recognize him. He spent so much time as someone else that his own face was now a disguise.

Once he was done, he closed the case and put it on the floor of the closet. Then he grabbed his room key and headed out the door to take a walk and get some fresh air.

No one paid any attention to him as he exited the hotel and stepped out onto the busy downtown sidewalk. He wasn't sure which way to go and he really didn't care. He knew the river was a block or so ahead of him and that restaurants lined the street he was standing beside. A block behind him was the street that ran in front of the state capitol—the same street Bull's club was on. He'd made a promise to stay away, though, and he always kept his word. Good or bad, you had to always keep your word or you weren't going to get jobs. So he strode to the corner and then across the street and down the side road to the river. He saw what looked like a park, so he began to walk briskly.

Most people would have enjoyed the shade and light breeze on a warm summer day, but not Lowell. He barely noticed them. He spent his time watching people and habitually changing direction and doubling back just to make sure no one was following him. No one was, but habits learned and perfected over more than a decade didn't just turn off. Those instincts had saved his life more than once, and they most likely would again. A man stumbled from behind a tree, bumping into him. Lowell's instinct was to grab the guy and drive him to the ground just to make sure the bump hadn't been done on purpose as a way to distract him. He'd actually reached out to grab the guy, but backed away and watched as the homeless man ambled on like nothing had happened. He didn't even look back, and Lowell checked that he had everything, ready to chase the guy down, but nothing was missing. It appeared to be an innocent encounter. Lowell continued on. When he passed under a bridge, he tensed, ready for anything, but nothing happened. "Damn it," he whispered to himself when he exited the other side.

He was so wound up in his job that he couldn't even take a simple walk in the park without seeing danger around every corner. At the next street, he walked out of the park and back toward the hotel. He needed to get the hell off the street. What he'd hoped would be relaxing had turned into an exercise in precaution and edginess. Along the way he found a coffee shop and stopped in, watching everyone's movements as he bought a large latte and took it with him.

As he headed toward the hotel, he saw Jeremy walking toward him with some of the guys he'd been at the club with the night before. None of them even looked at him twice as they passed, but Lowell stopped once they'd passed him and watched as Jeremy talked animatedly with his friends. On a whim, Lowell held back and then followed for a few blocks.

He knew how to follow people without being noticed. But he wasn't paying as much attention to the following as he was to the subjects he was following. The four guys laughed and joked with each other. Jeremy seemed quieter than the others, but just before Lowell got ready to turn and head back to his hotel, he saw Jeremy throw his head back and laugh deeply. Lowell tried to remember a more joyous sound or a happier sight. He couldn't, which was sad. He hadn't realized how much death and destruction he'd seen in his life, and he couldn't remember a time when he hadn't skulked in the shadows, disappearing from view until he was ready to strike.

Jeremy and his friends turned a corner, and Lowell turned around, retracing his steps until he arrived back to his hotel. He knew it was best not to get tangled up with anyone. Jeremy had a good life, with friends and people who cared about him. Lowell knew it would be best to walk away and not see him again. That would be the wisest decision for him and for Jeremy, but like Zach had rightfully said, Lowell was selfish, and he knew nothing came in life unless you went for it.

"Am I being a complete fool?" he asked himself as soon as he got back into his hotel room. This was a man he'd danced with and talked to a few times in a club. Why Jeremy had such a grip on his imagination, he wasn't sure. "No, it's best for both of us that I let this go." With that decided, Lowell flopped down and turned on the television. There was nothing else for him to do but wait for Bull's answer.

CHAPTER
FOUR

"YOU'RE REALLY going to do this?" Zach asked Bull. Jeremy had been invited over to their house, and the three of them were sitting in the living room. Bull had gotten out of bed a while ago, and Jeremy and Zach had returned from lunch with the guys.

"You don't understand," Bull told him. "I *was* him a few years ago, trying to figure out if there was a life beyond what I knew. Spook is the way he is largely because of the job he does." Bull sat down next to Zach. "I'm afraid to tell you that I doubt you would have cared very much for me if you'd have met me when I was still part of that life."

"So? That doesn't mean you're running some sort of mercenary rehabilitation service, and certainly not for him. He tried to take you away from me, and he came into what is now our home, and I know he would have used me to get to you."

"Yes, he probably would have," Bull said. "It's part of the job. Find an angle and use it to get what you need. It's one of the basics." Bull pulled Zach to him. "Do you have any idea how hard it was for him to ask for help? That's a sign of weakness."

Zach didn't argue, but he also didn't snuggle into Bull's side the way he usually did when Bull held him.

"What do you think?" Bull asked, turning to Jeremy.

"Me?"

31

"Yeah. You spent more time with him than anyone else. You also heard what he said in the office. You have good instincts about people. So what do you think?"

Jeremy tugged slightly at the collar of his T-shirt, which now seemed a little tight. "I don't know. We danced, and then he talked to me a few times at the table. I thought he was nice and I liked dancing with him." Jeremy tugged on his collar again. He was embarrassed to tell them that this Spook had made him hotter than anyone he could ever remember.

Bull turned back to Zach, whispering to him.

"There was something in his eyes," Jeremy said, and both Zach and Bull turned to him. "When he was talking to me, they were soft and warm, not hard like when he was in the office." Jeremy thought back to the night before. "When we were dancing, he looked at me the way Bull sometimes looks at you." Jeremy shrugged. "At the time I thought there might be something there, but now I don't know. He might have liked me or he might have been playing me to get to you."

"He didn't need to play you to get to me, and Spook would know that." Bull shifted on the sofa, and Zach handed him a small pillow, which he stuffed behind him.

"He did say he was waiting to speak to someone, but the guy was busy. Now that I think about it, he was probably referring to you." Jeremy smiled and nodded.

"We talked about this at lunch, and we all agreed that you should let it go," Zach said softly to Jeremy.

Bull snorted and then laughed. "Since when do you and your group of friends get to make Jeremy's decisions for him? And aren't all of you putting the cart way before the horse?"

"You didn't see them dancing," Zach said. "I did, and he had our Jeremy here half swept off his feet and partway down the aisle within minutes." Zach giggled. "Though I will admit the two of you looked hot together, and it did look like he was really into you. But it's Spook, and the guy isn't to be trusted."

"Come on, give me some credit. He was a guy I met last night, danced with for less than fifteen minutes, and talked with a few times. I think I can keep my head on straight enough to resist his charms." Jeremy grinned. "Besides, Bull asked me what I thought, and I told you. He didn't seem menacing to me, but that's probably part of his act as well." Jeremy shrugged and picked up the cup of coffee Zach had brought for him while Bull was getting dressed.

"These guys never look menacing. That's what makes them effective. They play everyone. It's a game," Zach said forcefully.

"Slow down, tiger. It isn't as though we aren't human," Bull said. "I know it's easy to think of what we did as heartless and of mercenaries as machines, but we aren't. We have feelings like anyone else, and while we do feel emotions, we're simply good at controlling them, unlike some cute people I know." Bull pressed Zach closer to him. "We also feel fear, and from what I saw last night, Spook is afraid. He was doing his best to cover it, but something has him running scared."

"But still…," Zach said.

"What concerns me isn't helping Spook, per se. It's what we'll end up getting involved with if we do help him. Whatever is enough to scare a guy like Spook isn't something I want anyone I care about getting involved with."

"I think I understand. But if he did those things to you and Zach, how can you help him?" Jeremy asked. He'd known Bull was a real stand-up guy, but this seemed incredibly nice for anyone, almost saintly.

Bull sighed. "It's hard to explain, but I'll try. Do you remember those guys from last night, the dancers?" Jeremy nodded. "Well, those guys, the ones taking their clothes off on stage, that's a job for them. Once the show is over, they go home to lovers, maybe go to college on Monday morning. They have parents and friends just like you. They aren't prostitutes or anything like that. They have people they love and who love them, just like anyone else. Backstage, they joke, laugh, fight, argue, and gossip just like you guys do when the four of you are all together. They're just guys, like anyone else. The only difference is that they are on stage and dance."

"Okay," Jeremy and Zach said together, and then they shared a quick smile.

"It's the same way for a mercenary. We make our living doing… well, sometimes some pretty dirty jobs. Sometimes we do things for some pretty disreputable people, and it's easy to get sucked into doing jobs that maybe you shouldn't, but because you have a reputation, once you've taken a job, you don't back out. And over time you learn things about certain people that they don't want known, so you make enemies. But you're still human, deep down. You want to be loved like anyone else, and you have families and, hopefully, friends. I get the feeling that Spook has no one, and that makes him vulnerable." Bull paused. "He's still a person, like anyone else, and he asked for my help. He took a real chance coming here, yet he still came and still had the guts to ask for help."

"Yeah, well…," Zach mumbled.

"Think about it," Jeremy said. "I'm sure he had weapons and stuff, and yet he didn't fight or anything. You yelled at him, and he barely flinched, except the few times I saw him look down. He could have hurt any of us, but he didn't."

"Jeremy's right. I could have searched him, but I knew I wouldn't find all his weapons. He's that good."

"I was wondering why you didn't," Zach said.

"He really wasn't causing any trouble. I just needed to know why he was there," Bull admitted. "I probably should have searched him, but backing him into a corner wouldn't help me get the information we needed."

"Well," Zach humphed, "he's going to have to prove himself to me before we'll help him."

"Oh, he does, does he?" Bull said with a twinkle in his eye.

"Yes." Bull ran his fingers along Zach's side, and Zach giggled and squirmed away from him. "Bull, that's not fair." Zach laughed, and Bull continued tickling. "Come on. I'm trying to be serious." He continued giggling and managed to squirm his way off the sofa and onto the floor. "Bull." Zach's scowl lasted for about two seconds.

Bull extended his hand and helped Zach back up. "Okay, Giggle Boy. Why don't you let me worry about how trustworthy Spook is?"

Zach caught Jeremy's eye for a second and then crossed his arms over his chest in a very Bull-like move. "Because you'll make your decision and go off and do whatever you've decided. But we're in this together. That's what you said a few months ago, and I'm holding you to it. Someone has to watch your back." Zach grinned. "And it's definitely going to be me, because no one is better at watching your backside than me."

Bull tugged Zach to him with a belly laugh, and suddenly Jeremy realized it was time for him to leave. He wasn't needed for this conversation, and those two needed some time alone to discuss whatever it was they were going to talk about when Bull eventually carried Zach back to bed. "I think I should be going." He stood up and carried his mug into the kitchen. "I'll talk to you guys later."

"Be sure to keep your eyes open," Bull said.

"I will," Jeremy agreed and headed for the door. By the time he left, those two only had eyes for each other, and Jeremy doubted they even heard the front door close. Jeremy shuffled down the walk to his car. He got in and drove across the river into Harrisburg. He tried to find parking near the place he shared with Tristan but had no luck. He found a spot a few blocks away. He locked up his old Tempo. There were a few things he needed, so he decided to walk the two blocks to the drugstore.

The first block or so was fine, but after that, sweat broke out on his skin and he began feeling light-headed. He only had a short distance to go, so he picked up his pace. His stomach began flipping and he felt his pulse pounding in his ears. His entire being focused on food. It was all he could think about and he had to have some, right now. Jeremy walked as quickly as he could. He stumbled slightly over a crack in the sidewalk, but hardly noticed it. He had to get to the store.

Jeremy's hands and arms shook as he finally reached the store. He grabbed the handle and pulled, but it didn't move. Jeremy lifted his gaze and wondered why it wouldn't open. He pulled again and the door didn't budge. Panic began to overwhelm him and he fell forward. The door went with him and Jeremy tumbled to the floor inside. He tried to get up, but couldn't seem to determine which direction that was. His vision was blurry and swimmy, so he gave up. At least the floor wasn't moving.

Someone took his hand. "Are you all right?" The words seemed like they were being said through a fog. Jeremy tried to follow them, but the fog only seemed to thicken. "Can you tell me what's wrong?" He felt a hand on his arm. "I need some juice now!" the voice snapped through the fog. Jeremy tried to answer but nothing came out. "Can you sit up?" the voice asked more gently. Jeremy was cradled and something pressed to his lips. "Go ahead and drink." He felt cold on his lips. Jeremy opened his mouth and a small amount of liquid dripped inside. He swallowed and more liquid touched his lips.

He was so tired, and he pulled away. "No!"

"You need to drink. Just take a few more sips." Jeremy did as he was told. It was orange juice; he could taste it now. Something deep in his mind kicked in, and he swallowed hard. He reached for what was in front of his lips and drank. He took in more and more. He'd done this before. "That's better. Just relax. You need to get some sugar into your system."

"How did you know?" a female voice asked.

"He has a bracelet," the man answered. Jeremy liked his voice. It was nice and mellow. Well, it was when he wasn't barking at people. Jeremy liked how it sounded when he was talking to him. "Drink some more."

Jeremy emptied the container and sat still. He could feel his system begin to work again. His blood raced in his ears for a few more seconds and then calmed. His skin began to dry and the jitteriness slowly dissipated. "I'm okay," he whispered as he realized what had happened.

"Get some of those," the man said. Jeremy didn't know what he was talking about. "And another juice."

Soon a bottle was pressed into his hand. Jeremy drank and slowly blinked his eyes open. The world had stopped spinning and the last of the fog was lifting. Someone pressed a bag of snacks into his hand.

"I'm feeling better."

"Good. Can you stand? There's a chair right over here." The man helped him up, and Jeremy took a few uneasy steps to the chair. He sat and drank some more. "Eat. It will help," the man said. A package crunched open and something was pressed into his hand. Jeremy ate the pretzel nuggets without thinking.

Feeling better now and with the edginess gone, he shifted and looked at his benefactor, but he didn't recognize him. "Thank you."

"You're welcome, Jeremy," the man said, and Jeremy leaned forward and looked closer.

"Do I… know you… from the club?" he asked haltingly. After he had one of these episodes, it sometimes took a while before all his neurons started firing again. He thought he knew the man from somewhere.

"Yes. We met last night."

He gasped and opened his mouth. It was the voice. "You're the guy I danced with last night. You're Spook." Jeremy colored as he remembered his behavior on the dance floor. Spook looked really different, but now that he knew who he was, Jeremy could see the similarities, especially in the eyes. "Is this the real you or a disguise?"

Spook didn't answer right away as he touched his face with the tips of his fingers. "This is the real me. Last night I had altered my facial features with prosthetics and stage makeup."

"Did you have to check?" Jeremy asked and ate some more of the pretzel things, then drank from the bottle of juice.

"Yeah," Spook answered softly after looking around. "I change my appearance often enough that I had to check and make sure I wasn't wearing anything. I'm not."

Jeremy nodded and drank the last of the juice. He was feeling better by the second. His blood sugar was on the way back up, thank God. He knew he was going to have a devil of a time of it for the rest of the day because of all the stuff he'd just eaten, but it was better than passing out... again. "Thank you."

"Does that happen often?"

"No. I was on my way here to get some toilet paper and I felt the low blood sugar coming on. I tried to get here so I could get something to eat. I usually carry things with me." Jeremy looked at the clerk, who fidgeted nervously behind the counter. "I appreciate your help. Ring up everything you gave me and I'll pay for it." He needed a few more minutes to make sure he was all right before walking home. Jeremy pulled out his wallet and handed the clerk a ten. She rang him up and brought back his change with a receipt. "Thanks." He always felt like a fool when this happened. He'd been diabetic for years and should be able to manage his blood sugar. Most of the time he could, but occasionally his body would do something crazy and send it into orbit or dropping like a stone, which was what had just happened.

"Are you really okay?" Spook asked him

"Yeah. I'm feeling better." Jeremy ate a few more pretzel snacks and then rolled up the rest of the package for later. He took a deep breath and released it slowly to let go of some of the tension that had built. These episodes always took a great deal out of him.

"You said you walked."

"Yeah." Fatigue was already setting in.

"I'll walk you home."

"That really isn't necessary," Jeremy said. "It isn't too far, and I'll be okay." He stood up and thanked the clerk again. Spook stood as well and walked over to the counter. He passed a bill to the clerk for any trouble, with his thanks, and then turned. He caught up with Jeremy as he was pulling the door open.

"I'll really be okay," Jeremy said.

"Fine. But I'm still walking you home."

Jeremy wasn't too sure how comfortable he was with Spook knowing where he lived. But then he shrugged. Spook could probably find his address quite easily regardless, so he didn't argue and started walking across the small parking lot. "Bull called you Spook. Do you have a real name?"

"Lowell. But no one uses it. I think the last people to call me that were my parents, but they're gone." The hitch in his voice was barely audible, but Jeremy caught it. He knew there was most likely a story there, but he didn't know Lowell well enough to ask, so Jeremy kept quiet. "I've been many people with many names for a very long time. Right now I'm not even Lowell. I have another name that I'm using. It's how I've lived for a number of years. In the real world, me, as a person, only exists in a few places."

"That's really sad," Jeremy said. "I mean, when I asked if that was your real face, you actually had to check. I bet that means you always have to remember who you're supposed to be. So Lowell, who you really are, gets lost."

"That's as good a way to put it as I've heard. But it's part of my job and what I need to do to keep being able to do my job," Lowell said.

Jeremy led them north and turned off the main road to a quiet street lined with older homes that had been turned into apartments. Parts of the city were really bad, but this neighborhood had maintained its character and a number of the buildings were still owner-occupied, at least in part, so that kept the area clean and the buildings maintained. "You told Bull you wanted to get out of the business. Is that true?"

"Yes. But I need to maintain my cover so I can be safe, at least for now."

Jeremy stopped at the corner and waited for the light to change. "Is someone really after you?"

"Yeah. I doubt they know where I am, and I intend to keep it that way. But they're most likely trying to find me. Not that it will do them any good. Their boss wants his money back, but it's long gone and untraceable to anyone but me. There's no way they can get at it even if they were to try to force me into it. There are way too many safeguards in place."

The light changed and they crossed. "How did you get started doing this?"

"I was in the military. Special Forces. And once I got out, there were no jobs, and I had skills that were in demand. I was recruited by a government contractor and ended up back in Iraq. Eventually, after I'd demonstrated what I could do, I was sent to other areas. Then I was offered other, private work, and that paid a hell of a lot more. I didn't set out to be a mercenary, but one thing led to another."

"But you aren't a mercenary, are you?"

"Yes and no. I eventually graduated to being a man who fixes things," Lowell said.

"You kill people for money," Jeremy asked, stopping just outside his building.

"I'm not an assassin, if that's what you think. The people I work for aren't Boy Scouts, but the people I take out are generally worse. I've worked for royalty, and I try to be particular about the clients I take. But this last one was a mistake." Jeremy paused. "I needed the money and I took the job for that reason."

"Why do you do it?" Jeremy asked.

Lowell didn't answer. "Maybe someday I'll be able to answer that question."

Jeremy nodded and turned to climb the steps into his building. "Thank you for the help and the walk home."

"You're welcome," Lowell said, and Jeremy caught his gaze. It was intense and directed at him. Jeremy shivered, even on the warm day. He swallowed hard and waited to see what would happen. Lowell moved closer. "I'm so glad I was there to help you. I mean, that it was me who was there to help when you needed it." Lowell smiled, and Jeremy's stomach did a little flip-flop. No one had ever looked at him like that. Jeremy had been with other guys—after all, he was the experienced one in their group. He liked to project that image, at least. But he'd never experienced this kind of intensity before. Zach had told him what it was like between him and Bull. Jeremy imagined it must have felt like this. Lowell moved closer, and Jeremy took a single step down. He was face-to-face with Lowell, and Lowell kissed him. It wasn't like at the club, all heat and energy. This kiss was softer and gentle, like Lowell really cared for him.

Lowell stepped back and said, "I'll see you later." He smiled, and Jeremy did the same in return.

Jeremy then turned and went inside, aware that Lowell watched him the entire way. He climbed the stairs to the second floor. He paused outside the door for a few seconds, smiling as the remnants of Lowell's kiss faded away. He heard Tristan playing a game inside. He opened the door to find Tristan and Kevin sitting on the sofa, battling monsters on the Xbox.

"How was it at Zach's?" Kevin asked, angling to the side and shooting.

"Fine. I was going to get TP at the drugstore, but had an episode." They paused the game and both of them leaped over the sofa.

"Are you okay?"

"Yeah. The guy from the club last night was there and got me some juice and something to eat."

"You'd just had lunch," Tristan said. "Are you sure you're okay?"

Jeremy smiled at his mother hen of a roommate. "I'm fine. He helped me and walked me home. But I forgot what I went there for, so you'll have to use newspaper."

"I bought some toilet paper yesterday," Tristan said. "It's under the sink." They drifted back to the sofa and started their game again.

"Could you turn down the volume? I'm going to lie down for a while." These episodes always made him feel like he'd just run a marathon.

"Sure thing," Tristan said, and Jeremy headed down the hall to his bedroom. He closed the door, emptied all the stuff from his pockets, and slipped off his shoes before lying on the bed. He was wiped out and fell asleep soon after closing his eyes.

HE WOKE some time later to his phone vibrating on the nightstand. He drowsily reached for it, if only to get it to leave him alone, and answered it.

"Are you okay?" Zach asked. "Tristan told me you had a problem at the drugstore. He said that the guy from the club helped you. Was that Spook?"

"Yeah. His name's Lowell. He was there and helped me after I'd passed out on the floor." Jeremy sat up and wiped his eyes with the back of his hand. "He stayed around and made sure I was okay, then he walked me home." Zach was quiet. "What?"

"Nothing," Zach said.

"We talked a lot when he walked me home. He told me how he got into the mercenary business and said that there's someone after him."

"Did he say anything else?"

"Just that he was the real him without a disguise and that his real name was Lowell."

"Yeah, sure," Zach snarked.

"I think he was telling me the truth," Jeremy said. He knew he couldn't convince Zach of anything, so he didn't press it. "Anyway, he got me OJ and some pretzels, held my hand, and helped me drink while we sat on the floor. He could have just left me there, but he didn't. He made sure I was okay, helped me drink, got me into a chair, and then walked me home. So since I've spent more time with him, I think I'm the one who gets to make judgments."

"Okay. God, I forgot how snappy you can get after one of these episodes. I just called to make sure you were okay."

"I am," Jeremy said more softly. "I just woke up and I'm still trying to get my head together." He felt bad that he'd barked at Zach.

"Are you coming to the club tonight?"

"No," Jeremy said with a yawn. "I think I need to take it easy, and drinking is the last thing I need right now. Quiet and some real food is probably best. You're welcome to come over if you want, unless the others are going out."

"That would be good. We can have a video-game marathon or something," Zach said.

"Cool. I'll see you in a few hours," Jeremy said and hung up the phone. He got up and left the room. The guys were still playing. They hadn't moved, and Jeremy would have thought they'd been in the same position the entire time except that there were more soda cans on the coffee table.

"Come on, Jeremy. I'm whipping his ass good," Tristan said, bobbing and weaving before the sound of gunfire echoed from the television, followed by an explosion and a thud. "Dude, I just killed you for like the millionth time."

"I hate this game," Kevin said, setting down the controller. "You go ahead and teach him a lesson."

Jeremy sat down and picked up the controller. The game started and he concentrated. Tristan was wicked good, but Jeremy was usually just a little better, and soon he had Tristan on the run, before gunfire, explosion, thud.

"He smoked you," Kevin said.

"Yeah, yeah," Tristan said and started the game again.

"Zach will be over in a little while. We can order pizza and stuff," Jeremy explained, concentrating mostly on the game. "He asked if we wanted to go to the club." He dodged Tristan and came up behind him, taking him out with a shout of triumph. "You guys can go if you want, but I'm not up to it tonight."

"I'm going with a game marathon," Tristan said. He got up, took the game out of the player, and put in another.

"What's this?" Kevin asked.

"Something more your speed," Tristan teased as the title *Dance Dance Revolution* came on the screen. Kevin pounced and the game was on. Jeremy got out of the way as the two of them tickle fought until Tristan gave up. Then he changed the game and they went back to playing.

Zach came over an hour later. "Was Bull disappointed that you weren't going to be there?"

Zach chuckled. "I think he's relieved. He says he's going to call Spook and talk to him, and we agreed that it was probably best if I wasn't around. Bull wants to make sure he's on the level, and all I want to do is rip his nuts off, so in Bull's words, I'm counterproductive."

All of them broke into laughter. "No doubt," Kevin said and stood up. "I'll order the pizza." He made the call, and Jeremy settled on the sofa with Tristan and they began to play. When Kevin returned, they reconfigured the game and played teams until the pizza showed up.

Jeremy turned off the game and turned on the television, finding a rerun of *Big Bang Theory*. They talked and ate as they watched, debating the merits of the characters like they always did. Each of them saw some part of themselves in each of the characters. When the show was over and they had finished eating, they played video games for hours, laughing and having their usual good time.

"Why do you keep looking at the door?" Zach asked.

Jeremy hadn't realized he was. "I don't know." He turned back to the screen, and Tristan put in a game. They played until all of them began to tire. Zach left to go home, and Jeremy made up the sofa for Kevin. Then he went to get ready for bed.

He cleaned up, checked his blood sugar level and then his phone for messages before climbing under the covers. But he couldn't sleep. He'd probably napped too long earlier in the day, and he wasn't as tired as he'd thought. His mind wandered, and of course it traveled back to Lowell. He'd been nice, and Jeremy hoped Bull agreed to help him.

CHAPTER
FIVE

"LOOK, THERE isn't some magic formula that I stumbled on to get these guys off my back and get out of the business," Bull said in his office in the club. Lowell sat in the same chair he had the night before, only this time under more comfortable circumstances.

"I figured that," Lowell said.

"First thing. My advice is to make sure you have no outstanding jobs or contracts. Stop taking more, and eventually you'll fade from memory for most people. There will be some who feel they need your special talents, and they'll be a little more insistent." Bull stared at him, and Lowell knew he'd been the agent of one of those people. "Are you sure this is what you want to do?"

"Yeah. I've got more than enough money squirreled away, and my agent has no idea where it is. The usual thing. Trust no one enough that they can hurt you." Lowell saw Bull nod slowly. "The thing is…."

"I know. You were a different kind of mercenary than I was, and you branched out into areas where I refused to go." Lowell nodded. Bull had never been the kind of gun for hire that he had become. Lowell hated the word assassin, but that was what he'd done over the last few years and what had made him decide that it was time to leave. "You have a lot of information that very powerful people would like to make sure doesn't ever see the light of day. I had some as well…." Bull leaned back against his desk. "I sealed the most damaging information and contracted with a lawyer to arrange to make it all public if anything happened to me. That worked for the most part, but there were still people who tried to pressure me back."

"I know. Some people just can't take no for an answer." Lowell couldn't resist, and Bull chuckled.

"Yeah." Bull's expression became serious. "I have to ask if this is some sort of game. I've been through enough and gotten out of this game, and I'm not going back. I'm also not running a mercenary reform service. If you want to leave the life, then you need to come up with a plan to do that. I've thought it over, and I'll provide what help I can. But I will not put my life here or the people I care about in danger. And I won't let you pull Jeremy into this."

Lowell nodded slowly.

"I mean it. Zach called and told me you helped Jeremy today, and that act went a long way toward persuading me to help you."

"I—"

Bull cut him off. "I know you like him, and Jeremy is a great person. He likes to come off as strong and as the leader of Zach's little group, but he's fragile, and you saw that earlier. Emotionally, Jeremy has been through a lot, and he doesn't need all of this. You came here to hide, and once you've decided what to do, we'll help you put your plan into action, but then you'll leave town and build whatever life you want. It's best if you don't start things here that you can't finish."

Lowell got the message loud and clear. "You're warning me off Jeremy?"

"No. I'm telling you not to hurt him. Think about where you are in your life and where you've been. Jeremy is a kid from Central Pennsylvania. He knows nothing about the kind of life we've led and the dangers it involved." Bull was becoming more forceful.

"Did Zach?" Lowell countered.

"No, and I have you to thank for bringing the impact of my former life into reality. I had hoped to spare him that, but you brought that into our kitchen. I'm just thankful Zach didn't run screaming for the hills."

"As I remember, he came through with flying colors."

"Yes, and now you're sitting in my office." Bull came closer. "I'm not going to tell you what to do, and I'm the last guy in the world to get involved in someone's love life. If you really like Jeremy and are good to him, that's one thing, but if you use him or hurt him, you'll have to deal with me. Do we understand each other?"

Lowell shook his head. "I've only danced with him and talked to him a few times. And today I helped him out at the drugstore. I…."

Bull smiled slightly. "Let's just say that you aren't as good at keeping your feelings hidden as you thought you were. At least not as far as Jeremy is concerned." Bull smiled, and Lowell found himself grinning like a cat. He had loved holding Jeremy in his arms while he'd been helping him, though seeing Jeremy on the floor of that store had set his heart racing in a panic. And the kiss on the stairs had been so sweet, it had touched his heart.

"Thanks. I'll keep that in mind," Lowell said.

"You do that," Bull told him. "Now, I have work to do, and you have some planning to do. I also recommend that you take clear stock of the people in your life that you trust. Make sure they are all people you would trust with your life. If they aren't, cut them off and make sure they have no way to find you. And that means your agent and handler as well. They are the ones with the most to lose by you leaving the business. You make money for both of them, so they aren't going to be happy."

Lowell had already thought along those lines, but it was good to have confirmation. "Yeah, I figured that."

"Good."

Lowell stood up and extended his hand. "I really appreciate this. I know it seems stupid of me to say this, but I trust you."

"Why?" Bull asked.

"I think because of the way you feel about Zach and how it shows. You love each other and the kind of relationship you have requires deep trust. So I guess if you can trust each other, then I can trust you." Lowell had never trusted anyone in his life, not really. He'd taken extra precautions to make sure no one was ever able to get close enough to him or his money to actually hurt him. It surprised him how easily he was willing to trust Bull and that he wanted to be trusted in return. What the hell was happening to him? He must be getting soft.

"That's good. But we don't trust you. Not yet." Bull glanced at the clock on the wall. "I need to get back to work."

"Are Jeremy and his friends going to be here tonight?"

"You don't know?" Bull asked.

"I kept my word and haven't been following them. I just happened to be at the drugstore this afternoon." Lowell hardened his gaze. He didn't like what Bull was insinuating. "We made a deal, and I stuck by it."

"Okay. And to answer your question, they're at Jeremy's playing video games. Apparently Jeremy was feeling a little under the weather, probably because of what happened this afternoon."

"Is he all right?" Lowell asked quickly.

Bull smiled. "Yes." He motioned toward the door, and Lowell left the office with Bull following him. Entering the club, he looked around. There were lots of good-looking guys dancing with their shirts off, having a great time. Lowell knew he could join the fray.

"Hey, wanna dance?" a guy asked from behind him.

Lowell turned around. A shirtless man, well built, with great eyes and narrow hips that disappeared into a pair of very low-slung jeans that left nothing to the imagination, looked up at him with an invitation in his eyes. He was just Lowell's type, and excitement ran through him for a second and then dissipated.

"Sorry, no thanks," he said. "I was just leaving." Lowell took a step forward, and the guy took his arm.

Lowell whirled around, instantly ready to take the guy out. "Do you want some company?" the guy asked. Lowell shook his head and turned. He needed to leave, but the guy was persistent. "We could have a real good time."

"Sorry, but you're not who I was looking for." Lowell headed for the door, calming himself as he made his way out of the club.

He strode down the sidewalk and to his car. He got in and drove straight back to his hotel and went up to his room. It felt so strange to him, and unsettling, that he hadn't wanted the guy at the club. The only person he really wanted was Jeremy. Lowell remembered asking his mother when he was thirteen why she'd never remarried after his dad had died.

"Your father was my one and only true love. Someday you'll meet yours, and then you'll understand." She'd smiled at him and wished him a quiet good night in that soft, warm tone she'd had. Lowell could still remember it, and he smiled to himself. He hadn't thought of that in a very long time. Was Jeremy the person his mother had been talking about?

Even if he was, maybe it was best to leave Jeremy alone and not let him get tangled up in his life. It wasn't one that would be good for anyone. Not even him any longer. But he felt drawn to Jeremy. Lowell got cleaned up and made sure his room was secured before getting into bed and deciding he needed to sleep on it.

In theory that was a good idea, but in practice it didn't work out so well. For most of the night, Lowell saw images of Jeremy in his dreams. He rarely dreamed. That was one thing Lowell had learned long ago to suppress. Dreams did him no good, especially the type he'd had when he was particularly tired, where he relived jobs he didn't want to think about. But tonight was different. He and Jeremy were happy. They had a good life and a house of their own. Lowell was happy and content. When he initially woke up, he blinked a few times and closed his eyes again. He wanted more of that happiness. But this time it didn't come. When he fell back to sleep, his happy dream shifted to a nightmare. His home was gone, and all Lowell kept doing was searching for Jeremy, but he couldn't find him. He could hear his voice, but Jeremy was always just out of his reach.

LATE THE following morning Lowell sat down at the desk in his hotel room and tried to figure out what he wanted to do. He had plenty of information on his computer that would make a terrific insurance policy. That wasn't an issue. He'd thought about that for quite a while, and he could use that if he had to. He liked the idea of simply not taking any more jobs and letting things just wind down on their own. That seemed like the wisest course of action.

While he was at it, Lowell checked a website he and Moonstone had used to trade coded messages during times of extreme secrecy. He found one and viewed the file. He didn't want to download it in case Moonstone could trace it. Apparently she was anxious for him to contact her. That was all the message said. Lowell disconnected from the site and closed his computer. Then he picked up a burn phone he'd purchased in New Jersey on his way here and called her. "It's Spook," he said when she answered.

"So you are alive," she said with a smile in her voice.

"I got your message."

"I sent it because I have a job. It's a big one and carries one hell of a payday." Lowell didn't say anything for a few seconds. That had always been the temptation. There was always one more job that carried a huge reward to tempt him to stay. He'd thought about leaving a few times before, and in every single instance, Moonstone had come up with some incentive for him to keep working. It was almost uncanny how she knew what he was thinking. "Do you want to hear about it?"

"Not right now," Lowell said after taking a deep breath. "I'm not taking any jobs for a while. You know what happened in New York."

"This one is on the other side of the world. You get on a plane and you're gone. No one can trace you now, and they certainly won't be able to once you're on the other side of the world. You'll simply disappear, and at the same time you can make yourself a huge pile of money. This is the big one. The leader of one of those small sheikdoms has a daughter who wants to marry someone completely unacceptable. You don't have to hurt anyone. The prospective suitor simply needs to disappear for a little while, until Daddy can marry his daughter off to someone who suits the family and his reputation. He's willing to pay a great deal to make his potential son-in-law a nonissue." She sounded thrilled, then she told him how much the job paid, and Lowell swallowed hard. Jesus....

He didn't respond right away. This was not what he wanted right now, but the lure of that much money was almost too much for him to turn down. Almost. "Let me think about it."

"Okay. But I need to know soon. I thought of you first for this one, but I have others I can offer it to."

"I said I'd think about it," Lowell responded and terminated the call. Then he pulled the power supply out of the phone and set it aside. He needed a chance to think and get some perspective. Moonstone had always been pushy, especially where money was concerned, but what she was suggesting was rather reckless. He had a place where he was holed up for now and he wasn't going to be found. Maybe it was the fact that Moonstone didn't know where he was that was bothering her?

The job offer and Moonstone, the people he was trying to get away from, the thought of getting out altogether... all of it raced through his mind. He needed to think about what he wanted.

Lowell was tired of room service, so he secured his things, grabbed his hotel key, then placed the "do not disturb" sign on the door. He snagged an elevator and left the hotel. He'd intended to go back to the park, but strode in a different direction. He told himself he wasn't going to Jeremy's, but he ended up there anyway and rang the buzzer out front. He was buzzed right in, which he thought strange, and Jeremy met him at the top of the stairs. "I saw it was you out the window," he said with a smile.

"I was out for a walk and thought I'd make sure you were okay. I had intended to get something to eat and was wondering if you'd join me. Unless you have to work or something." Lowell realized he didn't know very much at all about Jeremy. During their walk the day before, Jeremy had gotten him to open up about himself, which was something he never did, and Jeremy had told him almost nothing about himself.

"No, I don't have to work until tomorrow," Jeremy said. "And I was going to get some lunch, so, yeah, I'd like to go with you." Jeremy bounded down the stairs and nearly missed the last step. Lowell caught him and held him for a few seconds before letting him go once Jeremy had caught his balance. "There's a diner down the street if you want to go there." Jeremy was like a bundle of energy.

"That would be great," Lowell said and followed Jeremy out of the building and down the sidewalk.

"I kept hoping you'd come back last night," Jeremy said.

Lowell blinked a few times. "Did I miss something?" He would have loved to have done that, but he'd given Bull his word.

"I guess not. But since you knew where I lived, I thought you might…." Jeremy stopped walking. "God, I'm so dumb. Sometimes the guys… we seem to know each other so well that we just do things because we know that's what we do. Like Zach will sometimes just come over because he knows that's what we do. I forget sometimes that not everyone is like that. So did you talk to Bull? Is he going to help?"

"He said he'd do what he can," Lowell answered. Bull had been right—this problem was mostly his to try to figure out. He wanted to change the subject. "What kind of work do you do?"

"Boring stuff. I'm a software developer. I got my first job two years ago. I really like it, but the place is sort of old and does things like they've always done them. I've asked about using more modern development techniques, and they are changing, but slowly. My boss is cool, though. He's been pushing for us to do new stuff." For being what Jeremy said was boring, he sure sounded excited about it.

"Is that what you always wanted to do?"

"Sort of," Jeremy told him. "I always loved computers, and I could get them to do what I wanted pretty easy. I needed a job out of college, and Shoebox was hiring. But what I really want to do is be a game designer. There's nothing like that around here, though, and I need to pay the rent and stuff." He shrugged. "It's a good job and they treat me pretty well, so I figure I'll stay as long as they have something to teach me." Jeremy smiled at him as they approached the corner. "The diner is just up the block."

"What's that way?" Lowell asked pointing toward town.

"Restaurant row. There's lots of fancier places toward the center of town."

"Are you up for a walk?" Lowell asked.

"Okay," Jeremy said and turned to cross the other street. "What happened yesterday isn't usual."

"I didn't think it was," Lowell said and took Jeremy's hand. "I only wanted to make sure you didn't need to eat right away. My mother was an insulin-dependent diabetic for a number of years before she died, so that's how I knew what to do when I found you yesterday. Do you give yourself regular injections?"

"No. I have a pump." Jeremy lifted his shirttail. "It gives me a regular flow of insulin, but sometimes, like yesterday, my body starts to kick in and make its own. Then things get out of whack. I have what I call a cranky pancreas. It does what it wants, and though usually it does nothing, yesterday it decided to go into overdrive." Jeremy squeezed Lowell's hand. "I'm just glad you were there."

Lowell was only slightly taller than Jeremy, but much bulkier. Jeremy's hand felt delicate in his, and he knew Lowell could easily squeeze it too tightly and hurt him. "Do you go to the gym a lot?" Jeremy asked. "I know you wear loose clothes to hide it, but you're really strong. I could feel it the other day when we were dancing."

"I work out most mornings in my hotel room. I do the exercises I learned in the military. I've done them for years and I'm careful about what I eat. But as far as going to a gym, I don't usually do that. I'm all about staying in the background and trying not to be noticed. The fitness I do is designed to keep me safe and able to defend myself." Lowell shared a smile with Jeremy. "You told me at the club that you collect comic books. What sort do you like? I was always a huge *Spider-Man* fan. I loved how he could hide in plain sight. I also had a ton of *Invisible Man*."

"I think you took those to heart," Jeremy chirped, and Lowell laughed. "I love the *Fantastic Four*, *Superman*, and of course *Flash*, *Hulk*, and *Green Lantern*. I know it seems dumb to read that stuff as an adult, but I really love them, and so do my friends. Zach has been doing really well with his graphic novels. He based his hero on Bull. Tristan loved *Spider-Man* like you used to. Mostly, though, we collect the books and don't read them much. I guess that's stupid too. We don't have anything valuable, but we keep them all in plastic sleeves and care for them like they're each priceless."

"That's what I used to do too."

"Do you know what happened to them?"

"Not really," Lowell lied. He knew exactly what had happened to them—he just couldn't talk about it now. That conversation would open up a whole can of worms that Lowell was not willing to talk about. He'd buried that deep and kept it there. "I still pick one up every now and then."

"I went to a signing in Washington, DC, a few years ago and Stan Lee was there, so I have some signed by him. That's the heart of my collection. I brought two, and when he saw the copy of *The Flash* I had, he agreed to sign it and the newer one. We were only supposed to have one signed, but he did two for me and then talked to me for a few minutes before I had to move on." They crossed yet another street. "This is where all the restaurants begin. What did you have in mind?"

"Is there a place you've always wanted to go?"

"Yeah. There's Louise's just up the way. They're supposed to have the most amazing steak and seafood, but I can't afford to eat there, not even for lunch."

"Then let's go there," Lowell said, and Jeremy's eyes lit up.

"Tristan went there once when a salesman came to town at his work. He took the whole department there, and Tristan told me he had the best steak ever."

"Well, then, let's get you the best steak ever," Lowell said, and they continued down the street. He held open the door of the restaurant, and they walked in. The dining room was filled with patrons. Lowell gave their name to the hostess, who said it would be at least an hour.

"We can go somewhere else," Jeremy offered. He was looking a little peaked, and Lowell wondered how long it had been since Jeremy had eaten. He approached the hostess desk and handed her a hundred-dollar bill. Her eyes widened, and she took the bill and nodded. A few minutes later something opened up, and they were escorted to a table up front by the windows. He waited until Jeremy had sat down before taking his own seat.

"You do know that I'm not a girl," Jeremy said.

Lowell rolled his eyes. "I definitely know that." He sat down. "Taking care of the person you're with and treating them as though they're special doesn't mean that they're the 'girl.' It does mean that I'm trying to be nice and impress you so you'll like me." Lowell grinned. Jeremy stared at him for two seconds and then burst into a fit of giggles. Lowell shook his head and rolled his eyes again.

"Come on. You look so funny when you mug like that." Jeremy settled down until Lowell did it again, widening his eyes and tilting his head slightly as he made his cheesiest grin. Jeremy began giggling again. The sound was so adorably cute, and the more Jeremy tried to suppress it, the cuter it got. "I hate it when I giggle."

"Why? It's cute."

"For a teenage girl. I don't know why I still do it. Zach giggles all the time. In fact, that's how he met Bull."

"Oh?" Lowell prompted.

"Yeah. He was going to the club, and Bull was at the door checking people to keep them from bringing stuff in the club. Zach walked right up to him, held his hands in the air, and told Bull to frisk him. When he did, Zach started to giggle and squirm. Bull called him Giggle Boy after that. None of us realized it at the time, but that was the start of the relationship." The waitress approached the table and took their drink orders. "Can I have a cosmo?" Jeremy asked, half looking at Lowell.

"You can have whatever you want," Lowell said and ordered a gin and tonic.

"Bull and Zach are really good together, and Bull has been great to all of us. Last year at Christmas he rented this big van and took the four of us to New York because Zach had never been there at Christmastime. Zach was raised very religious...."

Lowell leaned closer. "How about we talk about you instead of Zach?"

Jeremy turned red. "Okay. What do you want to know? I was raised in this area. My mom and dad live in Florida, but they don't understand the whole gay thing. They love me and all. My mom and dad didn't think they could have kids and had given up. When my mom was nearly forty-five, she thought she was going through the change, and instead she was pregnant with me. The doctors and other people said she should end the pregnancy because it would be dangerous for her, but she wouldn't do it. Not so much because she wanted to be a mother, but it was against her beliefs. So I was born when she was forty-six. I graduated from high school when she was sixty-four, and right after that she and Dad moved to

Florida and I went to college. They were good parents, but they weren't really active parents. Growing up, I wanted to go swimming and do things with them, but they wanted to sit on the beach and read."

"That must have been hard. You were growing up, and much of that time your parents were planning for retirement," Lowell said. He could tell Jeremy felt cheated, but it could have been so much worse for him. At least his parents were around and he could talk to them.

"It wasn't so bad. I developed a close set of friends, which all changed when I came bursting out of the closet when I was seventeen." Jeremy made an explosion sound and waved his arms, nearly knocking over his water glass. "All this fabulousness couldn't be contained any longer, and let me tell you, the kids at school… now that was hard. But I had to be myself. I told my parents, and they were more than a little shocked. Not that they should have been, because I wasn't what you'd call a boy's boy. I liked music and was active in theater, doing the makeup and stuff. I loved costumes and dressing up, but I hated most sports and couldn't catch a ball to save my life."

"What did they do?" Lowell asked.

"They loved me, so they did their best to understand. I have to give them credit for that. My mom cried because she wasn't going to have grandchildren. For a long time my mother had said she hoped she lived long enough to see me have children. All her friends were grandparents, and she'd had years of people showing her their grandbabies." Jeremy shrugged. "Like I said, they did their best. Did your parents know you were gay?"

"No. I never told them. It was one of those things. The subject never came up, and I was in the military, so keeping quiet about who I was had become a habit, so I did it with everyone." Lowell hated talking about himself. It would have been easier to talk about his work, and that said something. But speaking of his family was the hardest thing in the world. Lowell had spent a lot of time in war zones, living in some of the harshest conditions on earth. He'd lived and fought in places where it broiled during the day and nearly froze at night. He'd had sand in places no one wanted to think about and always shook the hell out of his boots before putting them on because he had no idea what might have crawled into them. But talking about his family was something he couldn't do. Not yet.

"That's awful," Jeremy said. "Your family never knew who you really were. Mine don't understand, but at least they know who I am. Whether they like me is another story, but I don't hide from them."

Lowell chuckled as a realization hit him. "I hide from just about everyone. It's what I do." God, he'd turned morose all of a sudden. He never thought about shit like this, and in the last few days, he'd been thinking about all kinds of crap he didn't want to.

"Well, you don't have to hide from me," Jeremy said brightly. The server returned and set their drinks in front of them, along with a basket of bread that smelled heavenly. She offered to take their orders, but neither of them had looked at the menu, since they'd been talking nonstop. "I know you can't or don't want to talk about your job...."

Lowell sipped from his glass and stared hard at Jeremy. "It's not that I don't want to talk about it. But the more you know about what I've done, the more danger you'll be in." Lowell leaned over the table. "I've done some things that I'm not proud of, but I told myself I was doing it for a very good reason." He stopped. Why was it that he'd spent years talking to no one about what he did, and all of a sudden, with Jeremy, he developed diarrhea of the mouth and just couldn't stop talking? "It's best you don't know, just like I'm sure Bull keeps a lot of his past quiet."

"Yeah, he does." Jeremy took a drink and grinned. "So what do you want to talk about? Have you read any good books lately?"

"You smartass," Lowell quipped, and Jeremy grinned. "How often do you see your parents?"

"They come to visit in the summer. They'll be here in a few weeks. They stay with friends. For the last few years we'd go on a trip or do something together, but this year Mom and Dad said they were going up to the Adirondacks for a week or so, and I can't get the time off work. It's okay, though. Going on vacation with your folks isn't the greatest thing at my age." He sipped from his glass and grew quiet.

"So I guess that wasn't the best topic of conversation. What do you like to do besides comic books and video games?"

"Well, I told you I want to be a game designer. I have this idea for a game that's based around superheroes, and I'm working on one for Zach. We figured we could try to turn his novels into video games as well, sort of cross-marketing and stuff. I'm designing it now, and once it's done, I'll start developing it. Zach is writing the copy, and I'm going to do the development. It should be really cool. Tristan is going to help me too, and once it's done we're hoping Zach's publisher will be able to help us get someone interested in it." The server returned and took their orders. After she left, Jeremy said, "Pride is next week—do you want to go?"

"Excuse me?" Lowell asked.

"Harrisburg Pride festival. It's next Saturday. I was asking if you wanted to go… with me?" Jeremy lifted his glass and watched him over the top of it. And there it was, the sweet cuteness that made Lowell want to either laugh or kiss Jeremy until they were both breathless. Jeremy continued looking at him after he'd placed his glass on the table. Lowell leaned over the table and smiled when Jeremy did the same. Then Lowell kissed him lightly and sat back in his seat. "What is it?" Jeremy said after a few minutes. "What's that look for?" Jeremy picked up his napkin and wiped his face. "Is there something on my face?"

"No, you're fine. You're perfect," Lowell said softly. He could hardly breathe. How long had it been since anyone had touched his heart? He tried to remember and couldn't. He'd been closed off, *really* closed off, from everything and everyone for a long time.

"Then what is it? You look like you just figured something out."

He had, but he couldn't talk about it. Not right now. What if what he was feeling wasn't real? He had figured out something very important. It hit him that while he'd been working and making money, he hadn't been living. He'd gone from job to job and alias to alias, changing his appearance and then disappearing. But he hadn't been living. For over a decade he hadn't spent more than a single night with anyone, and he'd certainly made sure they didn't stick around after he'd gotten what he wanted. "It's nothing." Lowell swallowed around the lump in his throat. Their food arrived, and that gave him a few seconds to get his thoughts together.

"You don't have to go with me if you don't want to," Jeremy said, and it took Lowell a few seconds to realize that Jeremy was talking about his invitation, and that he thought Lowell didn't want to go.

"No, that would be fun," Lowell answered automatically, his thoughts circling in his head like a tornado. He'd been alone for a very long time and now that wasn't what he wanted. Jeremy was a great person, and Lowell liked him, but was it fair to inflict the life he had led on Jeremy? He could think of a million ways his old life could descend on them, and none of them were pretty. Hell, he was still in hiding trying to figure out how he was going to stay alive once his former client found him. His life was a huge pile of crap, and it was one he'd built all on his own. He needed to clean up his mess somehow, and it had to be done in a way that didn't hurt anyone else. But he wasn't sure that was possible.

"You don't look like you think it would be fun," Jeremy said.

Lowell forced a smile. "My thoughts were wandering." He took a bite of his lunch and watched Jeremy as he began to eat. He needed to spend a lot more time trying to figure all this out.

"How long are you going to be in town?" Jeremy asked.

"I'm not really sure. I was planning to stay a few weeks, but after that I hadn't made plans." He knew it probably wasn't a good idea to stay anywhere for too long. Hopefully Moonstone would be able to work her magic and get this whole thing taken care of. It wasn't as if his former client was going to be able to hire anyone else. Word got around quickly if you stiffed someone or didn't play by the rules. Yes, even in his profession there were rules. You didn't poach on someone else's job unless you wanted them poaching yours. There were also client and employer rules: you completed your job and they paid you. It was that simple. If you didn't complete, then you didn't get paid, but if you did and the client stiffed you, there were consequences. No one would work for you again, and worse, the client could end up at the business end of a contract themselves. The last rule was that once you were in, you didn't get out. And that was the one he was about to break. He'd played by the rules for years, and he'd done so ruthlessly, executing his contracts without remorse or second thought. Lowell had done some of the dirtiest jobs there were. He'd done things that had brought about regime changes in some countries. Hell, if he were caught in many places in the world, his life wouldn't be worth shit.

"Lowell, are you okay?" Jeremy asked.

"Yes," he answered. He needed to keep his thoughts in the here and now. He couldn't afford woolgathering. Alert and focused was how he'd always been, and he needed to continue that. What if he was discovered? Lowell needed to be at the top of his game, and he hadn't been. He'd been distracted for the last few days and he knew why. But that distraction could cost him everything. "I'm fine." He smiled again.

"Where did you grow up?"

"In Los Angeles. My dad worked for Boeing, making airplanes. He worked on the line that made 747s, and my mom stayed home until I was in school then she got a job as a bookkeeper in a small real estate office. My dad passed away when I was twelve, and my mother took care of everything after that. She worked really hard for a long time to make a good home."

"What about friends? Did you have a lot of them? I bet you went to the beach all the time."

"Not very much, no. I got a job and worked to help Mom out, and then after I graduated from high school I went into the service to try to help. After that, it was one thing after another, and here I am."

"You must really think I'm boring," Jeremy said. "With all the things you've done and stuff. All I've ever done is go to college and get a job."

"I don't know what you're thinking, but my life was never glamorous. James Bond and what you see in movies isn't real. There's nothing glorious or pretty about what I do for a living. It takes someone heartless and unfeeling. That's what I am. When I'm on a job, I feel nothing, and if anyone gets in my way I either go around them or I eliminate the obstacle." Lowell saw fear rise in Jeremy's eyes. "That's the truth."

"Then why did you help me yesterday?" Jeremy asked, draining his cocktail glass in a gulp.

"You needed it," Lowell answered. "And I wasn't Spook yesterday, I was me. But I have to tell you that if I'd have been on a job...." He didn't want to truly voice the thought that came to mind. He nearly said he would have stepped over him and kept going, but that would have been a lie. Yes, a week ago he might have done just that and used the confusion of someone passing out as a diversion to accomplish whatever goal he had. But if it were Jeremy, he wasn't sure he could do that. Hell, he *knew* he couldn't do that.

"You would have left me?" Jeremy whispered. He'd picked up his fork but set it back down.

Lowell paused and wondered if he should answer. It was probably best for Jeremy if he thought Lowell was heartless rather than developing feelings and finding out just what kind of person Lowell was. "I... no...," Lowell finally said as pain bloomed in Jeremy's rich blue eyes. That expression hurt worse than the last time he'd been shot. He looked down. He was in more trouble than he could possibly imagine. If all it took was a simple look from Jeremy to make him change his mind now, what would happen in a few weeks, when he had to leave? "I don't think I could ever leave you like that." He looked up from his plate and caught Jeremy's intense gaze. "You realize you aren't good for me."

"Why would you say that?" Jeremy didn't break his gaze, and Lowell found he couldn't, even though he probably should have.

"Because you...." Lowell swallowed. "Because I...." He wanted to snap at Jeremy so he'd stop looking at him like that. "Because you make me feel things I shouldn't. It would be best for both of us if we'd never met and if I simply left and went back to my old life."

"If that's what you want, then why don't you go?" Jeremy asked, his eyes blazing. "Maybe it is best if you simply leave." That was not the reaction Lowell had expected. "But can I ask you something? Are all mercenaries cowards?"

Lowell thought of himself as many things, but that he most definitely was not. "Excuse me?" he growled.

"Well, that seems like the coward's way out to me." Jeremy's voice was hard as nails and reminded Lowell of his first commander. "You say I make you feel things, and that scares you, doesn't it? And you'd rather leave than face what you're feeling."

"You don't understand," Lowell said. He needed to do this for Jeremy's safety.

"I understand plenty. You can tell yourself that you're doing this for me. Blah, blah, blah, whatever makes you feel better." Jeremy motioned around him exaggeratedly. "But the real reason is that you're scared of what might happen if you stay around. You might learn to care for me and then you might get hurt."

"I already care for you. When I saw it was you on the floor of the drugstore, I couldn't breathe for a few seconds. That's the problem. There are people who would use that against me, and they wouldn't think twice about hurting you to do it." Lowell stopped, looking down at his plate for a few seconds. He hated hurting him, but it was the truth. "I let my life get dragged down the rat hole. I don't want it to affect anyone else."

Jeremy sat still without talking for a few seconds. Lowell expected Jeremy to argue, but he didn't. He shifted on his chair and pulled out his phone, looked at the display, and pressed a few buttons. "Excuse me," he said and he stood up and left the table. Lowell figured he'd done what was right, and if Jeremy wanted to leave, maybe that was the best thing. He cared about the spitfire and the thought of him hurt bothered him as much as it would if…. Those thoughts did no good, and he'd taken every precaution to make sure nothing happened to what little remained of his family. He'd even stayed away to ensure it.

Lowell had pretty much lost his appetite. He lifted his glass with a sigh and drained the last of the alcohol. It burned going down, but didn't make up for the cold that had seeped into him. He turned and looked out the window. Jeremy stood by the edge of the sidewalk, still on the phone. He seemed to be listening rather than talking. While Lowell watched, Jeremy nodded, then he pulled his phone away from his ear and shoved it into his pocket. Lowell continued watching, expecting Jeremy to hail one of the taxis, but he turned and headed back into the restaurant. Lowell turned toward the door as Jeremy glided back inside. He came right to the table and sat back down.

"You're completely full of shit," Jeremy announced and picked up his knife and fork.

Lowell gaped. Words failed him. "Excuse me?" he managed to croak after a few moments. "I'm what?"

Jeremy took a bite of his steak and began to chew. "You know, this is really good. How's yours?" He grinned and took another bite. The server stopped by, and Jeremy ordered another drink. "The food here is as amazing as Tristan said it was."

"Are you high or something?" Lowell asked.

"No, I never do that stuff. Rots your brain."

Lowell could not get a grasp on where Jeremy was coming from or what he was thinking. "Let's go back to the beginning. I'm what?"

"I said you were full of shit, and you are."

"Who were you talking to?"

"Zach." The server returned with Jeremy's drink. "Thank you," he said with a brilliant smile and turned back to Lowell. "Zach said that Bull gave him that same line of crap when they first met. He said it was a cop-out you guys use because you're afraid of your own feelings." Jeremy's smile brightened. "Just what I told you earlier." Then his smile faded and he leaned over the table. "Ten minutes ago you were kissing me across the table, and twenty minutes ago you held my hand as we walked down the street. You were clearly having a good time, and so was I. Now I get this line about protecting me and crap." Jeremy's expression hardened. "I'm not some helpless little girl, or someone you need to protect or make decisions for. If that's what you think, then once we're done with this nice lunch, we'll go our separate ways just like you seem to want. I can live with that. But I've been making my own decisions and taking care of myself for almost six years now, and I'm more than capable of continuing to do that with or without you."

"Okay," Lowell said, putting up his hands. "I was trying to look out for you."

Jeremy shook his head. "I know you're bigger than me and think you need to watch out for the smaller guy. While admirable, it's still full of shit. I know what I want, and I'm able to make my own decisions."

Lowell swallowed. Jeremy would have made one hell of a soldier. "Then why did you call Zach?"

"I needed him to confirm why your eyes were so brown." Jeremy smiled. "So it's up to you. If you want to ride off into the sunset and say good-bye, you can do that, and I can't stop you. But if you don't, you better not go making decisions for me or do dumb things because you're trying to protect me. I'm not the helpless heroine from some Edwardian romance novel."

Jesus, he'd just been told. "I was only trying to…."

"I know what you're trying to do. But it isn't necessary. Just talk to me if you want to know something. Zach said Bull was the same way, and while there's nothing wrong with being protective, just don't try to make my decisions for me about what I do and don't want." Jeremy's expression softened.

"So am I forgiven?" Lowell asked.

"Maybe," Jeremy said with a wry grin. "I'll have to think about it." The look told Lowell that Jeremy was teasing. Lowell went back to his lunch, which was getting cold. "What's the most interesting place you've ever been? I told you Bull took us to New York for Christmas shopping and I've been to DC and to New England, but that's about it. Well, of course, Florida too. My parents traveled, but they tended to stay close to home. That is, until they retired. Now they love it in Florida and travel all over, just the two of them." Jeremy took the last bite of his steak. "I'm kind of jealous. I wish we'd have done stuff like drive to the Grand Canyon or Yellowstone when I was a kid. It would have been so beyond cool."

61

Lowell wasn't sure what to say. The places he'd been to were for work. He didn't do touristy things. But he also didn't want to throw a wet blanket on Jeremy's enthusiasm. "I went to Australia a few years ago. It was really cool. They have bats there with three-foot wings. They're huge and they swoop around the trees that have the fruit they like to eat. I saw kangaroos and koalas." Lowell didn't say that he saw them because he'd gone there to meet a client and the guy had them in his private zoo. It was pretty depressing now that Lowell thought about it, but he kept that to himself. That was one thing he was very good at, with most people, anyway—keeping his thoughts and concerns private. That was part of how he survived. "I wasn't there for very long."

"Did you see the Great Barrier Reef? I have always wanted to go there, snorkel, and maybe take diving lessons."

"I didn't. I saw mostly Sydney and a few outlying places." Lowell finished eating and drank his water.

"Do you ever sit back and wonder about the things you've done?" Jeremy asked. "If you did the right thing? If you had the chance, would you make the same decisions?"

Lowell lightly scratched the base of his neck. "I never thought of things in terms of right and wrong. I was hired muscle and I did what I was paid to do. The truth is that I never got close enough to my targets for long enough to get to know them. I located them, did what I was supposed to do, and got out."

Jeremy swallowed. "Did you always kill them?"

Lowell shook his head. "Sometimes I was just a hired gun, a soldier who fought for the client's cause or acted as a private bodyguard. Those were my early jobs. Once I learned how to disguise my appearance and I realized just how close I could get to people by seeming to disappear, I started getting different kinds of jobs." Lowell looked around. He'd been doing it since they arrived. "We should go. This is not a conversation for a public place." Lowell signaled the server, and she came over. He asked for the check, and she left, then returned a few minutes later. Lowell handed her enough cash to cover the bill and a tip, and then he and Jeremy got up and left the restaurant.

"Jeremy," Lowell began once they were on the sidewalk, "I'm not a really nice man. I can't tell you about what I've done, but think of some of the worst things possible and I've probably done it."

Jeremy paused. "Did you herd small children into a school and light it on fire?"

"No," Lowell answered.

"Did you attack small villages of women and children with poison gas?" Jeremy stopped. "I know—did you orchestrate the systematic killing of millions of people in the name of preserving the Aryan race?"

"Now you're being silly, and I was trying to be serious. I really am not a good person."

"Good and bad are subjective. If the Germans had won World War II, then we would all live in a different world and would think very differently about the Holocaust because we would have received very different information about it." Jeremy shivered. "I know that's harsh and scary as hell, but it's true. History is written by the victors. And I saw a glimpse of the person you really are when you held me and helped me drink orange juice on a drugstore floor. Maybe I'm wrong, and if I am, I can live with that. But… it's up to you."

"What do you mean?"

Jeremy stopped walking, and people passed on both sides of them. "I'm just some twink kid you liked the look of at the club and decided to dance with. But you said you want to quit, and if that's true, then it hasn't been that easy on you and you're not as heartless as you think. But it's up to you. You obviously wanted to change enough to come here and take a chance that Bull would help you. Are you just looking for a change in career or a change in your life?"

"How in the hell did you get so smart?" Lowell asked. "When I was in school I was the kid who sat in the back of the room and hoped the teacher never called on them. I was never very tall, but I was always big and…."

"You were the bully, weren't you?" Jeremy asked.

"I didn't think of it like that at the time, but I guess I was. I didn't steal kids' lunch money, but I did throw my weight around to get what I wanted sometimes. Mostly I was a shy kid. I played sports because it was what I thought I should do, but I wasn't very good. I was worse in my classes, so when I graduated, the military was my only option, and I was lucky they took me. There, I found a place where I belonged and skills I was good at." Lowell stopped. "What if this is all I'm good at?"

Jeremy chuckled and then laughed. "Please. We're all good at lots of things." He took Lowell's hand, and they walked along the sidewalk.

People noticed them, and Lowell broke the contact—not that he didn't want to hold Jeremy's hand, but he was not comfortable drawing attention, and Jeremy seemed to understand that without Lowell having to tell him.

Lowell brought the subject back. "So you were saying about good and bad."

"Oh yeah," Jeremy said. "I was saying that you can be who you want to be. You don't have to define yourself by what you did, but by who you are in here." Jeremy touched his chest. "You helped me, and I bet you never thought you would. You just did, and I think that a person's spontaneous reactions are a true measure of the kind of person they are."

Lowell wasn't so sure about that. His gut reactions had been either trained and drilled into him, or disciplined out of him, depending on if they were beneficial or not.

"Can I ask where this introspection came from?" Jeremy asked.

Lowell shook his head. "I wish to hell I knew. For years I worked and did what I was hired to do without thinking about it. I was like a machine, and if anyone got in my way, I dealt with them. Hence my visit to Bull and Zach some months ago. They'd gotten in my way. Only that time, I was the one who was dealt with." That was not one of the particularly brilliant decisions he'd made in his career. "I didn't think about things like good and bad. And I didn't question whether I was doing the right thing."

They approached Jeremy's building and stopped out front. "Then what changed?"

Lowell thought for a few seconds. He'd been trying to figure that out for the last few weeks. "It would be easy for me to say that my last job didn't go well and that was why I realized I needed to get out, but the truth is I don't know." That was a complete, bald-faced lie and he knew it. Lowell knew the reason he had to get out, but he wasn't willing to tell Jeremy or anyone. Maybe someday he could share that part of his life with someone, but not now. "I can say that I know I've made the right decision to get out."

"You did, huh?"

"Yeah." In the last few days, Lowell had come to realize just how alone he'd become. The person he interacted with most was Moonstone, a voice on the other end of a telephone connection. There was no one to do anything with, and as long as he continued to do what he did, there would never be anyone to share his life with. "But how I know is hard to say."

Jeremy looked up at the front of the building. "Tristan went with his boyfriend, Eddie, to visit Eddie's parents, so no one's home. Would you like to come up? I'd really like you to see my collection." Jeremy fidgeted from foot to foot. "I'll understand if you think that's kind of lame."

Lowell smiled. He hadn't been around comic books in a long time. "That would be nice." Jeremy nodded and pulled open the door. Lowell followed, and they went up the flight of stairs. Jeremy got out his keys and unlocked the door.

"It's not much," Jeremy said as they stepped inside. The apartment looked a few steps up from a bare-bones safe house. The furniture was nicer, there were rugs on the floor, and framed posters decorated the walls. Nothing matched, but the place was clean. Jeremy motioned to the sofa. "I'll be right back," he said and hurried away. Lowell scanned the room like he did anywhere he was. He located an escape route in case the front door was blocked. He figured he could go out one of the windows and down to the ground. They were on the second floor, and he'd made jumps like that before. He heard Jeremy in the other room and then his footsteps as he came back carrying a white file box. He plopped himself on the sofa and set the box on the coffee table. "These are the older ones I've got. The newer ones are in other boxes, but I thought these would be the most interesting." Jeremy opened the lid and gently lifted out the books.

They were all in plastic sleeves and had been stacked on top of each other to keep them from creasing or getting bent. "I had this one when I was a kid," Lowell said, when Jeremy handed him a *Spider-Man* comic. Lowell took it and admired the cover. He could remember the graphic on the front of Spider-Man flying through the air with a building collapsing behind him. "I can remember the day I bought it."

"Oh?" Jeremy prompted.

"Yeah. I'd gone to the store the way I always did, and I'd picked out this comic book. I carried it home along with a candy bar and a can of soda. When I came in the house, my mother was waiting for me with tears in her eyes. I was twelve, and she pulled me to her and told me that my father wasn't coming home. There had been an accident, and he was gone." Lowell swallowed hard. "That was it. I was twelve, and my dad was dead. We spent days going through all the funeral things. My mom had to go to work full-time, and I took care of Donny."

"God," Jeremy said.

Lowell handed the comic book back to Jeremy, and he placed it in the box. They looked through all of them. They found a few more that Lowell remembered. Jeremy's collection was quite extensive, with some complete and nearly complete series. It brought back lot of memories that hadn't come to mind in years.

"Who's Donny?" Jeremy asked.

Lowell closed his eyes and wished he hadn't divulged that information. He never would have around others. "He's my brother," Lowell answered. He wasn't going to continue down the path of questions that Jeremy would invariably ask. "Anyway, after that it was just us. Mom managed to hold on to the house, but she worked her fingers to the bone to do it."

"There's more to the story than that." Jeremy set down the comic book he was holding and looked so deeply into his eyes that Lowell became uncomfortable. He was usually the one to make others shift in their chair, not the other way around. "But I won't ask." Jeremy turned back to the pile of comic books and began putting them in the box. "Maybe this wasn't such a good idea."

"It was a fine idea," Lowell said and reached over to Jeremy. He touched his chin, and Jeremy turned back toward him. Lowell didn't think, he simply leaned forward and kissed him. Jeremy stilled, his lips tasting a little like cranberry. Lowell backed away slightly and smiled when Jeremy moved toward him.

When he kissed him again, Lowell had trouble controlling his urges. He'd gone for what he'd wanted for a long time, and every fiber in his being wanted Jeremy. He was so damned hot for him he couldn't stand it. After a few seconds, Jeremy paused and then pulled away. He hurriedly put all the comic books in the box and pushed the table farther away. Then he turned back to Lowell... and pounced. Lowell found his arms full of a hot live wire. Jeremy spread energy in every direction.

For years, Lowell had been in control of every situation, and when he wasn't in control, he was planning how to get it back. There was no way he was going to be able to control Jeremy. The kid was a handful, and at the moment, Lowell had his hands full of Jeremy's ass, and Jeremy squirmed and moaned softly, kissing him harder.

"Jeremy, I take it you like that," Lowell whispered against Jeremy's lips.

"Well, duh," Jeremy said, chuckling back. "I love sex, and, yeah, I like it when you touch me." He wriggled a little, and Lowell thought he was going to go out of his mind. Damn, the way Jeremy moved against him was more intoxicating than hundred-proof bourbon. Jeremy kissed him, and Lowell felt himself pressed back against the cushions. "Is this okay?"

"Duh," Lowell mimicked back, and Jeremy giggled before cutting him off with another searing kiss. Lowell had expected Jeremy to be reticent and a little inexperienced, even after what they'd done on the dance floor. Then, he'd been the aggressor, but Jeremy was surprising him in the most amazing way possible. "You aren't shy, are you?" he murmured, and Jeremy hummed his response. Words ceased as they kissed them away. Lowell held Jeremy close, enjoying his weight on top of him. Jeremy wound his arms around his neck and deepened their kiss.

"You taste like gin," Jeremy whispered. "It's a good thing I like it." He grinned quickly and then leaned forward to suck on the base of Lowell's neck. Damn, Jeremy knew how to kiss and just how to…. He squirmed when Jeremy hit that spot right at the base of his neck. A shiver went through him, and Jeremy must have felt it because he chuckled slightly.

"What is it?" Lowell asked when Jeremy paused.

"I like that I can make a strong guy like you quiver. It's pretty hot."

"Oh, it is?" Lowell said. Then he sat up and brought Jeremy along with him. He continued and set Jeremy on the cushions before scooping him into his arms. "Where's your bedroom?" he asked, his voice deepening.

"First one on the left, caveman," Jeremy answered. Lowell knew a giggle was coming, but he cut it off. There would be no giggling for a while. Lowell figured the next hour or two would be devoted to seeing how many throaty moans he could pull out of Jeremy.

He carried Jeremy down the hall. Jeremy made feeble protests, but Lowell kissed them away. He pushed open the bedroom door with Jeremy's feet and propelled them into the room. He set Jeremy on the bed and kissed him hard while working a hand under his shirt. He quickly found one of Jeremy's nipples with greedy fingers and plucked it lightly. Jeremy moaned into his mouth, pressing forward for more. "No words," Lowell instructed softly. "You can moan and groan all you want, the louder the better."

"You don't like dirty talk?" Jeremy asked.

"It has its place, but definitely not with you." Lowell lifted Jeremy's shirt and tugged it over his head. He was gorgeous, with defined but not bulky muscles. Sleek, like a runner or swimmer. Lowell loved that. He'd long ago figured out that people often liked what they didn't have. He stepped back, opened the buttons of his shirt, and shrugged it over his shoulders. Jeremy opened his mouth and then snapped it shut. Lowell smiled and leaned over him, climbing onto the bed.

He went straight for one of Jeremy's small pink nipples, licking it lightly. Jeremy moaned softly and pressed forward, greedily asking for more. Lowell gave it to him, wrapping his arms around his back and pulling them together, licking and sucking his skin until Jeremy let out a high-pitched keening sound. Lowell wondered if he was hurting him until Jeremy ran his fingers through his hair and pressed Lowell tighter against him.

Jeremy was obviously a complete hedonist. He seemed to revel in every sensation. Lowell was careful to make sure he was only giving pleasure. He liked variety in sex, and in his last few encounters, things had gotten very athletic.

Lowell loved the taste of Jeremy's skin. The salty richness was like a drug he couldn't get enough of. He licked and sucked his way across Jeremy's chest, teasing the other nipple before kissing and licking a trail down his belly. He loved how Jeremy sucked in his stomach, and the closer he got to Jeremy's belt, the more he thrust his hips upward. Without words, Jeremy was very explicit about what he wanted. Lowell licked the skin above the waistband of Jeremy's pants. Jeremy whimpered softly, and Lowell slipped his fingers beneath.

Jeremy gasped, and Lowell stopped, looking into his clouded eyes. He slid his hand farther, and Jeremy's eyes widened when he closed his fingers around his shaft. Jeremy was built more slightly than he was, but he was definitely not smaller. Lowell gripped him tightly, and Jeremy groaned. Then Lowell pulled his hand away and set his fingers to work opening Jeremy's belt.

Once it was open, he kissed Jeremy hard and stroked up and down his chest and belly. Jeremy writhed beneath him, and when Lowell slid his fingers beneath the band of his boxers, Jeremy nipped his lip slightly, not enough to draw blood, but enough to tell him just how nearly out of control he was. Lowell pressed the fabric downward, and Jeremy clung to him, shaking as he got the boxers off. Lowell felt Jeremy's cock strike his hand. He gripped it and stroked him. Jeremy pulled away from his lips and arched his back, letting loose with a deep, throaty groan, and began thrusting into his hand, harder and with near-jackrabbit speed. Lowell tightened his grip and kissed his way back down Jeremy's skin.

He ran his lips along Jeremy's length, and Jeremy greedily thrust forward. "Ahhhh," Jeremy cried, and Lowell gripped him tightly, stroking quickly. Within seconds, Jeremy's belly muscles clenched and released. He thrust upward, and Lowell watched as he clamped his eyes closed.

"Watch me," Lowell whispered, and Jeremy blinked his eyes open. His body shook and then stilled. With a soft cry, Jeremy thrust one more time and came on his chest and belly. His mouth hung open and he gasped and flopped back on the mattress.

"Can I talk now?" he whispered.

"Yes."

"Holy shit," Jeremy exclaimed and then took a deep breath. "That was amazing." Jeremy smiled. "And if you give me a few minutes, I'll be ready to go again."

Now it was Lowell's turn for a "holy shit." Oh, to be that young again. Jeremy sat up and hugged him tight before pulling him down on top of him. Jeremy kissed him, and within a few minutes, he was stroking Lowell's back and sliding his hands down beneath the back of his pants. Lowell was quickly getting the idea that Jeremy was going to border on insatiable, and he liked that.

Jeremy slid his hands around Lowell's side and along his belly before working his belt open. Lowell lifted his hips, and Jeremy took advantage. Lowell didn't want to break their kiss, but he wanted Jeremy's hands on him in the worst way. Jeremy began to squirm under him, and Lowell settled on the bed beside him, intending to hold him, but Jeremy had other ideas. He pushed Lowell onto his back and straddled his hips.

Jeremy laid his hands flat on Lowell's chest and stroked up and down. "I was wondering what you looked like under those baggy clothes you always wear." He carded his fingers through the hair on Lowell's chest. "Now that I'm in charge, I get to talk all I want."

Lowell's chuckle was cut off as Jeremy ran his hand over his nipples, bumping them with his fingers. "Dang, you're sexier than I imagined," Lowell said and pulled him forward, holding Jeremy still. "Why don't you help me get out of these pants?" he whispered. Jeremy giggled and jumped off the bed. Within a few seconds they were off and added to the jumble on the floor. Jeremy's excitement had returned, and he stalked over to the bed and began pulling at Lowell's clothes. Lowell helped him, and soon their clothes littered the floor.

Jeremy climbed back on the bed, throwing his leg over Lowell's hips. He worked his hips, sliding his butt over Lowell's length. Lowell pressed forward, aching for more sensation, and when Jeremy began stroking himself slowly, Lowell nearly lost it. He held Jeremy by the hips and thrust up against him.

"Do you like what you see?" Jeremy asked.

"Oh, yeah," Lowell whispered, his mouth going dry in an instant. Jeremy slid down his legs and gripped him, then started stroking his length. "I'm glad everything's proportional." He waggled his eyebrows and then leaned forward, sucking Lowell into his mouth.

Jeremy was gifted—there was no doubt about it. The way he knew just how to take him, and then the thing he did with his tongue, stole Lowell's breath away. He would have spilled national secrets or worse in order to get Jeremy to continue if he'd stopped. Thankfully, he showed no signs of that and hummed softly, a sexy serenade that only added to the sensation.

Lowell's eyes crossed and he did his best not to grab Jeremy's head and thrust deep and hard down his throat. He had to hold back and he needed to let Jeremy go at his own incredibly, frustratingly slow pace. Jeremy wasn't giving pleasure; he was pulling it from the very depths of their souls. Within minutes, Lowell swore he could see God, he felt so good. Jeremy gripped him hard and slipped his mouth away. Lowell growled low and deep, willing Jeremy to continue.

Jeremy grinned like the cat who'd eaten the canary. "You sure are vocal for a guy who told me not to say a word."

"That was so you'd feel me."

"Well, you'll feel me for days, I swear to God," Jeremy countered, and Lowell had little doubt that every time he closed his eyes he'd remember this moment with Jeremy and he'd feel him deep down inside. Lowell pulled Jeremy to him, cupping his small, tight butt cheeks and pressing their bodies together. He couldn't help flexing his hips, and Jeremy did the same, their cocks sliding along each other. Jeremy filled Lowell's ears with soft whimpers and shallow breaths. Lowell slid his finger along Jeremy's crease and pressed to his tiny opening. Jeremy started and paused.

"What is it?" Lowell asked, wondering what had suddenly taken the fire out of his firecracker. He moved his finger away, and Jeremy loosened up and returned to what he was doing. Lowell caressed his back and rear end, and soon Jeremy was pistoning against him. Everything flew from Lowell's mind except the rich scent and smooth feeling of Jeremy's skin on his. Soon he was flying with Jeremy, holding him like a lifeline. His entire body sang with the sensation, and soon he was on the edge. Jeremy whimpered in his ear, and Lowell tumbled over the edge with Jeremy not far behind.

It was nice to lie still, holding Jeremy and being held in return. Tenderness was not part of Lowell's life, or at least it wasn't something he'd experienced very often in recent memory. After a few minutes, Jeremy squirmed and then got up. He left the room, and Lowell watched his little butt bounce as he moved. Jeremy returned right away with a cloth and towel. Lowell used them to clean up, and Jeremy did the same before scooting out of the room again. He loved the way Jeremy moved and could watch him all day.

When Jeremy returned and climbed onto the bed, Lowell rolled onto his side and held Jeremy close, the warmth of their bodies mixing. "You know, it's okay if you don't like something," Lowell whispered.

"It isn't that I don't like it. I mean, I've never done… you know… that." Jeremy buried his face in the pillow.

Lowell's mind swam with disbelief. Jeremy had been aggressive and forceful in bed, almost tigerlike… that didn't seem possible. "There's nothing to be embarrassed about. But I don't understand."

"The guys think I'm this experienced guy. I've had boyfriends and stuff, but…." Jeremy swallowed. "That requires a lot of trust, and I never had anyone I trusted enough. I've never been inside anyone either. I figured it wasn't right to ask if I wasn't ready to receive. I love blowjobs, though."

"And, honey, you're good at them," Lowell said. Jeremy smiled and shrugged slightly. "So is the aggressiveness a way to keep control so nothing happens that you aren't ready for?"

"Nah." Jeremy grinned impishly. "I love sex, and I have to be honest, I had you whimpering like a little girl."

"You did not."

"I did too, and it was hot to have a strong guy like you whimpering and begging for more. That was way hot." Jeremy settled against him once again. "If you're disappointed…."

Lowell cupped Jeremy's cheek as warmth spread through him from head to toe. "I'm not in any way." Lowell kissed him and tugged Jeremy close, closing his eyes as he wondered what in the hell was happening to him. Sex was for relief, or it had been for so long. This was different, and he didn't know why. That scared the hell out of him, and he didn't know what to do about it. Fear in his profession was controlled and used to sharpen the skills. It kept him alive and helped keep his senses and reflexes sharp. He hated being afraid, so he used it to his advantage whenever possible. But this was a strange kind of fear for him. Usually when it reared its head, Lowell was trying to figure out how to get some distance from a dangerous situation. With this, he was afraid it would end. Everything ended; it always had. Sometimes it was best to end things rather than have them ended for you. Lowell shifted and moved away.

"Are you going to shoot and scoot?"

Lowell stopped. "What?"

"You know," Jeremy said as he lightly stroked his arm, "come and then go." He waved toward the door.

"That's a new one, and no, I was just shifting." Lowell got comfortable and tried to relax.

"Have you had many boyfriends?"

Lowell looked for a way to answer. "I guess I had a boyfriend once. It was just after I'd left the service. I'd gone to a bar because while I was in the army I played by the rules. That life was too important to me to give up for something as ridiculous as sex."

"If it was so important, why'd you leave?"

"I thought there would be more opportunities and I was tired of the political bullshit. I wanted to advance, but being good enough wasn't all that was required. I was stupid enough to think that I had skills people would want, so I looked for greener pastures and found only scorched earth. Anyway, right after I left, I met Harm at a club. We talked and really hit it off, and after a few drinks, we went back to his place and had a great night. He called me the next day and…." Lowell smiled at the memory. "The short version is that he was on leave and we spent the next week together. It was great. But he was still on active duty and was about to ship out. That was his last tour and then he was leaving the service as well." Lowell rolled onto his back and placed his arm over his eyes. "I honestly have no idea why I'm telling you all this shit."

"Because I asked and because I'm listening," Jeremy answered, and Lowell realized it was as good an answer as any.

"I don't think about this shit for years, and with you I remember it all and turn into a Chatty Cathy." All he wanted to know was what the hell had happened to him and why was everything turned on its ear? Jeremy didn't say anything, but when Lowell peeked, he saw Jeremy had propped himself on his hand and was watching him. "Do you really want to hear this?"

Jeremy nodded once. "Only if you want to tell me."

"I don't want to think about this at all," Lowell growled and then wished he hadn't. "I tried to find a job and ended up working as a bodyguard at a club. It was boring as hell after the action I'd seen, but it paid the bills."

"What happened to Harm?"

"He never came home. He was killed in action. Of course I didn't find out until weeks later, when I was asking a buddy about him. It wasn't like his family knew about me, or about him, for that matter." Lowell swallowed. "Then my mom passed away, and I had to figure out how to take care of things."

"So you became a mercenary?"

"Yeah. I got hired with one of the private contracting firms, and things progressed from there." And he'd never looked back, at least not until he'd made the decision to dance with Jeremy at the club. He'd just been killing time and figured he deserved some fun and maybe a frolic with a cute kid. Now here he was spilling his guts out. He was so screwed he had no idea what he was going to do. "So, yeah, I had a boyfriend of sorts once, but that didn't end well. None of my relationships end well, you have to know that. I don't have a good track record with any of them."

Jeremy didn't argue or say something trite. In fact, he said nothing at all. He simply moved closer to Lowell and placed an arm around his chest, his warm breath tickling the skin of his neck. What he'd ever done to deserve someone as understanding and intuitively sweet as Jeremy, Lowell didn't know, and would probably never know. But that fear was rising once again, and Lowell had no idea what he should do. The simple answer was to flee—get out of the situation and just go back to the life he understood and where the rules were known to him. He was sailing into uncharted waters. Like he always did, his mind ran through possible scenarios. All of them ended badly, and some of them ended in disaster. Those made him shudder. Usually his worst scenarios ended with him hurt or worse, but this time the scenarios almost all ended with something bad happening to Jeremy.

"I'm no Boy Scout," Lowell whispered, without realizing he'd said it out loud.

"What?" Jeremy asked drowsily.

"Nothing." He rolled onto his side and pulled Jeremy to him. The room was a little warm, but he was cold and more conflicted than he could ever remember being. He'd always done his job and that was where he'd put all his energy. He hadn't thought about the repercussions or if what he was doing was good or bad. Now, as he lay next to Jeremy, the things he'd done in his life all began to flash through his mind, and the picture wasn't pretty. It took Lowell a long time before he could push all of them back into their compartments and lock them up tight once again.

CHAPTER
SIX

"I'M NOT sure what to do," Jeremy said as he and Zach sat on the floor of his apartment, leaning back against the sofa while they ate Reese's Cups and watched television. Jeremy had gotten home from work an hour earlier. "We had a great afternoon on Sunday, but I haven't heard from him since."

"It's only Wednesday."

"Yeah, I know, but he seemed to be everywhere last weekend, and now he isn't around. I got the feeling when we were together that he was pulling away."

Zach nodded and hummed his agreement. "I wish I knew what to tell you."

"I like him," Jeremy said. "Inside, under the hard exterior, is a guy who's...." He searched for the words, but they failed him. "Sort of like Bull. I know you don't like Lowell, and I can respect that. But I see something in him, and I think it's the same sort of thing you see in Bull. He's hard and growly on the outside, but caring on the inside."

Zach shook his head. "I don't trust the guy, and I don't know if I ever will, but Bull explained that he's willing to give him a chance, so I'll do the same thing for you. But if he hurts you, then all bets are off, okay?"

Jeremy shrugged.

"What did you guys talk about? After you rocked his Casbah." Zach broke into giggles.

"We talked about all kinds of stuff. He told me how he got into doing what he does, about his first boyfriend. It's sad. He met him and they only had a week. Then the guy shipped out and didn't come home." Jeremy could still hear the pain in Lowell's voice.

"He told you stuff like that?"

"Yeah."

"Do you think it was the truth or a story he was making up? These guys have cover stories and aliases that are pretty thorough, and I'm sure he has a line for every occasion." Zach popped the last of his piece of chocolate.

"Where do you get this stuff?" Jeremy challenged. "And for your information, I'm not stupid, and I believe he was telling me the truth. There was too much emotion in his voice. He may be able to fake that, but I don't think so. He told me how his dad died when he was twelve and his mother died after he got out of the army and he had to take care of his brother." Jeremy spoke faster and faster and was getting angry.

"Hey, I'm only saying this because I care and don't want you hurt. You called me and asked me to come over because you wanted to talk, so there's no need to get huffy." Zach picked up another pack of Reese's and began unwrapping it.

"I know. I'm sorry." Jeremy reached over and hugged Zach. "I'm disappointed, I guess. He knows where I live and I'm sure he can find out whatever information he wants to know about me. So he could always call."

"I don't know. But he'll show up when he's ready," Zach said. "I still don't like him." Zach stood up. "Bull had to go into the club because he's auditioning some live music acts and won't be home until really late, so do you want to play some games or something? You need to get your mind off Spook. Remember, there's a good possibility that he may not show up again at all."

That hit a nerve, and Jeremy swallowed hard to keep from arguing.

"Hey, I'm just telling you the truth," Zach said. "I know he told you stuff, but that doesn't mean you really know him or have a clue what he's up to. Bull told me he thought he was sincere and all about wanting to get out of the mercenary business, but…." Zach shrugged and didn't finish his thought.

"It's nice to have my friends supporting me," Jeremy said, grousing a little.

"We are, and I am. I'm worried about you. I don't trust him. I don't know him well enough to like him or not, but I don't trust him and I don't know if I ever could. He threatened Bull, and while Bull may be willing to overlook that, I'm not sure I can." Zach stopped and calmed down. "But I know you like him and that's fine. You see something in him that the rest of us don't. All I'm saying is just make sure it's real."

"If he ever shows up again," Jeremy muttered.

"And if he doesn't, then it's his loss and not yours. Because if he can't see what a wonderful person and friend you are, then he isn't good enough for you, and there are plenty of other guys who will be dying to have you." Zach hugged him again. "Now let's do something besides talk about men. We need to get our minds off them."

"All right, what do you want to play?"

"I wanna shoot stuff," Zach said, as if Jeremy didn't know. Zach loved games like *Call of Duty,* so Jeremy put in the original version and they played for the next hour. Jeremy got immersed in the game and forgot some of his frustration. Zach checked his phone between games and got his messages.

"Is it something important?"

"Bull. He says he wants me to hear the bands. You can come with me if you want," Zach offered, but Jeremy wasn't in the mood.

"No, thanks."

"I'll stay if you want," Zach offered.

"It's not necessary. Bull wants your opinion. Go on and spend some time with him." That was part of what hurt. Jeremy wished he had a guy like Bull in his life, someone who asked his opinion and valued him for his mind and point of view the way Bull valued Zach.

Zach got his stuff, and Jeremy cleaned up. When Zach was ready, they said good-bye and hugged. Then Zach left, and Jeremy was alone in the quiet apartment. He turned on the television and settled on the sofa. Tristan came home a half an hour later, showered, and then rushed out again, saying he and Eddie were going out to dinner. "I probably won't be home," he added with a grin.

"Have fun," Jeremy called.

"I will," Tristan said and stopped at the door. "Promise me you won't sit home and wait for him to call or something."

"You did with Eddie, remember?" Jeremy teased.

"I know, and it sucked. Either he'll call or he won't. But don't hang around here like you have for the last two days. Go out and have fun. Kevin is around—give him a call and see if he wants to come over or go out to the club. Dance and have a good time. It won't be busy, so you can just relax and have some fun." Tristan rushed back and hugged him. "You're my best friend and I want you to be happy. I hate it when you aren't your usual self. You've been quiet and standoffish, and that isn't like you." Tristan hugged him again and said good-bye before leaving the apartment.

Jeremy watched television for a little while longer before deciding that Tristan was right. This wasn't him. He wasn't a mopey person, and he hated being this way. *So what if Lowell wasn't interested or what the hell ever.* He wasn't going to sit around and wait by the phone like some fifteen-year-old. He was going to go and find something to do. He grabbed his things and turned out the lights before hurrying out and down the stairs.

On the street, he wasn't quite sure which way he wanted to go. He wasn't interested in going to the club and he wasn't hungry. So he opted for the bookstore. They had a comic book section, and he figured he could poke around to see if there was anything new. He walked to the block between Second and Third. There was a neighborhood tucked between the more major streets, and he loved walking that way. The houses were small and older, with pretty yards and lights hung in the trees. For him, it was a small, magical place hidden in the center of the city.

He walked through the neighborhood, looking around and smiling. Once he came to the cross street, he headed up a block and pulled open the door to the store. Perry, the guy behind the counter, said hello, and they talked for a few minutes. Then Jeremy wandered to the back and perused the selection. He passed over what he'd seen already, looking for anything new.

He jumped when someone touched his shoulder. Jeremy turned around, expecting Lowell for some reason. Maybe it was the way the touch settled gently on his shoulder. But he found Kevin standing behind him. "I thought I might find you here," Kevin told him. "Tristan said he was going out, and then Zach called a little while ago. It seems our mother hen, Zach, was worried about you and thought you might want some company. He suggested I try your usual spots."

"You didn't need to come looking for me. I'm fine." Jeremy smiled. "But I'm glad you're here." It was very nice to have some company. "Were you looking for something?" He swallowed when Kevin continued looking at him. "They have some great Batman books right there."

"Thanks," Kevin said, but he didn't turn away.

"You're staring," Jeremy said and turned to look behind him to see what Kevin was looking at so intently. "Is something wrong?" he added in a whisper as two other guys started leafing through the displays nearby.

"No. I was just wondering if something was wrong with you. I've noticed that you've been quiet and unapproachable, and the last time that happened was just before you got the flu last year, remember? You were so sick, and you got this same way then." Kevin had decided about a year ago that his true calling was in health care. He hadn't been sure he could do it, but he'd gone back to school after a few years away and had attacked his classes with gusto. Everyone was proud of him, including Kevin's parents, who after seeing his dedication had started chipping in to help out, especially after Zach had moved in with Bull. Kevin had let the apartment he and Zach had shared go and he was living alone in a tiny place while he worked for the summer. His lease was up in the fall, and Kevin hadn't decided what he was going to do yet.

"I'm feeling fine," Jeremy told him. "I've been a little preoccupied for the last few days. But nothing is really wrong."

"Well, something is. Zach said you got busy with that Spook guy. Are you really interested in him, or was it a ride on the wild side?" Kevin bumped his shoulder and giggled at his own joke.

"I like him, I think," Jeremy answered honestly. "But I think I'm dumb for even considering that there might be more to it than just some fun. Yeah, he told me stuff, but Zach thinks it was all an act. I thought he was telling the truth, but who the hell knows or cares." Jeremy's voice got louder, and he looked around before lowering it to a more private level. "I'm beginning to think that Zach might be right and...."

Kevin shook his head and looked up from where he'd been perusing the books. "I think you need to follow your own heart rather than listening to Zach all the time. He found someone and he's happy, so it's easy for him to give advice to everyone else." Kevin turned back to the stack of comic books. "I know he means well, but he forgets what it's like for the rest of us. We go out and try to meet people, but we only see the same people over and over again." He continued fingering through the stack.

"That's one you don't have," Jeremy said, realizing that Kevin wasn't really watching. He pulled out the book and handed it to Kevin, who smiled and took it before setting it down on top of the display. "You weren't really looking, were you?"

"I guess not," Kevin said. "There's an old song about 'looking for love in all the wrong places,' and I'm really thinking that's what we've been doing. It isn't like the guys who come to the club are interested in anything more than a quick hookup and then they're on to the next guy in line." Kevin picked up the comic book. "I want more than that, and I think that's what you're looking for too. Lightning struck for Zach and he found Bull there, but I guess I don't think that counts, since he didn't snag one of the guys at the club. He fell in love with the owner, and there are only so many of those." Kevin turned away again.

"What? You're trying to tell me something, but I'm not getting it." Jeremy turned Kevin around. "Are you in love with me?"

Kevin gasped and then started to laugh. "God, no."

"Thank goodness for that," Jeremy said more bitchily than he intended. Kevin hip-bumped him lightly, and then both of them started laughing. "So who is it that you…." Jeremy paused. "Are you saying you like Harry?"

Kevin went back to looking through the stacks.

"You do, don't you?"

"Yeah. I think he's hot, but he hardly comes out of the office except to talk to Bull and watch things in the club. Then he goes back without really talking to anyone. I've tried to get up the nerve to go over and speak to him, but I've wimped out so many times now, I think it's hopeless." Kevin stopped moving and rested his hand on the top of the comic books.

Jeremy understood. Harry always kept his distance. He watched everything, and though Jeremy had heard him talking about being with other guys, it all seemed rehearsed, like he was saying what he thought he had to say. "I don't know what's up with Harry, but the next time you see him, go ask him to dance. What can it hurt?"

"I don't know. I'm starting to think it's hopeless and I should let go of this… I don't know what to call it, but I keep thinking about him, though he's hardly said two words to me except for the few times he's stopped by the table when we're all there."

"So talk to him. Or you could ask Bull about him first, see what the deal is," Jeremy suggested. He wanted Kevin to be happy. "Can I ask why you like him?"

Kevin shrugged and then smiled, which turned to a chuckle and then a deep laugh. "I have no fricking idea. Why do you like this Spook guy?"

Jeremy joined in Kevin's mirth. "Same answer, different guy." The people in the store were looking at them, and Jeremy figured Perry was going to come over to find out what the hell was up with them any second, but he didn't care. "Come on, let's put all this talk of *men* behind us and have a good time, okay?"

"Yeah," Kevin agreed, and they turned back to the stacks of comic books, looking through and debating, almost arguing, the merits of the various characters and superheroes. They laughed, joked, mock fought, and picked at each other for the next hour. And it was just what Jeremy needed—something normal and fun. Why was it that their love lives always seemed to turn them every which way? It had happened to Zach and Bull, and now it was happening to them. "You know, sometimes men suck."

Jeremy turned to Kevin. "And not in a good way," they said together and broke into peals of laughter. Perry walked over and joined them.

"You two seem to be having fun," he observed.

"Just dissing men," Jeremy told him.

Perry was definitely not the stereotypical kind of guy you would expect to own a center city bookstore, let alone one that stocked a lot of comic books. For one thing, he was dreamy-looking, with huge blue eyes and long blond hair that damn near sparkled in the sun when it shone through the windows. Women would kill for his color hair. He was tall and lanky, with a smile that could stop traffic. Jeremy had asked him why he worked here and had been surprised to learn that he owned the place. He'd started the business after college, and once the big chain stores moved in, he'd branched out into areas that they didn't carry—one of them being comic books. "All right. I hope I'm not included."

"Nope. I should have been more clear. We're specifically dissing men who we're interested in but who don't seem to have a clue," Jeremy clarified. Perry was straight, as far as he knew, but a really cool guy. At one time or another, all four of their group had made eyes at Perry, and he hadn't seemed to notice any of them. However, there was still doubt in Jeremy's mind, because while Perry never seemed interested in guys, there were never any girls around either, and Lord knew when Perry walked down the street, women turned to watch. "So, how are things with you?"

"Fine," Perry said with a smile. "Business is good and I've been thinking of expanding. The building next door is going to go up for sale, and I was thinking of buying it and adding a coffee shop with some baked goods too. My mom is thinking of retiring from her office job, and she has been baking for years. She asked about me adding some things like that to the store, and I think it's a good idea."

"So do I," Jeremy piped up. "That would be great. This area needs something like that, and it would fit in the neighborhood. Are you going to build an entrance through the store, or would you keep the two separate?"

"I haven't decided," Perry said. "I have to get the building next door first, but I'd like to be able to join them together. Either way, I'll probably wait to see if the idea works. How are you guys doing? Other than the man troubles," he added with a smile, and Jeremy saw Perry glancing at Kevin occasionally, so maybe Perry wasn't as straight as he'd thought. Jeremy excused himself and went to look at the collectibles section. He kept an eye on Kevin and noticed that Perry stuck around for quite a while and rarely took his gaze away from Kevin. So much for his gaydar, but if Kevin and Perry liked each other, then so much the better.

Perry couldn't stay too long and left to help a customer at the register. Jeremy returned to where Kevin was gathering up the few things he wanted to purchase.

"You're really subtle, you know that?" Kevin asked.

"Come on, he kept looking at you, so I thought that maybe—" Jeremy tilted his head toward Perry.

"He has a girlfriend," Kevin told him with an impish grin. "Apparently he was looking at me because he heard that I used to work in a coffee shop when I was in high school, and he wanted to know what I thought of his idea and talk about some of the ins and outs of running that kind of business." Kevin rolled his eyes. "You're such a matchmaker."

"I...." Jeremy looked toward where Perry was talking with the customer and tried not to chuckle. "Okay, I'm sorry." Jeremy hadn't found anything he wanted to buy, so he accompanied Kevin to the register. Kevin paid, and they both said good-bye and left the store.

"Do you want to come to my place, or we can go to yours?" Kevin asked, and Jeremy motioned in the direction of his place and they began to walk. "So tell me about this guy," Kevin prompted after a while.

"I'd rather not," Jeremy said. "I've talked about him and spent enough time wondering if he'll call or come by. I think maybe it's time to chalk the whole thing up as a mistake and move on. If he calls, I'll listen to what he has to say, but...."

"Come on," Kevin said, and Jeremy was sure he was rolling his eyes. "You never let things go like that."

"Thanks...," Jeremy groused lightly.

"No, it's a good thing. You're loyal and you stick things out to the end. It's one of the things that make you special. So don't change that." Kevin put his arm around Jeremy's shoulder. "I think we've been talking about this stuff so much that we're all making each other crazy. None of us can make your decisions for you, and while we all care about each other, neither Zach, nor me, nor Tristan knows what you want or how you feel."

Jeremy nodded and said, "You realize we're beginning to sound like the girls did in high school. Come on, let's get home." Jeremy looked around and realized it was starting to get dark. The downtown area was safe enough, but Jeremy picked up his pace just a little. They walked the few remaining blocks, talking a little and paying attention to what was around them. He and Kevin arrived at his building, and Jeremy unlocked the outer door. They walked up the stairs, Jeremy opened the apartment door, and they went inside.

Someone had been inside—Jeremy knew it. The window in the living room was open, and he didn't remember leaving it that way. Even though the apartment was on the second floor, they didn't keep windows open when they weren't home. "What's wrong?" Kevin asked.

"I don't know. I think someone has been here." Jeremy wasn't sure if he should go farther inside. *What if whoever it was was still here?*

"I don't hear anything," Kevin said and looked around. Before Jeremy could stop him, Kevin stepped inside and walked down the hallway toward the bedrooms. Jeremy waited and hoped like hell nothing happened. Jeremy saw him open the doors, so he finally joined him, peering inside. The rooms looked the same, but yet it felt like they weren't. He stepped into his own and peered around. The small closet door stood ajar, and Jeremy knew he had left it closed. He always kept the door closed.

"Someone has been here. The closet is open."

"Is anything missing?" Kevin asked. Jeremy shook his head. It didn't look like it. "Maybe Tristan came home and needed to borrow a shirt or something. There's nothing messed up." Kevin left, and Jeremy heard him in Tristan's room. "This looks to be okay," he called and then joined him back in his bedroom. "I think you're imagining things."

"But I don't remember leaving the window open, and—"

"Why wouldn't you leave the window open on a day like this? It's warm, and the window was probably already open and you forgot to close it," Kevin offered logically.

Jeremy knew Kevin was probably right, but he couldn't shake the feeling that someone had been here. But why anyone would break in and not steal stuff was beyond him.

"You're right," Jeremy said. "What do you want to do?" They ended up watching television, ordering pizza for a late dinner, and gabbing until late in the evening. More than once Jeremy checked his phone for messages, but there were none.

"I need to get home," Kevin said. "We both have to work." Jeremy nodded, and Kevin got his things and got ready to go. "Do you know if Tristan will be back?"

Jeremy shook his head. "He's been spending more and more time at Eddie's." He sighed. "Now I know how you felt when Zach started dating Bull." It was difficult not to feel a little abandoned. Jeremy was happy for Tristan, but things seemed to be happening awfully fast. They hadn't been dating that long, at least not as far as Jeremy was concerned.

"At least I'd met Bull. None of us have ever seen this Eddie. For a while I was wondering if he was a figment of Tris's imagination, but then I've seen that happy smile on his face when he gets back, and no imaginary boyfriend is going to do that." Jeremy laughed. "I told him the last time I saw him that we all wanted to meet this Eddie and that if he didn't bring him around next weekend, I was going to follow him and introduce myself."

"You didn't?" Jeremy said, gleefully appalled.

"I did. And I asked him if he was ashamed of Eddie and that's why we'd never met him. Tristan promised we'd meet him at Pride this weekend."

"I asked Lowell if he'd go with me, and he said he would, but I doubt that's going to happen," Jeremy said.

"Then you can stick with me and we'll have a good time," Kevin said, and Jeremy nodded. Kevin checked his watch and began cleaning up their mess.

"I'll get that. You go on home before it gets too late," Jeremy said. "And call me so I know you're okay." The whole thing with thinking someone had been in the apartment still had him a little spooked. Kevin promised he would and left the apartment after giving Jeremy a hug. Jeremy closed the door, locked it, and finished cleaning up and throwing away all the trash. Once he was done, he settled on the sofa until it was time for him to go to bed. He felt better once Kevin called to say he'd made it home okay.

Jeremy still kept hoping Lowell would call, but he didn't, so he got cleaned up and went to bed. He'd turned out the lights and rolled over when he heard Tristan come home early and wondered if everything was okay. He heard him moving through the apartment and then using the bathroom. Then Tristan's door closed quietly, and Jeremy closed his eyes and finally went to sleep.

He woke to the sound of gentle rain as well as a buzzing sound that took a few minutes to register as the front door of the building. He checked the clock and wondered who in the hell could have stopped by at this hour of the morning. He had to get up anyway, and his alarm went off as he pushed back the covers, as if to reinforce that fact. He slapped it silent and got up to find out what was going on. He'd almost reached his bedroom door before he remembered to pull on shorts.

The buzzer rang again and he opened the apartment door. The automatic door release was now out of order, so he walked down the stairs. The windows in the front door were opaque. Jeremy could see movement on the other side, but not enough to identify who was there. It was a stupid choice of the landlord to put in glass like that, but he'd probably gotten the glass cheap. Jeremy pulled open the door and saw Lowell standing on the stoop, drenched from head to toe. "What are you doing here?" Jeremy asked and then motioned for him to come inside. "And why are you soaked to the skin?" Jeremy closed the door after him, and Lowell dripped on the old carpet in the entry, shivering quietly. "I don't think I have any clothes that will fit you except some shorts, but come on up." Jeremy wasn't sure what to make of this, but he wasn't going to let Lowell catch pneumonia.

Lowell squished as he climbed the stairs behind Jeremy, and he tried to stay away from the drips and wetness. Once inside the apartment, Jeremy closed the door and hurried to his room. He found a pair of shorts and a T-shirt someone had given him from a concert. He usually wore a medium and even they were sometimes big on him, but this was a large and the one time he'd put it on he'd swum in it. But he figured it should fit Lowell.

"What's going on?" Tristan asked with a yawn, peering around his door. "Oh," he said. He must have seen Lowell.

"If you want to get cleaned up first, go ahead," Jeremy said, and Tristan nodded and then disappeared back in his room. Jeremy grabbed an extra towel from the bathroom and hurried into the living room. "Take off the wet stuff and put this on. It isn't much, but it's dry."

"Thanks," Lowell said and stripped off his wet shirt and shoes.

Jeremy handed Lowell the towel. "What were you doing out in the rain at this hour?"

"I've been working to put together my insurance policy, the way Bull suggested. I was able to get a lot of the information I needed. I've also done a lot of thinking. I spent most of last night trying to run things through in my mind." Lowell absently rubbed his chest with the towel, and Jeremy saw him shiver. He seemed absent and his speech was a little halting.

"Why don't you go into my bedroom and change out of all this wet stuff? There's an empty clothes basket in the corner. You can put them in there and I'll run them down to the laundry room and put them in the dryer." Jeremy checked the clock on the Blu-ray player and wondered if he should take a personal day at work. It was already going on seven. He decided he'd better, because this was probably going to take more than a few minutes, and he would otherwise have to hurry if he was going to make it on time.

Lowell walked down the hall and went into the bedroom. Jeremy made his phone call. While he was on the phone, he heard the shower start. When Lowell came out of the bedroom, Jeremy took the basket of wet clothes and grabbed some quarters from his dresser before hurrying to the basement. He wrung out the sopping pants, shirt, and underthings before throwing them in the dryer and starting it. He left the basket and went back upstairs. Tristan was out of the bathroom and dressed. "Where's Lowell?"

"I think he went in your room," Tristan said with a yawn. "Oh, man, I was out too late last night." The scent of coffee began filling the room. "I made some extra." Tristan went back to his room and returned a few minutes later, ready for work. He poured some coffee in a travel mug, said a quick good-bye, and left. Jeremy found Lowell in the bedroom, sitting on the edge of the bed.

"Your clothes are in the dryer," Jeremy explained, and Lowell nodded. "Do you want to tell me what's going on, and why, after what we did, you stayed away? You made me feel like a boy slut. I thought you liked me, but no call, no nothing…."

"I really thought it was best," Lowell began.

"Here we go with that again."

"You can't understand, and I don't want you to." Lowell paused. "You have a life that's good and it isn't tainted by all the things I've done in my life. And believe me, the more information I add to my insurance policy, the more I remember all the things I've done. There aren't seven deadly sins, there are really eighty, and I've done them all at least twice. Anyway, I got a lot of what I needed together, and I found a place that will house it for me and help me put my plans into action. It took more time than I expected because it wasn't simple, but the plans are well on the way."

"That's good, but it doesn't explain the game of 'keep away.'"

"I really thought that if I disappeared, it would be best." Lowell turned and lightly stroked Jeremy's cheek. "I can't expect you or anyone to understand."

"So you came by this morning to say good-bye," Jeremy said flatly. "If that's what you did, then fine, say it and go. Maybe you're right. Maybe you aren't good for me. Hell, I don't know what's good for me sometimes, but obviously you have a lot more experience and information than I do." Jeremy's voice dripped with sarcasm. "I have got to be completely out of my mind."

"Why do you say that?"

Jeremy stood up and began pacing the small area between the bed and door. "Because I'm having an argument with someone who's made his living killing people." Jeremy stopped and stared deeply at Lowell. "How do I know you won't lose your temper and take me out? Maybe I should have my head examined for even being in the same room with someone like you. After all, assassins and all are coldhearted people who don't feel anything for anyone." Jeremy made his voice as hard as he possibly could.

"I'd never hurt you," Lowell whispered.

"See, I knew that. I always knew that," Jeremy said.

"I know you're upset. But it's because I don't want to hurt you that I've been doing all this and why I stayed away. I kept thinking if I was gone, then you'd be safe. And that's the best thing possible. I can be happy if I know you're safe and that for once in my life I truly did the *right* thing by someone else."

"I think a lot of that is because you're afraid. I know you don't trust easily." After all, it wasn't lost on Jeremy that Lowell had never told him his last name. Jeremy knew for Lowell that required a high level of trust that wouldn't come easily to someone who'd spent his life in the shadows. "But I have to ask how much of this is concern for me and how much is because you're afraid of getting hurt?" Lowell didn't answer. "I thought so."

Lowell growled and stood up, holding Jeremy's shoulders. "There is very little in this world that I'm afraid of. I've stared at death more times than I can count. I was shot at in two wars and hit in one. I've looked down the barrel of a gun at another man and seen him fall when I've pulled the trigger, then gotten paid, and I felt nothing when it was done. Targets have gotten so close I could smell them, and they didn't even know I was there. I didn't let them hear me breathe and as soon as they turned, they dropped. Many times in my life it has been kill or be killed, and a lot of the time it was just kill. That's what I was hired to do. But fear… I never knew real fear until I met you. I can deal with getting hurt. I've been hurt physically and emotionally more times than I can count. What I can't deal with is *you* being hurt." Lowell took a deep breath and held it. Then he released it very slowly. "Not even the first time I was in combat and there were bullets everywhere and shells exploding all around have I felt such fear as the thought of something happening to you."

"But why?" Jeremy asked. "Why me?"

"I don't know, except that you woke something in my heart that I thought was dead and gone forever. But I think the more important question is why would you want someone like me in your life? You have everything going for you. Why would you turn your life upside down for me? That's what I really can't understand and don't want to happen. I made a ton of mistakes because I did what I thought I needed to. You don't need to pay for those mistakes, and anyone in my life will pay in some way or other," Lowell told him earnestly.

"Is that why you were wandering around early in the morning in the rain? To figure out how you were going to tell me this? Because you probably could have called and saved yourself a bout of pneumonia and me days of waiting by the phone." Jeremy reached around Lowell's arms, knocking his hands off his shoulders. Then he grabbed Lowell's shoulders. "You're under the impression that your decisions and what you want are the only things that count. I've got news for you—what I want counts as well." Jeremy gave Lowell a shove; he took a step back and then fell onto the bed. "I think it's time to get it through your head that I can make decisions for myself. That I have a right to make my own decisions, and if I don't understand something that involves me, you need to explain it to me." Jeremy climbed on the bed and straddled Lowell, staring down at him. He knew they were in a very sexy position, but he was too angry at that moment to really care. "Do you think I want to come home to someone in my kitchen the way Zach did when you paid him and Bull a visit? No, thank you. But what I do want is to come home to you in my kitchen maybe making a little dinner for the two of us."

Lowell's eyes widened. "You think I can cook?"

"That's not the point," Jeremy countered, rolling his eyes. "I do appreciate you thinking about me and all, but how about talking to me too? You don't have to take the world on your own shoulders. My mom told me that the best part about having someone was that they were there to help carry the heavy stuff."

Lowell nodded, and Jeremy moved closer. He could feel his heat through the thin clothes they were wearing.

"I'm trying to protect you," Lowell said. "I don't want you to come home and find someone waiting for you or wonder if someone has been in your house while you're away. I do that every single day."

Jeremy went stock-still.

"What?" Lowell asked.

"That happened last night." Jeremy shifted off Lowell and sat on the mattress. The amorous thoughts that had begun to creep into his mind were gone in an instant, and Jeremy's smile slipped from his mouth.

"What happened?" Lowell asked quickly. "Tell me everything."

"I was at the bookstore downtown where I get comic books and stuff, and I met Kevin. We joked around for a while and then walked back here. When I came in, I thought something was off. The window was open, and I thought I'd closed it before I left. My closet door was cracked open, and it's always shut, because otherwise if the wind comes up, it blows it open and it hits the wall. You don't want that in the middle of the night."

"Show me what was different," Lowell said, his body instantly filling with tension and then relaxing in a forced way. Jeremy got off the bed and led Lowell to the closet door.

"It was open like this," Jeremy explained and cracked the closet door. Lowell examined the door and then the inside of the closet. He looked around the rest of the room as Jeremy stood back. Lowell came right up to him and leaned close. Jeremy tensed as his warm breath tickled his ear. "Was anything else moved or touched? Don't answer, just point."

Jeremy hadn't noticed anything.

"There are marks in the dust on the top of your dresser. Have you moved anything lately?" Jeremy answered by shaking his head. Lowell went back over to the dresser and began moving things. He smiled after a few seconds and motioned him out of the room. "What about the living room?" he asked, and Jeremy quietly explained about the window being opened. Lowell knitted his brows together and checked out the casing. Then he wandered through the living room, looking at things, then carefully picking them up and putting them back down. He checked behind pictures and continued looking around. He also checked Tristan's room and then the bathroom. "Go get dressed and we'll get some coffee. I also want to call Bull," Lowell whispered into his ear. Jeremy nodded and went into his bedroom. "Is the laundry room at the bottom of the stairs?" Lowell asked out loud.

"Yes. I can get your clothes for you, though. They should be dry."

"No, I'll get them," Lowell said. Jeremy had finished dressing and returned to the living room. Lowell left the apartment and returned with his dry clothes. He pulled off the ones he'd been wearing, set them on the sofa, and dressed quickly. Then he settled on the sofa and turned on the television. Jeremy wondered what was going on, but he sat down too. "Get some umbrellas if you have them and move very quietly. Take your phone and anything else you'll need for the day with you. But first, come here…." Lowell pulled him close and started kissing him. Jeremy was so confused he wasn't sure what was happening. Lowell got more intense and gently pressed him back on the sofa. While his touch was nice, it felt mechanical and flat, not like the other night. "Get up and close the window and drapes in a hurry, smile and giggle in that cute way you have when you do it." Lowell kissed him again, and Jeremy giggled like he'd been told. Then he got up, closed and locked the window, and pulled the drapes.

"God, sweetheart, come here. I want you so bad," Lowell said in a bedroom voice as he got up off the sofa and silently moved through the room. Jeremy was confused as hell. He got his things and listened as Lowell made soft noises just like he had the night they'd been together. This was obviously acting, and Jeremy wondered if Lowell had been acting when they were together. He suddenly felt very cold and wondered if he wanted to go anywhere with Lowell. He thought he knew what was right and when he was being played, but obviously he didn't. Maybe there was a lot more of this Spook in Lowell than he'd thought. Hell, maybe Lowell was all Spook, and he'd been a fool to believe otherwise.

CHAPTER
SEVEN

LOWELL CONTINUED his banter. He could see that Jeremy was upset, but his entire attention was focused on getting them out of the apartment. Between the television and his banter, he hoped he'd thrown off anyone who might be listening, and there was no doubt in his mind that someone was listening. Why, he wasn't sure. Lowell hadn't thought it was possible that he'd been found, but that was now a distinct possibility. He'd only been to Jeremy's a few times, though, and not in days. Something else was going on, and he needed some time to figure out what it was. He also needed some help, and the only person he could turn to for that kind of help was Bull.

He finished their little "encounter" and turned down the television. Then they quietly left the apartment with the television still on. He led the way and went into the laundry room, where there was a back door to the building. As soon as they were outside, they both put up their umbrellas, and Lowell led them down the back alley toward one of the main streets. They hailed a cab and got inside. Lowell gave instructions to take them to his hotel and settled back on the seat. "It's going to be fine. I won't let anything happen to you," he whispered in Jeremy's ear. This was what he'd been afraid of all along, that his life would somehow intrude on Jeremy. He deserved better than this.

"What's going on?" Jeremy asked, and Lowell glanced toward the driver. Jeremy nodded his understanding, and Lowell pulled out the phone, looked up Bull's number, and made the call, hoping he would answer.

Thankfully, he got Bull. "Jeremy needs your help," he began.

"What's going on?"

"I'm not sure. But can you come to my hotel? I need to explain where we can't be overheard." He explained which hotel, and Bull said he'd be there as soon as he could. "Call me at this number, and we'll meet you." He didn't want to say the room number to the driver. Lowell had learned to hold everything as close to the vest as possible. He hung up and tugged Jeremy to him. "Bull is going to join us in a while."

Jeremy nodded and leaned close, but his body was filled with tension. Lowell knew Jeremy was getting a good dose of what his life was like. This was exactly what he'd wanted to keep him from. The cab ride didn't take long, and they got out at the hotel. Lowell paid the driver in cash, and then they hurried inside.

A crowd of business people packed the lobby. The hotel he was staying in was very nice, and as Lowell had found out, connected to a downtown shopping center and office complex, so there was always a lot of traffic in the lobby area. That made it relatively easy to come and go without being noticed. They reached the elevators, and Lowell pressed the button for the twelfth floor. "I'll explain everything once we're in the room," he said on the way up. Lowell led the way down the hall and slipped his keycard into the lock. The light turned green, and he opened the door, walked inside, and instantly scanned the room for anything that might have been disturbed. Jeremy followed him in.

He got Jeremy seated in one of the chairs and checked that everything was set. Then he took out a frequency detector and checked that no one was listening before closing the curtains. "Okay, someone put some listening devices in your apartment. There's one in your room on the television and one in the living room on the side of the poster frame above the sofa. I suspect there's one in the other bedroom as well."

"Why?"

"That's what I mean to find out."

Jeremy gasped. "We were talking. They heard everything you said."

"No. They heard a bunch of static and a garbled mess because I turned on this." Lowell pulled out his phone. "I developed an app that sends out interference. I always turn it on when I'm in a strange place. But I turned it off once you told me what you suspected because I didn't want whoever bugged your place to know that I knew the listening devices were there. It's been on since we left your place."

"Why would the people who were after you bug my place?" Jeremy asked.

"I doubt this is connected with me. The person who placed the bugs knew how to get into the apartment pretty well. They must have come in through the window, been disturbed, and not been able to close it when they left. Whoever did it didn't want you to know they had been there, but they did a pretty amateurish job of it. I could have placed those bugs in much better places and you would never have known I was there." Lowell sat on the edge of the bed and leaned closer to Jeremy. "The thing I want to tell you is that you have good instincts. You thought something wasn't right when you came into the apartment. Don't dismiss that feeling. It wasn't as though you thought someone might have broken in and had been worried about it the entire way home. You went in and felt something was wrong." Jeremy nodded. "In the future, if that happens, turn around, leave, and call someone right then. Don't investigate on your own. Call me, call Bull, call the police, but don't take any chances."

"Okay," Jeremy agreed. Lowell's other phone rang, and he dug it out of his pocket.

"Bull, we're in 1210," Lowell said when he answered the phone, and Bull told him he'd be right up.

"You said you don't think this is connected to you. If not, then who bugged my apartment? Why would you think that? People didn't bug my place before you got here, so it has to be your fault," Jeremy said.

"One question at a time." A knock sounded on the door, and Lowell got up and walked over. Through the peephole he saw Bull in the hall. Lowell opened the door to let him in. He half expected Zach to be right behind him, but Bull was alone.

"What did you do to Jeremy?" Bull asked, scanning the room.

"I'm okay, Bull," Jeremy said. "Someone bugged the apartment."

"It was an amateurish job. They picked the window lock and left two listening devices that I know of. There's probably a third in the other bedroom, but I didn't look long enough to find it." Lowell sat on the arm of the chair next to Jeremy and placed his arm around him.

"So explain fast why this isn't your fault," Bull said, crossing his arms over his chest.

"Okay, first thing, this was amateurish by our standards. Two, there's no way anyone could have followed me here. I've been off the grid for days. The cells I'm using are burn phones. The only one that isn't is off network with the SIM disabled. My handler doesn't know where I am, and that has her worried. No, there's something else going on."

Bull didn't look convinced.

"Come on, we all know how to disappear when we want to," Lowell said. "I'm better at it than anyone. The people on my last job think I was José, and I had the complexion and heritage to match. Each client thinks I'm someone else. I look different, and none of them have a clue about the real me. No, this has nothing to do with me and everything to do with either Jeremy or Tristan." He turned to Jeremy. "Is there anyone new in your life besides me? A new friend or someone from work that you've been hanging around with lately?" He kept his voice soft. He didn't want Jeremy to think he was accusing him of anything.

"No. The only new person in my life is you," Jeremy answered.

"What about Tristan?" Lowell asked, glancing at Bull.

"Eddie," Bull said and Jeremy nodded.

"Tristan's new boyfriend," Jeremy supplied. "None of us have met him, and we all think that's strange. Kevin told Tris that he expected to meet Eddie this weekend at Pride, but…."

"What is it?"

"It's not like Tris to keep secrets like this. We all know each other's business. These guys are my best friends in the world, and we've seen each other through breakups, job interviews, layoffs, and everything else you can imagine. It's what drives all our boyfriends crazy, but why our friendship is so strong—because we love each other and we trust each other. But Tris has been pulling away since he met Eddie. We've all noticed it. Tris has been all happy and smiley, so none of us wants to interfere and rain on his parade. But something isn't right, and it's getting worse. We all meet the boyfriends and… like I said, Tris seems distant."

"Okay," Lowell said as he hugged Jeremy a little closer.

"I'm sorry I blamed you," Jeremy whispered.

"What do you want to do?" Bull asked. "Because either this Eddie has bugged Tristan and Jeremy's home or… what? Eddie has enemies who are looking for him and they've connected him to Tristan?"

Lowell shrugged, and Jeremy shook his head.

"Do you know where Tristan met Eddie?" Lowell asked Jeremy, who shook his head again. "What *do* you know?"

"Tristan came home a few weeks ago and said he'd met the greatest guy. His name was Eddie and they were going out on Saturday. They've gone out a bunch since then, and then they always go over to Eddie's. None of us has ever seen him." Jeremy chuckled. "We all thought for a while that he was a figment of Tris's imagination or something, because Tris hasn't had anyone in his life in a long time." Jeremy shifted in the chair, moving over, and Lowell sat next to him until he'd worked Jeremy onto his lap. "I hate to say anything. It feels like I'm ratting out Tris or something."

"You aren't. There's something going on. It may be nothing and Tristan simply wants his privacy. But someone did break into your apartment, and we need to find out what for." Lowell looked at Bull. "Any suggestions? We could follow Tristan the next time he and Eddie go out together. Let Tristan lead us to him."

"Right, and in the meantime, some guy is listening in on everything I say or do in the apartment. Maybe I could take up throat singing or symphonic underarm fart noises to annoy the guy," Jeremy wisecracked nervously. Bull stepped closer. "Maybe we could just ask," Jeremy added.

THANKFULLY, IT had stopped raining when they left the hotel. Jeremy was a bundle of nerves, and Lowell had asked if he wanted to wait at the hotel, but he insisted on going with them. "You don't have to say anything. Let us do the talking."

"Okay," Jeremy agreed and they rode the rest of the way in Bull's car in silence. When they arrived, they got out, and the three of them climbed the stairs and entered the apartment. The television was still on. Bull walked over to it and turned it off. Jeremy closed the door, and the room became quiet.

"How do you want to play this?" Bull whispered. Lowell shrugged, and a second later Bull's deep voice boomed through the room.

"Whoever placed the bugs, I'm talking to you. We know you've wired the apartment for sound, and we're in the process of tracking the signals to you... and we will." Damn, Bull sounded threatening as hell. "You picked the wrong people to mess with. I spent a long time in the military and then worked as a mercenary. I've hunted down and taken care of men for a hell of a lot less than this. So if you want to come out of this with your skin intact, you will do the following. One, you will come to Bronco's on Third Street at six tonight and ask for Bull. Two, you will be prepared to answer any and all questions we have, and I better get some answers. Three, you will show up or else the bugs you planted will be turned over to the police and we'll let them help us hunt down your scrawny asses!" Bull motioned, and Lowell went into the kitchen, got a plastic bag from one of Jeremy's drawers, and used it like a glove to remove the bug. He did the same with the one in Jeremy's room. Bull looked in Tristan's room, and they were able to find one in there as well.

"Will you get a plastic container?" Lowell asked Jeremy. He pulled one out of the kitchen cupboard, and Lowell placed the bugs in it, added some flour, and sealed the lid. "It's good now."

Jeremy slumped against him. Lowell hugged him close and helped him to the sofa. "Are you okay?" Lowell asked softly.

"Is this what your life is like all the time?" Jeremy asked.

Lowell glanced at Bull for a second and saw what he expected to.

"Yes, sometimes. I tried to tell you it isn't pretty. People do terrible things to each other. This was relatively tame, and it's part of why I want a different life." Lowell touched Jeremy's chin. "The thing is, and Bull will tell you, it's hard to leave it behind totally. The people we worked for have a lot of money, and because of that, they think, and often are, above the law. Part of what we did was equalize that. But these people don't often take no for an answer." Lowell lightly kissed Jeremy and then hugged him. "You have to decide what you want. You've said you want to make your own decisions, so this is the first one. Do you want me in your life?"

He was terrified of the answer he'd receive. Jeremy was upset and scared. While Lowell was convinced it had nothing to do with him, there was the very real possibility that some intrigue would show up eventually, and it was likely to be more complicated and more dangerous than this. "You don't have to answer right now, but I want you to think about it."

"I'll leave you two alone," Bull said.

"No, I don't want to stay here until you figure this out."

"We have to, hon. What if Tristan comes home and doesn't know what's going on?" Lowell asked. Jeremy nodded, but Lowell could tell he wasn't happy about it.

"I could call him," Jeremy offered, looking up at him with big, pleading eyes.

"He isn't going to believe you. Tristan is going to have to see for himself. If he's in love with Eddie, then he's going to need proof. Otherwise he'll just get angry with you, and that won't help anyone. I'll stay here with you, and somehow I doubt that after that announcement these people are going to come anywhere near here. As I said, these were relative amateurs."

"I'll stay if you want," Bull offered and took a seat in the chair off to the side of the room. He settled in almost immediately and closed his eyes. Lowell knew he'd be awake in a second if anything happened,

"Come on," Lowell said, helping Jeremy to his feet. He took him by the hand and quietly led him to his bedroom.

"Lowell, I…." They walked in the room, and Jeremy sat on the edge of the bed.

"It's all right. Try to relax and not think about all this, if you can." Lowell sat down next to him. "If we're right, this had nothing to do with you."

"But what if you're wrong?" Jeremy asked. "What if this isn't because of Eddie, but something else?"

Lowell had thought of that. "Then we'll figure it out together and deal with it. I promise." He took Jeremy's hand and squeezed it. "I'm going to make some lunch. You haven't eaten in a while, and I don't want you to feel bad. If you want to lie down and rest, go ahead. I shouldn't be too long."

Lowell didn't want to leave, but Jeremy needed some time alone to think. A lot had happened in the past few hours, and he needed a chance to process it. Lowell had dealt with many fast-evolving situations, but this was a first for Jeremy, he was sure of that.

Lowell left and went into the kitchen. He found some basic things for simple sandwiches and made Bull, himself, and Jeremy each one. He left Bull's on the table next to his chair and carried the others into the other room.

Jeremy hadn't moved.

Lowell handed him the plate, and he took it, but barely acknowledged anything else. "You need to eat."

Jeremy picked up one half of the sandwich and nibbled on it slightly. "Is this really what things were like for you?"

"No," Lowell answered. How could he explain that what he did was very different, particularly because he'd always done it alone? He didn't work with others, and his jobs often involved more danger. He realized that this was Jeremy's way of trying to figure him out, but there was no way Lowell could ever make Jeremy understand. And he didn't want to— he hoped Jeremy never saw or experienced anything like what he'd done. "Let's just say this is tamer and leave it at that."

Jeremy nodded and ate a few more bites. "Why are you doing this?"

Lowell turned toward Jeremy. "Doing what?"

"Helping me? You don't have to, you know," Jeremy said.

Lowell touched his chin very gently, and when Jeremy turned, Lowell kissed him. He had no words for the feelings that swelled within him or the near panic that had overtaken him when he'd realized what had been placed in the apartment and that Jeremy might be in danger. They broke apart, and Jeremy stared at him for a few seconds and then turned away.

They ate the rest of their lunch in silence. Lowell wanted to ask Jeremy what he was thinking about, but was afraid of the answer. He'd never been this scared of anything in his life. It was very possible Jeremy would reject him.

When they were done eating Lowell took the dishes and carried them back into the kitchen. Bull's plate was empty as well, and Lowell wondered if he'd eaten in his sleep because his eyes were closed and it didn't look like he'd moved, but the sandwich was gone. He placed the dishes in the sink and went back to check on Jeremy. Lowell pushed the bedroom door open. Jeremy lay on the bed, eyes closed. Lowell watched and waited to see if he was asleep. Jeremy didn't move, so he leaned against the doorframe and watched him for a few minutes. Jeremy was an angel—one who got his heart racing and pulse pounding. He watched Jeremy for a while and thought about joining Bull in the living room. But instead he took the chance and stepped into the room.

Lowell climbed onto the bed, and instantly Jeremy curled to him. Lowell put his arm around Jeremy, and he snuggled closer. He wasn't tired, but he'd lie here with Jeremy for as long as Jeremy wanted him to. Jeremy didn't say anything, but for now he didn't need to. Lowell brushed the hair off Jeremy's forehead and kissed him lightly. Then he settled on the mattress to listen.

There had been many times in the service when he'd been on guard duty. The men in his unit needed to be safe and they needed to sleep. That required someone to watch over them, and Lowell had spent many nights watching over his compatriots, just as they'd done with him. But Lowell had never stood guard over anyone who meant as much to him as the smaller man sleeping next to him.

"It's okay, Lowell. I'm not going anywhere."

He wasn't sure what Jeremy meant exactly, but Jeremy took the hand Lowell had draped over him and held it tight. For now that was enough, but only time would tell what Jeremy's true feelings and desires were, especially in light of all the drama.

LOWELL MUST have dozed off. He hadn't meant to, but Jeremy felt so good next to him and he was content. The apartment was silent, and Lowell wondered what had disturbed him. Jeremy moved in his arms and then rolled over to face him. Jeremy cradled his cheeks in his warm hands and looked into his eyes. Lowell held still without blinking, wondering what Jeremy was searching for. He didn't move, and then Jeremy leaned closer and kissed him. It certainly felt like Jeremy had found what he wanted, especially as Jeremy deepened the kiss.

"You seem better," Lowell whispered.

"Is Bull still in the living room?"

"I believe so. Do you want me to check?" Lowell asked and moved away to get up.

Jeremy pulled him back. "No. That just means that you have to be quiet."

"Me…," Lowell said indignantly. "As I remember, you were the one who was particularly vocal." Jeremy cut off the argument, and Lowell didn't care whether he won or lost. All he cared about was the slightly sweet taste of Jeremy's tongue as he lightly sucked on it. The kiss deepened, with the two of them dueling over who would control their kisses. Lowell pressed Jeremy onto the bed, using his strength to win the silent argument. Not that Jeremy seemed to mind as he wound his arms around Lowell's neck and held him so tight there was no way he could stop.

Not that the thought entered his mind. Their kisses paused only long enough for Lowell to pull Jeremy's shirt over his head and to get his own off. The rest of their clothes ended up on the floor very quickly too, and Jeremy wound his legs around Lowell's waist, telling him exactly what he wanted. In the back of his mind, Lowell didn't think this was a good idea at a time like this, but there was no way he could stop. Not now.

Lowell stroked down Jeremy's back and took his firm buttcheeks in his hand.

"I'm ready, Lowell," Jeremy whispered.

Lowell swallowed hard. He knew what Jeremy meant and what it signified.

"Not now, sweetheart," Lowell murmured into his ear. "Before we do this, I need to prepare you and make you scream for me, and I can't do that right now. I want to so badly, but I will not hurt you for anything." He pulled Jeremy into a kiss and pressed them together as he stroked lightly up Jeremy's side and over his chest, lightly teasing Jeremy's small nipples until he arched his back beneath him. Then Lowell gently brushed his fingers over Jeremy's opening, teasing him a little. He'd meant what he said. He wasn't going to go any further, but he loved the small whimpery sounds Jeremy made in his ear when he was happy, and, Lord, the man was ecstatic now. He knew he should quiet him, but Bull could certainly ignore any sounds that came out of this bedroom, at least for the next little while.

Lowell wanted him to be happy and to let go of some of the strife that had been bothering him. Lowell shifted slowly, tasting Jeremy's sweet, smooth skin as he slid downward. Jeremy moaned softly when Lowell licked his nipples and giggled a little when Lowell swirled his tongue around and in his belly button. Lowell stroked up and down Jeremy's chest and continued on, caressing his pelvis before encircling his cock with his fingers. Jeremy stilled, and Lowell smiled before opening his mouth and sucking Jeremy hard and deep. Jeremy whimpered at first.

"That's... God...," Jeremy whispered between clenched teeth. Lowell smiled and did it again, burying his nose in the light curls at the base of Jeremy's cock. He inhaled deeply and shuddered at the rich scent of the person who mattered most to him. He would do just about anything to see that Jeremy was happy. "Lowell...." Jeremy sat up and laid his hands flat on the mattress, pressing his hips forward. Lowell sucked harder and let Jeremy have his way.

He lifted his gaze and was nearly shocked into stillness. Jeremy had thrown his head back, his mouth hanging open in ecstasy. Lowell continued moving, bobbing his head slightly before sliding his lips away and letting his tongue tickle the underside of Jeremy's shaft. When he pulled his lips away, Jeremy whimpered, and when he sucked him deeper, gripping him with his lips, Jeremy groaned deep and long. He wasn't sure which sound he liked best, so he continued on and on until Jeremy began sounding a bit hoarse. Then he added his hand to the mix, stroking and sucking until Jeremy filled the room with soft whimpers. Lowell knew he was close and increased the pressure and pace until Jeremy stilled and came, with Lowell swallowing every salty-sweet drop.

Jeremy collapsed back on the bed, and Lowell smiled as he simply watched Jeremy breathe. He was relaxed, smiling slightly in contentment. That had been what he wanted. But within a minute Jeremy was tugging him down on the mattress and sucking him. Jeremy went slowly at first, teasing him until Lowell thought he would fly apart. He whispered encouragement that Jeremy seemed to revel in. "Damn...," Lowell breathed as Jeremy sucked all of him. He gripped the bedding in desperation as Jeremy sucked and bobbed for all he was worth, and when he did that thing with his tongue around the head and along the shaft, Lowell could take no more. He managed a small groaned warning before his passion got the better of him and he tumbled into heavenly oblivion.

Jeremy released him, and Lowell pulled him into his arms, holding Jeremy while he tried to catch his breath and slow his racing heart. "Do you really think this is going to be okay?" Jeremy asked after a while.

"I stopped trying to predict the future a long time ago, but Bull and I will do our best to see if we can't find out what's going on and put a stop to it. I promise." He hoped it was one he could keep.

BULL REMAINED with them until he had to go to the club, and if he'd heard anything from the bedroom, he gave no indication when they joined him later in the day. Tristan got home from work about five, and after some persuasion from Jeremy, he agreed to come with them to the club. Jeremy took Lowell's advice and told Tristan only that they were meeting someone and that he'd need him for support. They took Jeremy's old car to the club and parked around back. Bull let them inside, and they sat at one of the tables. Bull offered them each a drink, but only Tristan took him up on the offer. Jeremy was too nervous, and Lowell wanted his senses and reflexes as keen as possible. He wasn't sure if their little message would be acted on, but shortly before six, someone pounded on the front door. "You two stay here and be prepared to make a run for that door right there if anything happens," Lowell instructed seriously.

Tristan opened his mouth, and Jeremy shook his head. Like a fish, his mouth snapped shut. Lowell looked at Bull and joined him, standing back slightly so Bull could pull the club door open. Three men stood outside. Two were large with dull eyes, and the third was clearly the leader. Instantly, Lowell sized them up and figured he could take them all out in less than ten seconds with the weapons he had on him at the moment.

"You left a message, and I thought I'd answer," the leader said.

Bull stepped forward. "I don't know who you are, but you made a huge mistake."

"I think you made a mistake getting into my business." The man took a step forward, and Lowell saw him better. He was well dressed, with an expensive haircut. "Boys...." He didn't move, but the other two did. Lowell snapped his boot and hand forward at the same time and the one nearest to him went down like a sack of wet cement. Bull did the same, and then Lowell stared at the remaining man, who was at least three skin shades paler.

"You made a mistake," Bull reiterated. "Now, as I said in my message, I want some answers, and you're going to give them to me. I'm sure anyone who travels with muscle like that has things the authorities would be very interested in, and we're also sure they could easily trace the listening equipment to you and your men. A federal offense, if I'm not mistaken." Bull took a single step back and brought a chair forward without taking his eyes off the man. "I suggest you have a seat and tell us what we want to know. Then you can be on your way, along with what's left of your men."

He did not look pleased but he sat down slowly. "I'm a businessman," he began, and Lowell knew exactly what kind of business he was in.

"Name," Bull barked.

"Just call me Julio," he said with a slight Spanish accent.

Bull glanced at Lowell briefly and then back at Julio. "I know who you are. What I want to know is what you and yours want with them?" Bull growled and motioned toward where Tristan and Jeremy sat. Lowell could tell they were both afraid, but Jeremy held himself erect in his chair and looked straight back at them. Tristan looked on in confusion, which was to be expected.

Julio didn't answer, so Bull moved closer. "You may think you have connections and muscle, but you haven't got shit compared to us. Your men are thugs. Ours are assassins who can reach you anywhere on this earth, so you better drop the tough-guy act and simply tell us what we want to know."

"I know you think you're armed," Lowell said and approached him, removing a knife and gun before Julio could move. "I know all the tricks because I've used them." Lowell prowled around the drug dealer. He knew exactly what he was. The man smelled of the stuff—rot, filth, and decay covered by a suit and cologne. Lowell had been around people like this long enough to know the type damn well. "I've killed men like you with my bare hands and they never saw it coming."

"You can't—" Julio began.

Bull stepped forward and duct-taped his arms to the chair.

"If you think anyone is going to come looking for you or give a rat's ass if you disappear, you got some more thinking to do. I've got witnesses who will all say you struck at me first and you're a lowlife drug dealer. So I suggest you start talking fast," Lowell spat.

"I was just protecting my turf. The little fag's boyfriend—" Julio gasped when Lowell grabbed his hair, yanking his head back.

"You be respectful, or *this* fag"—Lowell turned Julio's head so he could see him—"is going to mess up that pretty face of yours so bad your mama won't recognize you."

"The boyfriend of the gentleman in the blue at the table over there," Julio corrected, and Lowell released his hair with a snap of his wrist. "His boyfriend is trying to muscle in on part of my territory, so I sent my boys over to try to gather some information. No one was hurt." He looked down at the men still lying on the floor. Both were moaning now and beginning to move.

"Just stay down if you know what's good for you," Bull told them, and one stopped moving. Bull kicked the arm out from under the other one, and he banged his nose on the floor and stayed down. "You got the stupidest muscle I've ever seen."

"So they were supposed to bug the apartment," Lowell said. "That doesn't seem like the style of a guy like you. Making your rival pay in blood is more like it." Lowell looked over at the table, saw Jeremy pulling

Tristan into his arms, then turned back to Julio. "What did you have planned?" Lowell snarled.

Julio's veneer of confidence was definitely slipping, his lower lip trembling as he realized just how much trouble he was in. Guys like Julio didn't play by the rules, but they counted on others doing so. That went out the window with him and Bull.

"Tell me!" Bull snapped.

"We haven't been able to get a line on where Eddie has holed up, but we got wind that he was seeing the—" Lowell knew a slur was on the tip of the slime's tongue, but it didn't come out. "We knew he was seeing the kid over there and figured if we bugged the place we could get a handle on him. Didn't do anything. Static, and all we heard was some dudes going at it." He shivered, and Lowell was ready to have at him again. "Then we heard the television for hours until we got your message."

"What are you going to do now?"

Julio held up his hands. "Nothing."

"You got that right. You stay away from them and us. This club is off-limits to you and everybody else who deals in that shit. You stay away from us and ours, and we'll let you live. Don't forget we still have the bugs you planted, and I'm willing to bet the authorities can pull the fingerprints of your associates, there, off them. As for Eddie, I don't care what you do to him. He's all yours." Bull jerked the tape off Julio's arms and backed away, and Lowell did as well.

Julio stood slowly and straightened his clothes, his pride and machismo falling back into place. "You can't see what's coming all the time." He smiled.

"Neither can you. I can drop you with a shot from a quarter mile away. You won't hear it or see it. You'll just be dead. Do you understand me?" It was clear to Lowell that Julio got the message loud and clear this time. Julio cleared his throat and nudged the men on the floor with the toe of his shoe. "Get up! We're out of here. They aren't worth it."

The men groaned as they got up off the floor and pushed their way out of the club. Both were unsteady on their feet.

"You go see to them while I make sure our guests have left," Bull said after locking the doors and stepping away from the glass in case they were even stupider than they looked. Lowell hurried back to where Jeremy and Tristan sat. Tears rolled down Tristan's cheeks, and Jeremy was really upset as well.

"It's going to be okay. It's better you found out now rather than later," Lowell said.

"But I liked him and… why do I always attract the losers?"

"Hey," Lowell said. "Guys like that are masters at letting you see what they want you to see until it's too late. How do you think they get their customers? They give them samples and party with them until they're hooked, and then they take them for everything they have, including their self-respect and their bodies, until there is nothing left. That's what they do, and that's what he was using on you."

"But I should have known. How could I not?" Tristan held on to Jeremy.

"The other thing they do is isolate you from your friends and the people who love you." Lowell paused to let that settle in. "I bet he told you that you were the most precious person in the world to him and that he wanted you around all the time. He gave you gifts and made you feel special, but hated whenever you looked at anyone other than him. Am I right?"

Tristan nodded and hugged Jeremy closer. A stab of jealousy went through him, but Lowell pushed it back. This was a friend helping a hurting friend, nothing more. "Yeah," Tristan said, sniffing, "but I love him."

"No, you don't. You loved the way he treated you."

"It's the same thing," Tristan argued.

"No, it isn't. Because before long he'd show his true colors, and you'd be wondering where the wonderful boyfriend you thought you had went. What you'd be left with was a man who was using you like he uses everyone else. I know I sound harsh, but you're better off with friends like Jeremy, Bull, and Zach than you are with the likes of Eddie or anyone like that. They truly care about you." Lowell hoped he'd gotten through. There was nothing more he could say, so he stepped back to let Jeremy comfort Tristan. He saw Bull return and walked over to where he stood near the bar.

"They're gone. How is he holding up?"

"As well as can be expected. He was really taken in by the guy."

Bull pulled out his phone. "I'm calling Zach, and if I know him, he'll call Kevin, and all three of them will do what they do to help him feel better." Bull watched them at the table and then pulled out his phone. "I've been with Zach for well over a year now, and I still don't understand the dynamic of the four of them. They argue sometimes, spend hours together, and they might even go without seeing each other for weeks at a time, but in the end, they are always there for each other."

"It's the twink version of *Sex and the City*," Lowell said. "And I wish I had friends like that. Things might have been different if I'd been surrounded by people who loved and cared about me, no matter who I was or what I did. Unconditional love is priceless and incredibly rare." He caught Bull's eye and saw him nod before making his call.

The employees started to arrive and prepare for opening. Lowell got out of the way. He didn't want to intrude on Jeremy and his friends, so he took a table a little ways away.

Zach and Kevin burst into the club a few minutes later. Zach stopped to close the door behind him before racing over to his friends. The three young men soothed and hugged Tristan, babbling like brooks, but in a way that seemed to calm all of them. After a while, Zach left the group and walked over to where Bull was working behind the bar. The two of them talked earnestly, their faces very close together. When they were finished talking, Zach headed back toward his friends, but detoured to Lowell's table. Zach plopped himself on the chair across from him. "It's no secret that I don't trust you, and I'm not really sure I like you, but Bull told me what you did for Jeremy and Tristan, so maybe you aren't as bad as I thought." Zach looked over at his other friends and then back at him. "I'm glad you were there for them."

Lowell nodded. He knew Zach was going to be a tough nut to crack. He was small but fierce and protective as hell of the people he cared for. Lowell respected that. It was a trait he understood. He said nothing and Zach stood and went back to join his friends. They leaned closer and had what looked like some meeting of the minds. Jeremy motioned him over, and Lowell stood and joined them.

"Tristan and Kevin are going to go home with Zach for the night. And I was wondering if you'd be willing to stay with me?" Jeremy asked. Lowell could understand him not wanting to be alone in the apartment. This was not the first time he had found listening devices. He remembered the ones he'd found in his room in Nassau years ago. It had unnerved him because he'd realized just what he'd said. The entire mission had had to be replanned because of what had been revealed. In the end it had worked out, but not without additional effort. The feeling of being spied on had not gone away for a long time, though. In his business that was a good thing—it had made him more cautious. For someone like Jeremy, he figured it would simply be disturbing and creepy for a while.

"Of course," Lowell said. Once those decisions were made, things moved pretty quickly. They all agreed to call each other to make sure everyone got home safely. Bull offered to drive Zach and Tristan, but Zach assured him that they would be fine. Bull still walked them out to their car.

"Are you ready to go?" Lowell asked Jeremy once Bull returned. Jeremy nodded, and Lowell led the way to Jeremy's car and drove to the apartment.

Jeremy was quiet the entire ride. What bothered Lowell most was the way he didn't look at him. When they arrived, Jeremy looked around in every direction before unlocking the door to the building.

Lowell followed him inside, vigilant as well until they were inside the apartment with the door closed and locked. "Has anyone been here?" he asked quietly. "I have the blocking app turned on."

Jeremy shook his head but said nothing. Lowell wanted to hold him, but Jeremy moved away and sat on the sofa, then turned on the television. "There's food if you want anything. I'm not hungry," Jeremy announced without looking away from the screen. Lowell went into the kitchen and managed to put together a halfway decent meal based on what was there. A trip to the grocery store was sorely needed, but he managed an omelet and brought a plate to Jeremy. He took it and ate a few bites while Lowell finished what he had.

"You need to eat and stop thinking so much," Lowell said. He wondered if he should simply pick Jeremy up and take him to bed. He wasn't sure how Jeremy would react to that, and if it wasn't what Jeremy wanted, Lowell didn't want to come off as a predator or something.

"That's easy for you to say," Jeremy retorted, but he did eat some more. Lowell left him alone. If Jeremy needed some time, then he would give it to him.

"I don't know what I did to upset you," Lowell began once he'd washed and dried the dishes. "But you need to talk to me. You asked me to stay, and I will, but sitting there silently is not helping."

Jeremy looked up from the television and stared at him. "Is that how you treat people? The way you treated that guy in the club? You had him duct-taped to a chair and I saw how harsh you were, and you looked...." Jeremy shivered. "I don't know if I want to be around someone who can do that. All he did was…." Jeremy's voice trailed off, and he put his hands over his face.

Lowell was confused. "I needed to get some information from him to help make sure you and Tristan were safe. Did you…?" Shit. Lowell realized that Jeremy and Tristan hadn't heard everything. They'd been on the far side of the club, and with the fans and other background noise, they must not have heard exactly what was being said. "I know how things must have looked, but it was to protect you and Tristan. Bull and I did what we had to do, and… yes, the way you saw me at the club is part of who I am. I can be a badass of the worst order. But you understand that Julio, the guy at the club, is just as bad or worse than Eddie. He only understands force and strength, so I had to make sure that was what he saw."

"But what if I make you mad? Will you—" Jeremy stared down at his plate.

"Jeremy, I don't have a temper. What you saw was controlled the entire time. I never lash out at people the way you're thinking. And we aren't going to have a fight and then I'm going to flip out and hurt you. I know what you think you saw, but you didn't hear what was being said, did you?" Jeremy shook his head. "That's good, believe it or not."

"How can you say that? You didn't look in control to me. You looked angry."

"I was. But what you saw was not a result of that anger. The way I acted was carefully thought out to make sure we would get the information we needed. We did, and we put the fear of God in the weasel. I truly believe he'll leave you and Tristan alone, and I'd be very surprised if he ever sets foot anywhere near the club again." Lowell wasn't getting through to him. "Do you trust Bull?" Jeremy nodded. "And you know that he'd never hurt Zach, but he'd do anything to make sure he was safe?"

"Yes, of course. But it wasn't always like that. They had time to get to know each other and…."

"That time is up to you. But, honey, you have to understand that I would never hurt you. I'd hurt myself before I'd hurt you or allow someone else to hurt you." He wasn't sure what else he could say. Lowell grew quiet and sat next to Jeremy on the sofa. At least Jeremy didn't pull away, but he didn't reach for his hand or touch him in any way either.

"I need to try to reconcile the person I saw at the club and the one I thought I knew," Jeremy said eventually. "I don't know if I can."

"Jeremy, I've told you a number of times about the things I've done and what I did for a living. You knew I could be extremely tough and very aggressive. It's what I had to be to survive. I'm sorry if I frightened you. But I had to make sure you were safe. That was my only goal and purpose."

Jeremy stood up and stepped away from the sofa. "I'll get you some blankets and stuff."

Lowell could feel him pulling away, and while it hurt like hell, he knew it was probably for the best. Jeremy wanted to make his own decisions, and Lowell had known from the start that when he did, there was a very real possibility that he would choose to walk away. Jeremy had been right about something else as well: he had been afraid. He'd allowed himself to develop deep feelings for Jeremy. Hell, the smaller man had stolen his heart, and Lowell hadn't even been aware of it. Jeremy put a blanket and pillow on the arm of the sofa.

"I need some time." Jeremy stood still for a few seconds. He leaned forward slightly and then straightened up again before saying good night and leaving the room.

Lowell made sure the doors were locked and the place was secured before settling on the sofa. He knew he wasn't going to sleep, not for a single minute, and it had nothing to do with being on guard and everything to do with the fact that his heart, one he would have doubted he had before meeting Jeremy, ached like hell. But Lowell knew he had to be prepared for Jeremy to turn his back on him. In fact, he wondered if that was already happening.

CHAPTER EIGHT

JEREMY DIDN'T sleep worth crap. After he got dressed in the morning, he saw that Lowell hadn't either. All night long, whenever he'd fallen asleep, he'd dreamed of people breaking into his apartment, strangers hiding in bushes, or mysterious phone calls. Basically, his imagination had run on overdrive. Most of it, he knew, was him being dumb, but he could not shake the sight of Lowell yanking on that guy's hair and knocking those men out. It had really bothered him. Lowell had told him what he'd done and all that, but that had just been words—seeing it was a completely different matter.

"Are you getting ready for work?" Lowell asked him as Jeremy started a pot of coffee. He so needed it.

"Yeah," Jeremy answered. He didn't know what to say and felt really awkward. "You want some?" He poured a second cup and carried it to Lowell, who was folding up the blanket. Lowell placed the pillow and blanket on the over the arm of the sofa and took the mug.

"I'll be ready to go when you are," Lowell said gently and then sipped from the mug. Jeremy watched Lowell and drank his coffee. "I think I understand how you feel."

"Maybe," Jeremy said. "A lot has happened in the past week. I met this guy on the dance floor at Bronco's. It turns out he's a great dancer, and everything else." Jeremy tried not to blush, but did anyway. "But, hey, it turns out he's a gun for hire, and there could be people after him, so he's laying low in town. Oh, and let's not forget that he's the same guy who threatened my friends Bull and Zach. So please forgive me if I need a little time to figure all this out. Hell, I don't even know your last name." Jeremy set down his mug. "I don't know what to think. It's like I've been living in a movie or something, and yesterday the film ended."

"This isn't a movie," Lowell said.

"I know, but it's felt like one to me. You came in and swept me off my feet, but I need to figure out what's real. I know I'm sounding a little dumb because I'm not explaining this right, but I need a little time. I need to know if I can trust you and rely on you." Jeremy paused. "The funny thing is that instinctually I think I can, but I have to know if there's more to it than that." Jeremy held his head for a few seconds. "I just need time to think."

"Okay," Lowell said. He set down his mug and pulled out his wallet. He took out a card and looked around the room, then picked up a pen from the coffee table. "Here's a number that I'll be sure to answer. Call that when and if you want to talk to me." Lowell handed him the card and turned toward the door. "Please use that number if you see or even feel that something isn't right. I'll be in town for a little while longer." Lowell took a step back and then moved toward him again. He leaned down and kissed Jeremy lightly.

Jeremy blinked when Lowell pulled back. He wanted to say something, but stopped. The kiss felt like good-bye, and he couldn't stop his fingers from touching his lips. He watched as Lowell turned and walked toward the door, opened it, and left the apartment.

Once the door clicked closed, he looked down at the card. There was a phone number and a single word: Cartwright.

WORK HAD never gone by so quickly. Jeremy had been a computer programming fool. He'd kept his head down all day and didn't want to stop. Every time he did, he thought of Lowell and the card he'd been carrying in his pocket since Lowell left that morning. It felt to him like it was his last connection to Lowell. He knew it was stupid. All he had to do was call, but doubts still plagued him. He thought of calling his mother, but she and Dad had never understood, not really. So instead, when he was done at work and had turned off his computer for the evening, he called Zach and drove over.

Zach met him as he pulled in. "You really need to get a new car, dude. This one is about ready to fall apart around you."

Jeremy nodded and chuckled. "Eventually." It was an old conversation. "I wanted to talk."

"I sort of figured," Zach said and motioned toward the backyard.

Jeremy carefully closed his car door and followed Zach around the side of the house. "You are going to think I'm a total dork, but I don't know what in hell to do about Lowell, and it's driving me crazy."

Zach pushed open the gate, and they stepped into a mini Eden. It seemed Zach had been spending a lot of his time in the yard. Flowers bloomed everywhere, and there wasn't a weed to be seen. It was idyllic and beautiful. Jeremy followed Zach to the patio. "I know."

"How can you?"

"Because you're never this indecisive. You got the job offer and took it. When you and Tris had to move, you found the place and told Tristan it was perfect for you guys and had the lease signed in a day. You're never wishy-washy." Zach sat back, stretching out his legs. "You know I don't know what to think about the guy, but he went up in my estimation yesterday. He stood up for you and Tris. He didn't have to."

"But the things he did… I saw them." Jeremy couldn't get that out of his head.

"So you saw him being tough. Bull is tough when he has to be. If that's got you squeamish, then you definitely shouldn't be with him. Not that I ever thought he was a great catch. Bull is tough-looking, but he has a heart of gold, I know that. I somehow doubt Spook has that same heart. Bull told me he's been doing dirtier jobs for a lot longer than Bull was, so I figure his heart is probably tainted." Zach stood up. "I'm going to get some tea. Do you want some?"

Zach walked away, and Jeremy seethed. "Come on, he helped me when I had that low blood sugar, and he's been there through this whole apartment-bugging incident." Jeremy followed Zach. "How can you say he doesn't have a heart? He's very caring, and you just said that he stood up for us, so how can you think that? He does, and I think I care for him!"

"How can you be sure?" Zach sniped back as he pulled open the patio door.

"How can anyone be sure? I know what he did. You told me. But that was a while ago, and he was working. He explained that, and I believe him."

Zach walked behind the breakfast bar and leaned over the top. "Then why are you asking me?" he said with a smile. Jeremy paused and Zach shrugged.

"You son of a bitch, you were baiting me."

"Of course I was, you idiot. You knew what you wanted, but you had to come to it yourself. My opinion doesn't really matter. Bull seems to have forgiven Spook, and if he can, then I'm willing to consider it, especially after what he did for Tris." Zach backed away and opened the refrigerator.

"He gave me his phone number," Jeremy said and pulled out the card. "And his last name—his real last name." The full impact of what he'd just said made him step back. Lowell trusted him enough to tell him his real identity.

"What is it?"

Jeremy shook his head and put the card back in his pocket. "You don't wanna know."

"Come on." Zach poured two large glasses of tea.

"No, it's something he trusted me with, and I'm not going to betray him. He's spent years hiding behind various identities and faces. This is part of his story that's his to tell."

Zach handed him a glass of tea, put the pitcher back in the refrigerator, and then closed the door. "Let's go back outside." Zach grabbed his glass and pulled the sliding door open. "So have you decided what you're going to do with the number?"

"That's the funny part. I think I always knew, but I wanted to be sure. He's...."

Zach laughed as they walked to the chairs in the shade. "Do you think I expected to end up with my Bull? Love happens when it happens, and you need to grab onto it with both hands." Zach sipped his tea. "If Spook... Lowell makes you happy and he treats you right, then I guess I can try to move past it."

"Thanks, you're such a pal," Jeremy chided, and Zach rolled his eyes before they both broke into a fit of giggles. It felt good to laugh.

"So are you going to call him now?" Zach asked. "If you've made a decision and you understand where he's coming from, then call. That mopey look you had when you got here was just pathetic, and if the way he keeps looking at you whenever he's around is any indication, I'd say he was probably looking pretty mopey too. It isn't a good look for you, and on him I bet it's *ghastly*." Zach descended back into a fit of giggles, and Jeremy pulled out the card and his phone and dialed the number. It rang a few times and then went to a generic voice mail. He wasn't sure what to do, so he left a brief message. "It's Jeremy. Please call me back." Then he hung up, half expecting his phone to ring right away. But nothing happened. "He said to call this number if I needed anything or thought anything was strange, and he'd answer."

"Maybe he's out of service range or something," Zach said.

Jeremy wasn't so sure, but he sat back down and picked up his glass. Now that he'd made up his mind, he wanted to see Lowell badly. Hell, he wanted to do a hell of a lot more than see him—he desperately wanted to feel him. To think he'd relegated Lowell to the sofa the night before when he could have had him in his bed… if he hadn't been such a butthead.

"Maybe," Jeremy echoed. He needed to change the subject for right now. "How is Tristan holding up? He was really upset yesterday. If I get my hands on this Eddie, I'm going to wring his neck."

"Well, Tristan is doing okay. When he got up this morning, he was so angry he called the police and asked if they were looking for Eddie. Apparently they were. Tristan told them where they'd been meeting. Tris called a while ago from work to tell me that the police have picked him up and that Eddie is 'everything Lowell said he was last night and more.' Apparently Tristan got quite a rundown from the authorities on Eddie's activities."

"Poor Tris," Jeremy whispered.

"Yeah. It turned out Tristan wasn't the only guy Eddie was seeing. It's just a mess, and he's torn up as hell, but he'll be okay. He found out what Eddie was before he got in too deep, and even he admits he was well on his way."

"Where is he now? I haven't heard from him."

"At work. I'm not sure if he's planning to come back here or go home. He said he was going to call, but he hasn't." Zach bit his lower lip nervously. "When you get back to your place, have him call if he's there.

I'm worried about him. He's been through a lot. I know talking to the police wasn't easy, and he's bound to bounce between relief and regret."

"I'll ask him to call. I promise." Jeremy was worried about his friend too. They'd all been worried about Tris for a while, but this was more focused. He checked his phone again and then shoved it back in his pocket.

"It isn't going to ring any faster if you stare at it."

Jeremy shook his head. "You'd be worried if Bull didn't answer his phone when he'd told you he would. Remember what he and Lowell did last night? What if Julio decides to try to get even?"

"They can take care of themselves. I worry about Bull because I love him, but he really can, and I'm sure Lowell can as well." Jeremy finished his tea and set the glass on the small redwood table next to his chair. "Why don't you try him again?" Zach prompted.

Jeremy did, but got the same message. He put his phone away and finished his tea.

"You're just being impatient, and that's cool. He'll call," Zach said.

Jeremy knew Zach was right, but he wanted to talk to Lowell. "I should get going," he said and stood up. Zach pulled him into a hug.

"Call me when you get home," Zach said, and Jeremy smiled. "I know I'm the mother hen of the group, so just humor me. A lot of stuff has happened over the past few days, and I just want to make sure everyone is safe."

"Okay, I'll call." Jeremy said good-bye, then headed around the side of the house and back through the gate. At his car, he waved to Zach, who was standing by the gate, and then got in.

The drive was familiar, but he kept looking in his rearview mirror, especially as he crossed the bridge. A blue sedan had been behind him since he'd made the first turn out of Zach's neighborhood. Lowell had said that if he felt something wrong to go with his instincts. He dug out his phone and called again. This time the phone rang and didn't go to voice mail, but no one answered. He set it aside and continued, entering the bridge over the Susquehanna. There were only so many ways into Harrisburg, and a lot of people were going the same way he was, but that car stayed there. Once he got across, he continued into town without turning off to go home. Instead, he made his way toward Bull's club, reached for his phone, and called Bull.

"Bull, I think I'm being followed," he said, a little panicked. "I'm not sure, but this car keeps going where I'm going."

"Come to the club and park in the front. We'll see what's going on," Bull told him, and Jeremy made the turn and pulled up to the club. Bull stood out front, waiting for him, watching the cars as they passed. "Which one was it?"

"You wouldn't have seen it. It continued going straight when I turned," Jeremy said.

"Was it the same car the entire time?"

"Yeah," Jeremy answered with a nod.

"Did it look like anyone was trying to hide, falling back and then coming up again?"

Jeremy thought for a second. "No, it was just there."

"Okay. Pull around to the back, and I'll meet you and let you inside. I think your imagination is working overtime. But I'm glad you called and that you're keeping an eye out. If someone was following you, it isn't likely they would stay in your line of sight the entire time." Bull went back inside, and Jeremy pulled around to the back of the club. Bull was waiting for him by the door, and he stepped inside. "What did this car look like?"

"It was dark blue. I think a Toyota," Jeremy said. "I'm not really good with cars." The club always looked and felt strange whenever he was in here before it was open. Minus the dancers, milling guys, and music, it was just a big space with tables. It was actually kind of sad and lonely.

"Did it have a dent on the front fender?"

Jeremy's eyes widened. "Yeah."

Bull chuckled. "That's the guy up the street. He works evenings at the capitol." Bull put a hand on his shoulder. "Don't worry about it. I'd rather have all of you watching who's around you than getting into trouble, especially after the past few days." Bull looked around. "I keep expecting to see Spook—I mean Lowell. You two have been joined at the hip lately." Bull led him toward the bar. Jeremy sat on one of the well-used barstools. Bull pulled him a beer and passed it over to him. "Only one because you're driving, but you earned it."

Bull leaned over the bar and waited while Jeremy took a sip of the dark brew.

"I called him on the number he gave me special, but he didn't answer," Jeremy said.

"Okay…," Bull said.

Jeremy placed the glass back on the bar. "Lowell gave me the number and he told me his last name. At least what I believe to be his real last name." He lifted the glass again. "I think I screwed up, Bull. I freaked yesterday after what I saw you guys did, and I took it out on him. I saw him hurting that guy and I kept wondering if he'd hurt me like that. My mind got all turned around, and I panicked and told him I needed some time to think. The thing is, he left."

"He respected your wishes," Bull observed, and Jeremy nodded.

"He's always done that. He helped me when I needed it, and after some smothering, which I now understand as protectiveness…." Jeremy searched for the words. "He's respected what I've wanted and he hasn't pushed. That should have been a clue." He took a large gulp and swallowed it, warmth spreading through him. The beer was rich, sweet, and strong, with a bite at the end to finish it—just what he needed.

"I don't know what to say."

"I know. The fact that he did what I asked him to, though it was clear that he wanted to stay and for me to understand, that says a lot about him."

"I can tell you a few things that I know about Spook. I call him that on purpose. Spook has a reputation for being tough and thorough. He rarely fails at what he sets out to do. Spook is strong, smart, cunning, and ruthless. He has to be to survive. He's also impulsive and maybe too tenacious for his own good, as Zach and I found out firsthand." Jeremy nodded, wondering where Bull was going with this. "But believe it or not, he has a reputation for being honest. He wanted what was his, but didn't take what he hadn't earned. I think that's why he came after Zach and me, because we were standing in the way of what he thought was his."

"I understand," Jeremy said, staring down at the bar.

"No, I don't think you do. Those same traits mean that Lowell will care for you, protect you, and, I believe, cherish you. He's strong and ruthless when he has to be. You saw that. But what you have to understand is that he was that way to protect you and Tristan. I was there and I agreed. Hell, if that guy had been messing with Zach, he would have gotten a hell of a lot worse than that. Lowell showed restraint I probably wouldn't have. He was in control the entire time."

"That's what Lowell said," Jeremy mumbled. Then he pulled out his phone and tried the number again. This time the call was answered. "It's me," Jeremy said.

"You're safe?" Lowell whispered.

"Yeah. I'm with Bull."

"Don't say where you are. Stay with him and don't go anywhere alone under any circumstances. I can't talk right now, but please stay with Bull." Panic was clear in Lowell's voice. It was controlled, but clearly there.

"What's going on? Are you all right?"

"Someone didn't take the news of my retirement very well, and they're trying to make it permanent. I'm leading them away from you and the people there."

Jeremy heard a sharp sound in the background. "Was that a gunshot?" he asked, nearly falling off the barstool as he tried to stand.

"Stay with Bull, please," Lowell begged.

"I will," he said as he heard movement and yelling. "I love you." All he heard in response was dead air. Jeremy stared at the phone, and Bull touched his hand. Jeremy lowered the phone to the bar, picked up his glass, emptied it, and passed it to Bull. "Go ahead and fill it up again. I need it."

"What happened?" Bull asked.

Jeremy related the short conversation. "I heard a gunshot in the background," he said, shaking a little. He sat back on the stool because he wasn't sure how much longer he would be able to stand up.

"I heard what you told him. Is that how you really feel?"

"I think so. I heard the distress in his voice and my chest clenched. It was instinctive," Jeremy whispered. "But yeah. I guess I do. I just hope he heard it." He hoped Lowell came back to him. Jeremy closed his eyes and sat still, one hand still resting on his phone while he listened to Bull fill the glass. When he heard Bull set the glass in front of him, Jeremy reached for it and began to drink. He was so lost in worry and misery he could hardly

119

think, so getting drunk off his ass sounded like a great idea. It was Friday and he didn't have to work tomorrow, so what the hell.

"That's the last one, and I'm not letting you drive. Call Tristan and find out how he's holding up. Harry should be here in a few minutes, and then I'm taking both of you to our house. You can stay there until we know more about what's going on."

Jeremy's hands shook as he emptied the glass. He knew he'd drunk it way too fast. The beer was too rich for chugging, but he didn't care. He stayed at the bar while Bull continued his work. He was too miserable and worried to do anything else. He'd been such a fool, and now he might not get to see Lowell again to tell him that he did understand and knew what he truly wanted. Zach had been right—he'd been wishy-washy and indecisive, and that might have cost him his last chance to spend time with Lowell.

Eventually he picked up his phone and called Tristan. Thankfully, he answered right away. "How are you holding up?" Jeremy asked him.

"As well as can be expected," Tristan responded without any enthusiasm whatsoever.

"There's some shit going down that's pretty intense. I don't have details, but Lowell said to stay with Bull, so he's going to bring me over there. He wants both of us to go stay at his and Zach's place. He says it's safer there."

"God, our lives are falling to shit," Tristan muttered. "I'll have my stuff ready to go. I could use some time with you guys." He hung up, and Jeremy got off the stool. The room swayed a little, and he wondered just how strong that beer had been. He took a few steps and steadied himself on the bar. Bull returned and laughed at him.

"Come on, lightweight," he teased. "Let's get you to the car. When was the last time you ate?"

"Lunch, I guess," Jeremy said and then hiccupped. Bull helped him sit back down and went behind the bar once again. He passed over a napkin with some peanuts on it. Jeremy took a handful and shoved them into his mouth. Then he took another. He was suddenly very hungry and finished what Bull had given him. After a few minutes he felt better and much less swimmy.

"Harry just got here, so let's get you home and then back to our place. Stand up slowly," Bull instructed. Jeremy was steady on his feet, so he grabbed his phone and followed Bull out the back door. He got into Bull's car and rode to the apartment. Tristan was waiting and hurried out as Bull finished parking.

"What's all this about?"

"I don't know any more than I said on the phone. Lowell said to stay with Bull and he's taking us there." Jeremy hiccupped again.

"You've been drinking—you always hiccup when you've had beer," Tristan said. "And you didn't wait for me."

"Let's get your things and get going," Bull said, and they all hurried inside. Jeremy got a small bag and packed some clothes for overnight. He hoped this wouldn't take longer than that. As an afterthought, he added a second change of clothes and then his kit from the bathroom to the bag before joining Tristan and Bull in the living room. "I checked all the windows out here. Are they locked in both your bedrooms?"

"Yes," the two of them answered together. That struck him as funny, and Jeremy began to giggle, which quickly morphed into tears. Bull gathered him into his arms and held him while he blubbered all over him.

"What if he doesn't come back?"

"It's going to be fine," Bull soothed before adding, "I knew I should never have given you that second one. They're way too strong." Jeremy wiped his eyes and stepped away from Bull. He needed to get under control. He wasn't a baby, and yes, he probably shouldn't have filled his stomach with beer.

"Let's go," he said, and they left the apartment. Tristan locked the door behind them, and Jeremy managed to make it down the stairs and to the car without tripping. Bull put their bags in the trunk, and they all got inside.

Bull drove like a bat out of hell. Okay, he always drove like that, but it seemed more urgent at the moment. Bull called Zach and told him they were on their way, and he met them in the driveway. Zach carried their bags into the guest room, and Jeremy found himself in the backyard, sitting in the same chair he had been earlier.

His life seemed surreal. A few weeks ago he was a normal gay guy doing normal things like going to the club, dancing, and hoping to get a little action. Now he had a boyfriend who had people after him. "You know, this is all your fault," Jeremy said as soon as Zach came into the backyard. "If you hadn't fallen in love with Bull, none of this would have happened."

"Don't blame me because you're a tool," Zach countered good-naturedly. "You were the one who had him in your arms and let him go."

"I'm not talking about that," Jeremy argued back. "I'm talking about all of this." He waved his arms around him grandly. "If you hadn't been ticklish and giggled like an idiot when Bull searched you that first time we went to the club, you wouldn't have him. And Spook would never have come into your lives, and he wouldn't have shown up to make me fall in love with him and then disappear so I can worry like hell about him!" Jeremy's anger rose quickly and he jumped to his feet.

Zach stared back at him, lips pressed to fine lines. "Are you done? Because that's a load of manure if I ever heard one."

"Of course it is. I'm being dumb, and Bull plied me with beer." Jeremy slumped back in the chair. "I have no idea what I'm saying, and I feel like an idiot for yelling at you. Of course none of this is your fault. You fell in love."

"So did you, if what you were yelling about was the truth," Tristan said as he came out of the house and closed the patio door. "It seems this particular week is extremely hard on hearts. Maybe the damned thing will be over soon and we can get back to normal—miserable and alone." He schlumped to the wicker love seat and collapsed into it.

Zach rolled his eyes and went back into the house, and Jeremy went to sit next to Tristan. "It will be all right."

"I loved him, you know," Tristan whispered. "And I feel like I've betrayed him and then shoved a knife in his back." Jeremy held Tristan. He'd heard that the best way to put aside your own heartache or worry was to comfort someone who was hurting worse.

"I know you did. But this is for the best and you know that. He would have broken your heart in the end, or worse, you'd end up like one of those people you see in movies, broken and wondering what happened when everything falls apart."

"It wasn't going to be like that," Tristan said, pulling away. "I would never let it get that far."

"It already was. I live with you and never see you like I used to. That night we went to the club was the last time, and before that it had been weeks. He was separating you from your friends and the people who care about you so you would be dependent on him." Jeremy kept his voice level and soft, even though his anger from earlier threatened to spill over. He hated what had been done to Tristan, and even more, he was angry that Tris couldn't see it or wasn't willing to see it. "I know it hurts, but tomorrow it will hurt less, and eventually you'll find someone better."

"I don't know about that," Tris whispered.

"I do," Jeremy said. "I know that because you're my best friend, among the best friends I've ever had, and I don't have losers for friends. There is someone out there who will love you and care for you like no one else on earth. The way Bull does for Zach." He almost added "the way I care for Lowell," but couldn't do it. Not now. "It's what you deserve. It's what we all deserve. But we have to recognize it when it happens."

"Are we talking about you now?" Tristan asked.

"Yeah, I guess so," Jeremy admitted. "Sorry."

"No. We can commiserate," Tristan said. Jeremy continued holding him until Zach returned from the house.

"I put a casserole in the oven. It will take a little while to heat up. It's one of the ones Bull's mother made the last time she was here and put in the freezer, so we have to make sure there is some left for him when he gets home." Zach carried a tray of glasses and set it on the small table.

"He didn't stay?' Jeremy asked.

"No. He had to go back to the club, but he said to stay here and not wander out. He also said that he would have his phone on and to call the police if anything happens that seems out of the ordinary." He passed out glasses. "It's iced tea, since someone has already gotten tipsy. I also have crackers and cheese so all the beer you had doesn't go right to your head." He handed Jeremy the plate and set the tray aside.

Jeremy munched a little and drank his tea. None of them seemed in a chatty mood, so they all sat quietly, which was so unlike them. Jeremy thought about Lowell and checked his phone a few times. He assumed Tristan was alternating between anger and regret, while Zach simply sat there quietly.

"This sucks," Tris said after a while. "You guys are really bringing down the party."

Jeremy and Zach both laughed. "Look who's talking," Zach quipped. "You haven't exactly been a barrel of monkeys. Come on, let's go inside and we can get dinner on the table." Zach gathered the empty dishes on the tray and carried everything inside.

"I'm sorry about Lowell. I hope everything works out," Tristan said.

"Me too," Jeremy whispered. He wasn't sure what was going to happen next. "Lowell knows how to take care of himself."

"Yeah, but he doesn't have friends like you guys to watch his back for him," Tristan said, and Jeremy nodded. That was part of what really bothered him. Lowell was out there somewhere, alone. And while Jeremy knew he couldn't help, he still wished he could be there to watch Lowell's back and be there for him. Was that love? Jeremy had never been in love before, but he was pretty sure that was what it meant. And right now it sucked, because he couldn't tell the object of his affections what he wanted to. What bothered him most was the thought that he might never be able to.

CHAPTER NINE

LOWELL TOOK a deep breath as he boarded the train going east. He'd managed to evade the men who'd been after him, and he needed a chance to relax and get some rest. Thankfully, he'd seen one of the men he'd caught a glimpse of before he left his place in New York. He'd grabbed his things and used his secondary route to get out of the hotel. They had clearly been looking for him, but didn't know what he looked like. He spent the night in a fleabag motel and was up at first light. He'd have no trouble getting away, he knew that. What had taken time were the careful breadcrumbs he left to ensure that whoever was after him would think he was heading west and away from Jeremy and his friends here.

The damn thing was Lowell was *so freaking good* the assholes nearly caught him while he was on the phone with Jeremy. One of them took a shot at him, but his aim sucked, and he'd jumped down the stairs in the park behind the bus station, glad no one else was nearby. He'd been able to zip back inside, buy a bus ticket, but conveniently miss the bus. Then when he'd seen some of the men take off after the bus, he'd ducked into the bathroom, and while ensconced in a stall, changed his appearance by quickly shedding the jeans he'd been wearing for khaki shorts and trading his button-down for a T-shirt. He also pulled a flattened bag out of his current one, transferred his things, and collapsed the old bag into the new one. After putting on a ball cap and sunglasses, he was set to leave. He walked right past two of the men without them realizing it was him, but he got a good look at them. He even managed to hang back enough to listen to their conversation while he waited for a cab. They had no idea who they were dealing with.

"Watch everyone. They said he could change his appearance," the taller of the two men said. He had a scar on his cheek that would make him easy to recognize anywhere.

"Why do they want him so bad?" the stockier of the two asked. Their conversation wouldn't have been audible to most people, but to Lowell they might as well have been shouting.

"Money. It's always about money." The other man nodded, and they continued milling around, watching everyone, but by then Lowell had slowly descended the stairs and gotten into a cab. He got out at the capitol and walked around the building before hailing another cab to take him to the train station. He'd bought a ticket and was now on his way to take care of business and put an end to all of this. Lowell settled into a seat and watched the platform carefully, ready to make a run for it if he saw any of his pursuers, but no one showed up. The doors closed and the train began to move. He sat back and rested for the first time in twenty-four hours. He wanted to close his eyes and try to sleep, but instead he thought about Jeremy. He wanted to give him a call, but it was best that no trails whatsoever led back to him. He had to keep him safe. That was what mattered.

A phone vibrated from deep in his bag. He pulled it out and saw a message from Jeremy: *RUOK*. He could almost feel the panic and concern behind those four letters. Just before the end of their last call, he had heard what Jeremy had said, and it had taken all his willpower not to stop in his tracks in that moment and marvel in wonder. Hell, to hear someone say those words to him was almost worth getting killed.

He typed a *Y* and sent the message, then turned off the phone and removed the battery. He shouldn't have left it on at all, but he'd been afraid Jeremy was in trouble. It was a burn phone, so no one would be able to trace it, but someone had some pretty deep and creative resources if they'd been able to trace him to Harrisburg, a town where he'd had no previous connections other than a business encounter more than a year earlier. Lowell had spent the last day, when he wasn't occupied with saving his skin, trying to figure out exactly who was doing this.

The logical person was his last client, but this was a lot of effort and money to spend to soothe his pride. No, Lowell had come to the conclusion that there was something else going on, and as he rode, the picture became clearer and clearer. The train had Internet access, and since there was no one nearby, he booted up his computer, activated his security software, and checked one of his mailboxes. There was a message file from Moonstone, asking him to contact her. He left a file as a response saying that he was occupied at the moment and would contact her soon. Then he disconnected from the site and made one more verification. Pleased that everything important was where it was supposed to be, he disconnected and decided that all he could do was wait. He still had three hours to wait, think, and plan.

An hour and a half later, they were calling for a stop in Philadelphia. He gathered his things, along with his ticket stub, and exited the train. He got change and found a pay phone, hoping like hell that Jeremy had his phone with him. He would only get one shot to make this call and then he'd have to board the train again.

The terminal was huge and grand, with what had to be fifty-foot ceilings. It was from the glamour days of train travel. It took him a while to find a pay phone tucked back near the bathrooms. He put in the money, dialed, and waited for instructions. After adding more change, his call connected.

"Jeremy," Lowell said softly. "It's me."

A sniffle followed a sigh. "Oh, God, you're really okay." Was Jeremy crying?

"Yes, I'm fine. I don't have much time. I wanted to call because I needed to hear your voice." It was the truth and at the moment he wasn't ashamed of it. He had someone who cared, and for that reason alone, he had to put an end to this so he could have a life. Maybe *they* could have a life. "Listen, they found me there and I had to leave. I'm sorry I wasn't there when you called earlier."

"Bull helped me and I'm at his house." Jeremy paused for a split second. "I heard shots the last time. Were they shooting at you? Did you get hit? Do you need help? Tell me where you are and I'll get there, no matter what."

"Yes, there was a shot, but it missed, and thank God no one else was around. I'm out of town and that's all you need to know. I'd love to have you with me, but not under these circumstances. I don't want you hurt." His instinct was to protect Jeremy at all costs, and he had no idea how much what he had to do was going to cost him, but it would be worth it if in the end, he had a chance to have Jeremy in his life. "You have to promise me that you will stay safe. It's what I'm counting on more than anything. I know Bull will do his very best. I don't think you're in danger, but I didn't think they could trail me there either, and they did."

"Who are they?" Jeremy asked urgently. "Do you know?"

"Yes. I think I've figured the whole thing out. I know who they are and I know how to deal with them. I just need to find them, and I will. But it may take time." A phone dinged in his bag, but he ignored it. "Please be patient." He looked at his watch. "I'm almost out of time. But I'll contact you if I can." His heart was racing and there was still more he wanted to say. "Use that phone number I gave you. I'll know who any message is from. Be general and say as little as possible. You did great last time."

"I will," Jeremy said. "I'm sorry I freaked out."

"Don't be, sweetheart." Where this particular endearment had come from and how it had slipped into his speech, he wasn't sure. But it was how he felt. He'd always thought attachments like the one he felt for Jeremy constituted a weakness, so he'd avoided them. But now he realized his attachment to Jeremy was also a strength. "I'll get this done and come back."

"Okay," Jeremy said. "I'll hold you to that." The phone line beeped and a voice told him to deposit more money. He'd used all the change he had.

"Jeremy, I—" The line disconnected.

He wanted to slam the phone back into the receiver, but calling attention wouldn't be good. He placed the handset where it went and turned back toward the main terminal building. People were returning to the train, so he got in line, showed the conductor at the top of the stairs his ticket stub, and descended back down to the level of the tracks.

He found a seat on the train and sat down. Only then did he pull out his other phone and look at the message. A set of long numbers—GPS coordinates—flashed on the screen, and he smiled. Lowell booted up his computer, making sure the security encryption was in place before entering the coordinates into a web page. The application gave him the exact location he needed. Lowell closed everything, turned it all off, and took out the batteries. He wasn't going to take any chances. He knew his information could be wrong or that his quarry might be messing with him.

There was always the possibility that everything could fall apart. But he had to do this, and if this was going to work, secrecy and stealth were his best (and only) weapons. If he pulled it off, he'd be done and maybe he could start a life of his own.

After a while, the train left the station, curling around and heading north toward New York. It was getting late. Night had already fallen, and Lowell watched the lights outside the windows for a while before closing his eyes. He was safe for now. He'd watched around him and was sure he hadn't been followed, at least not this far this fast. There was little doubt that his ruse wouldn't fool them for long, but by then his trail would be getting colder and colder. He sighed and let go of some of the tension, but not his diligence.

He passed through Trenton and then Newark before finally stopping at Penn Station. But all he did was change trains and continue his journey east well into the night.

It was in the small hours of the morning that he pulled up at a small white house in a quiet suburb on Long Island. There was nothing remarkable about it. The ranch house looked much like all the others in the development. But this one was special. Very special. Lowell could feel it. The house was dark, but he knew that was an illusion perpetrated so none of the neighbors would suspect anything. Lowell didn't go near the house. He just needed to know where it was, and he smiled. The end was in sight. Lowell turned and walked away and back toward the main road. Now he simply had to wait.

HE WAITED out the rest of the night at a cheap motel next to a Walmart and thought about many things, particularly the life he'd led and even the possibility of going back to it. That would be the easy decision; he knew that. He was so tempted. But the one thing that stopped him was Jeremy. His thoughts kept coming back to him. Lying on his motel bed, staring up at the ceiling, he remembered Jeremy's touch and replayed the concern in his voice from their last phone call. Lowell wanted a chance with Jeremy. He knew that was what he was doing this for. Life held no guarantees, but a chance with Jeremy was worth the risk. Jeremy's smile made his heart skip a beat, and being with him settled his mind and made him want to be the best he could be.

Lowell didn't sleep much, not that he'd expected to. He got up early, dressed like a UPS deliveryman, and went back to the house after "borrowing" a truck. During the day it looked just as normal as it did at night, but it wasn't normal. The ruse was an old one, but most of the time the simplest things were the best. He held a package in his hand as he walked up the front walk and rang the bell a little after eight in the morning. He waited and didn't fidget or look around nervously. He figured there was likely hidden surveillance, so he needed to look as though he belonged.

After a few minutes the front door opened and a woman in her midfifties greeted him in comfortable clothes, like she was spending the day taking care of the house. "May I help you?" she asked in a voice he knew well.

"We need to talk, Moonstone," he said levelly, staring at her, and watched her expression change from relaxed to concerned in an instant. "You and I have business we need to talk over, and I don't think you want to do it on the street."

She stepped back and he walked inside. "How did you find me?" she asked as she closed the door.

"I think there are more important issues to discuss than that. I found you just like you found me. I found the bit of code you hid in your messages and I turned your own trick back on you. That was pretty clever of you, and damn brilliant of you to make me think Estevez was after me when it was you all along. You sent the men to my place in New York." Lowell looked around the house, instantly assessing routes for a quick exit. This was someone he'd trusted at one point, but he wasn't sure how far she'd go.

"Is this your real face, Spook, or another of your disguises?" she asked, changing the subject.

"It's me," he said with a slight smile.

"You know I have you on film," she said.

"Of course, Danielle." Lowell watched as a crack appeared in her confidence and was quickly shored up again. Hearing her real name must have come as a shock to her. Once he'd figured out what was going on and where she was, he'd been able to follow the trail past the alias she'd used to purchase the house to her real identity. All it took was someone who knew where to look. And he did. "I have pictures of you as well." He paused and let that sink in. "Now, let's be civilized about all this."

"So you know who I am."

"Yes. It was remarkably easy once I had a few key pieces of information." Lowell smiled as he set the prop package on one of the white, high-backed chairs and sat in one of the others, then waited for her to do the same. "You didn't leave much of a trail, but I put together what there was, and of course let you lead me here."

"What do you want?"

"I want you to call off your dogs," Lowell said. "I could have taken them out and left a trail right back to you. But I just sent them on a wild goose chase." He smiled. "Eventually they'll pick up my trail, which will lead here." Moonstone sat down on the edge of one of the chairs. "All of the information I have has been included in a nice little insurance policy. If anything happens to me, it will all be released." Lowell sat back. "You had to know I was getting ready to hang it up and you weren't happy."

"Of course not."

"I made a lot of money for you, and you weren't in the mood to recruit someone new." The picture had come clearly into focus over the past few days. It hadn't right away, but as the pieces came together, the information Lowell didn't have filled in nicely. "Is that why you sent the men to my place? To scare me so you could come to the rescue with a job that would take me safely away to the other side of the world?"

"It damn near worked," she muttered and then sat back slightly. "Okay. Yeah. I sent the men after you. They weren't going to hurt you, just shake you up and get you moving. I've gotten the feeling you were getting tired, but you have good years left, and with the money I was making, I could retire when you did and head off to Florida or some other beach without a care in the world."

"You made plenty and you had to get greedy," Lowell countered. "I wasn't going to rat you out. You knew that. So instead you risked everything for a chance at, what, keeping me in the fold? Please." There really was no honor among thieves. Jesus, what had he gotten himself into? All these years he'd told himself he was doing his job, what he was paid to do, and in his mind that had given him distance. He always delivered and only took what he was entitled to, nothing more. Lowell had never thought of himself as one of the bad guys. Until he looked in the mirror and saw Moonstone staring back at him coldly enough to freeze water in Phoenix.

"Business is business. You know that," she retorted.

"Well, your business is going to be done if you don't call off the troops. I'm through. I'm not ratting anyone out, but I've done my last job." Lowell stood slowly. "And you'll have done your last job unless you cooperate. Do you think I just happened to find out where you live? I followed all kinds of trails, like your money trail to those goons. They were sloppy, and I'm good." He reached into his pocket and tossed her a cell phone. "Lifted it off one of the men in Harrisburg. It isn't a burn phone. Used it to get everything I needed on him and then back to you. Took about an hour. So, you see, all that money you've been socking away, it's been waylaid. Or at least part of it has."

"You son of a bitch!" she yelled.

"Now, come on. You know me better than that. I never took what wasn't mine and I'm not starting now," Lowell said levelly. "But you are going to do what I want if you ever want to see it again. Do you understand? I am not going to spend the rest of my life wondering if I need to watch my back because of you." He was a cynical guy and very careful of the people he let anywhere near him, but to have let this jackal this close to his business and this close to him was frightening. He'd spent his life watching out for threats on the job and from the outside, when the real threat had been so much closer. Damn, why hadn't he seen it? Because, just like Tristan, he had been kept off balance and his attention elsewhere. "Do we have an agreement?"

He waited, wondering if she was going to go ballistic, but her expression calmed. "Fine!"

"Good." He extended his hand, and she reluctantly shook it. "Never forget that I have enough on you to send you away for a long time." Lowell stepped forward. "But that isn't how I'll play it. I know how much you charged whom, and I'll be sure to turn you over to some very nasty people and let them have at you. If you double-cross me, the law would be way too soft on you."

Another crack showed in her veneer.

"We both have a past that we need to keep hidden, so as long as you don't throw stones, I won't either. And just remember, the next time I pay you a visit, you won't see it coming. I could be your mailman, the guy who mows your lawn, the gasman, you name it. I won't look like this or sound like this. Hell, I could even be a customer or a rival. So don't try to pull anything." Lowell crossed his arms over his chest. "Now call off your dogs and put an end to this."

Moonstone stood up, and Lowell followed her through the house. She opened a door in back to what had once been the family room. Lowell suspected that from the outside, if he were to walk around the house, he'd see normal windows with lowered blinds, but from the inside, it was a completely different view. The room was filled with computers, servers, and a communication center that would make NASA jealous. He followed her down the two steps and into the room. "This was how I nailed down your house." She stopped and turned around. "You use three times as much power as your neighbors. I suggest you watch what you're doing, or you'll find yourself on the radar of the police, because they'll think this is a drug house."

She gaped at him. "You have to be kidding—something as stupid as that?" She sat at the desk and put on her headset. Lowell wandered around the room, looking at the equipment and listening. As he did, a lot more of the picture dropped into place.

"You're a smart woman," Lowell said and turned around. "I bet all this runs the websites we all use to communicate." My God—it was practically the whole mercenary network. The information was here, but she could run the traffic through a number of foreign countries to the point it would be untraceable, with one host passing the traffic off to another, changing regularly.

"Don't touch anything," she snapped, and Lowell stepped back.

"Make the call," he growled. She was stalling, and Lowell wondered why. He went back into the house and straight to the kitchen, where he found a pitcher and filled it with water, then returned to Moonstone's lair. "Water will do none of this any good." Now he had her undivided attention. She'd gotten up to follow him but stopped in her tracks. "It won't take much on any one piece of equipment, so I suggest you finish our business and I'll be on my way."

Lowell saw her reach for the drawer beside the desk, and he tipped the pitcher, water running into the top of the server cabinet. She yanked out the drawer, and he dumped the rest of the water. Sparks flew everywhere as equipment shorted out, followed by the wiring. The lights blinked, went out, and came back on for a second. Lowell dove for her legs as she reached for the gun. He grabbed her, and as she went down, the gun went off. Pain bloomed in Lowell's thigh. He cried out, but held her down as light grew in the room. Lowell looked over his shoulder as he saw flames licking the walls on the far side of the room. Moonstone might have built one hell of a place for herself, but she certainly hadn't done it up to code. Sparks were coming from the walls as the older wiring overheated.

He grabbed Moonstone's hand and banged it on the floor until she released the gun and it skittered across the floor.

"You bastard, I should have had you killed when I had the chance." She kicked at him, connecting with his thigh, and Lowell screamed but held on to her. The flames continued to build, a roaring sound in his ears as the heat grew and the ceiling caught. He didn't have much time. Moonstone got to her feet and looked around. She spotted the gun and dove for it. Lowell scrabbled to her, grabbed her foot, and yanked her backward. She slid along the floor.

Somehow, Lowell got purchase with his good foot and heaved her headfirst toward the fire. She screamed when the flames caught her clothes and hair, and then she did what she shouldn't do: she ran and tripped on the steps, her feet flying out from under her. Moonstone flailed her arms and went down hard onto the floor, the flames roaring around her, snuffing out her screams.

He had to get the hell out of here. The whole house was going to go up, and the fire department would get here any minute. Lowell was not about to try to explain a gunshot wound to anyone. He hobbled past Moonstone as the flames leaped across the room behind him. He got out of the room and closed the door. At least the heat abated, but the door would only last so long. There was no way he could go out the front door like this. His pants were soaked with blood. He found a side door in the kitchen, unlocked it, and went out.

He heard voices out front, so he headed toward the back. He made it to the garage and slammed the door closed. He yanked the old curtains off the window and fashioned a bandage of sorts that he wrapped around his leg, then yanked what was left of his pant leg over it. A Cadillac sat in one of the stalls next to a Toyota Corolla sedan. He pulled open the door of the Corolla, thanking the stars it was unlocked. Expertly, Lowell used the tricks of the trade to get the car to start and looked behind him. "Fuck." He needed to open the garage door. Shifting his gaze to the visor, he sighed with relief. Never in his life had he been so glad to see a garage door opener. He pressed the button, and the door slid open. Lowell put the car in reverse and slowly backed out of the drive and into the alley. He closed the garage door and began to drive calmly out toward the main road. He didn't want to attract any attention. He turned left, away from the front of the house, and continued moving. Fire trucks sounded in the distance, getting closer. Lowell pulled over and let them pass as they came toward him. Once they were gone, he picked up the pace and drove the long way around to the motel, which was just a few blocks from Moonstone's now blazing house. He parked in the Walmart parking lot next door. Thankfully, his leg had stopped bleeding, but he hurt like hell and it burned like a son of a bitch. He got out of the car and remembered to wipe down the areas he'd touched. The bandage seemed to have prevented him from leaving a blood trail.

It was still early and there were just enough people around for him to blend in. He limped back to his room at the motel. He grabbed his bag and went right to the bathroom. He sat on the toilet and ripped the pant leg before gingerly removing the makeshift bandage. There was plenty of blood, but thankfully the bullet had missed the bone and appeared to have exited his leg. The flesh was torn up, and the muscle most likely shredded, but at least there wasn't a bullet buried inside him.

He was running out of tricks he could pull from his bag. He cleaned the wound as best he could and got it wrapped in a clean bandage made from the roll of gauze he carried in his small first-aid kit. With that done, he changed into the clothes he'd worn the day before, because that was about all he had left, and sat on the edge of the bed, waiting for the light-headedness to pass. He gathered the bloody clothes, shoved them into the plastic motel laundry bag, and stuffed it into his duffel. He'd dump them once he was away from here. When he felt steady again, he got up and drank some water. Then he made sure there were no telltale signs of anything before leaving the room. He'd prepaid for the room for another night, just in case, so he didn't go by the front desk.

His luck was with him when he saw a taxi dropping people off in front. He got in and asked the driver to take him into the city. When the driver initially balked, Lowell handed him a hundred and said he was late for a business meeting and that he'd give him another when they got there. The driver's eyes widened and he took the money, and they were off. Now all Lowell had to do was not pass out and look normal for the rest of the ride and he'd be home free.

It wasn't to be, at least not without great effort. Traffic was a bitch, and the ride took forever. By the time the driver got him to Times Square, Lowell could hardly keep his eyes open, and when he did, the world swam in circles. On sheer willpower he got out of the cab and paid the driver his extra hundred. The man was thrilled, and Lowell headed into the bustling hotel.

The lobby was a madhouse. Lowell scouted the area and found a men's room tucked in a quiet alcove near an empty conference room. He dumped the bag of clothes in the trash, pushing them way down. No one would ever notice. When he checked himself in the restroom mirror, he looked awful. Then he checked the identities he had and went back out to the lobby to get a room. He used the last ID he had with him and was given a room on the twenty-third floor. The elevator nearly made him throw up, but he got off and down the hall to his room, nearly falling inside when the door opened. He got inside and closed the door, then collapsed on the bed.

Lowell knew he needed help. When he'd gotten into these rare situations in the past, he'd called Moonstone, but that was over and she was gone. So he pulled his bag along the floor and managed to dig out his phone. He dialed and waited for an answer. "I need help."

CHAPTER
TEN

JEREMY RAN around the apartment gathering clothes and shoving them into a bag.

"You're going to miss Pride," Tristan said. He thought Jeremy was being crazy and had told him so, bluntly.

Jeremy stopped. "I know you think I'm nuts. You made that plain. But there will be another Pridefest next year." He went to his dresser and pulled out a couple pair of jeans before returning to his bag. "You have no idea how hard it was for Lowell to do what he did."

"But you don't know what you'll be getting mixed up in," Tristan countered. "What if he's being pursued and you're going to get involved in a mess like that?"

Jeremy paused for a second. He'd thought of that. "Lowell wouldn't have called me. He needs help and he sounded very weak. You don't have to drive me to the train station if you don't want to. I can either walk or take a cab."

"Don't be dumb. Of course I'll take you. But I just don't understand how you can do this." Tristan was still hurting, and Jeremy figured that was part of it. "You don't know what he's done."

"He told me he took care of things and that it was over," Jeremy said and swallowed hard as Tristan stared at him. "That was his way of saying he needed help so he could come back here."

"You really love him, don't you? And not like I loved Eddie, but deep-down love." Tristan sat on the edge of the bed, near Jeremy's bag, and it tilted slightly toward him. "I can see now how Eddie was treating me. I couldn't at the time, but I'm starting to understand. He was nice, but I would never run off to New York because he called and said he needed help. Not that he ever would have asked." Tristan looked down at the floor.

"It took a lot of trust for Lowell to call, and I have to trust that he wouldn't put me in any danger."

"But how can you do that? Trust someone you only met a few weeks ago…. How do you know that Lowell is the right one?"

Jeremy stepped in front of Tristan. "All I can say is, you'll know. I know it sounds corny and as clichéd as anything I've ever said, but it's true. You'll know. The guy will touch your heart first, and then… the other stuff."

"But he was touching the other stuff first. I remember you guys on the dance floor."

"I didn't mean that literally. More like how you feel. It's hard to explain, but believe me, you'll know when it happens. Maybe Eddie seemed flashy and cool, but there was nothing on the inside."

"And there is with Lowell?" Tristan sounded suspicious.

"Yeah, there is, and I'm sure there's more to it than I know now. Lowell holds what's in his heart very close. He doesn't wear it on his sleeve and he doesn't share it easily. But he shows it. When I needed help, he was there. Even when I made him sleep on the sofa because I was a fool, he was still there. I think that's what love is. I used to think it was all about being hot for each other, and that's part of it, but so is just being there. I guess you gotta have both." Jeremy moved to the side and zipped his bag closed.

"Maybe," Tristan admitted. Jeremy picked up his bag, and Tristan followed him out of the room. "You got your phone? 'Cause you call me right away if you need anything." Tristan pulled him into a hug. "I know I've been a self-centered prick lately, but I'm here if you need me."

"I know, and you've been hurt. We all forgive and forget," Jeremy said as Tristan released him. He took a quick look around, ran through his list of things he needed, and then pulled open the apartment door.

TRISTAN TOOK him to the station, and Jeremy worried the entire four-hour train ride to New York. Lowell had sounded so very weak and tired on the phone. He tried calling, but the phone went right to voice mail, so he wasn't sure if it had been turned off or something worse, so he stopped calling and stared out the window all the way past Philadelphia and into New York. When he got to Penn Station, he got off the train and walked quickly toward Times Square. In their brief conversation, Lowell had told him where he was staying and the room number. Jeremy found the hotel and took the elevator up to Lowell's floor. Once he found the room, he knocked on the door and waited.

No one answered. He tried it to see if it was open, but of course it wasn't. Jeremy had started to look around to ask someone for help when he heard the lock and the door cracked open.

"Jeremy," Lowell said in a tired whisper. He opened the door further, and Jeremy went inside.

The room was dark and smelled stale. Lowell closed the door, and Jeremy saw him sway slightly. He dropped his bag, took Lowell around the waist, and led him back to the bed. Once he got him lying down, Jeremy turned on one of the lights so he could see what had happened.

Lowell looked terrible—pale with dark circles under his eyes—and the room smelled sour, like a sick person had been holed up there.

"I brought some supplies, but you're going to have to try to help me," Jeremy said to cover the gasp of shock that threatened to well up.

"I'll be okay now that you're here," Lowell whispered very softly.

Jeremy wasn't so sure and was scared as hell. From the looks of him, Lowell needed a doctor, but Jeremy knew the suggestion would be met with resistance, so he got some towels from the bathroom, laid them under Lowell's leg, and carefully removed the bandages.

As soon as he saw Lowell's leg, he couldn't stop the gasp and turned away to avoid being sick. He held himself together only because he knew losing it was not going to help Lowell. "I'll do everything I can to help you, but you have to promise me something."

"Huh?"

"You have to promise me," Jeremy persisted.

"What do you want me to promise?" Lowell asked warily.

"First, that you're truly done," Jeremy said.

"I am done. There's no going back now. That's not to say that my old life won't intrude sometimes on my new one. But I'm done." Lowell sounded weak, but confident nonetheless.

"And second, you have to promise to tell me everything. I know it won't be pretty or something you're proud of, but I have to know it all.

That is, if you want us to be together. If you don't, and after this you want to disappear and start clean somewhere else, like near your brother, I'll understand." He'd thought about this the entire train ride. "There can't be any secrets between us going forward. If you can't do that, say so now. I'll help you out all I can and then leave." Jeremy knew putting his cards on the table was risky, but he had to know.

Lowell sighed. "Sweetheart, I'll tell you everything you want to know, and not to get you to help me, but because you need to know it all." Lowell rolled slightly on the bed. "I got a good look at myself today, and it was… ugly." Lowell put his arm over his eyes. "I'm afraid you won't want me when you know, but I'll tell you everything."

Armed with that promise, Jeremy got a washcloth and carefully cleaned the dried blood off Lowell's leg. Once he'd done that, he could see that the bullet had gone straight through. It wasn't as bad as Jeremy had thought at first, but the skin was red and inflamed at both the entry and exit points. He needed to get the wounds cleaned and wrapped again. "I brought some alcohol and I need to clean the wounds, but it's gonna hurt." It was going to sting like hell. "I'm assuming that since the bullet went through, it didn't hit the bone."

"You're right. They're flesh wounds," Lowell whispered. "They bled a lot, and that's why I'm so weak."

Jeremy got a cloth and put some alcohol on it, then cleaned the area around the wounds. Then he poured some where the bullet had gone in. Lowell jumped half out of his skin, but said nothing at all. Jeremy had expected a scream, but Lowell remained quiet, even as deep lines of pain creased his face. Jeremy dabbed at the remaining alcohol and then cleaned the other side. Both wounds were clean and round, the bullet having passed right through. "I hope I'm doing some good," Jeremy said. At least the wounds were clean. They bled a little again, but what came out was red and seemed clean, which he thought was a good sign. Jeremy then wrapped Lowell's leg and got him settled on the bed again. "How long have you been here?"

"Since I called you," Lowell answered tiredly.

"Okay. I'm going to try to find you some food. Since there isn't much in your bag for you to wear, I'm going to get you some loose clothes that will hide the bandage. I can't stay too long, though. I have to get back to work by Monday." Jeremy knew that didn't leave them much time. But he had no choice. He couldn't stay any longer because he needed his job.

"Just go, but don't be gone too long."

Jeremy straightened the bed and gathered up the things he'd used. In the bathroom he rinsed out the washcloth and towels to get as much blood out of them as he could. Then he hung them up to dry and returned. Lowell's eyes were closed, and Jeremy straightened the bedding and did his best to make Lowell comfortable. He found Lowell's room key and took it with him before leaving and venturing out into the city.

He'd only been to New York once before, but there were stores nearby. He found light sweatpants at a sporting goods store and bought a pair in large. They were bulky and loose, which was perfect. He also got a plain T-shirt and some socks. He hoped Lowell could still wear his shoes. Then he went in search of food and found a small market a few blocks away. He bought chicken noodle soup and juice for Lowell and something more substantial for himself to eat. Then he hurried back to the hotel before everything got cold.

Lowell was asleep when he came into the room. Jeremy sat on the edge of the bed in the dark room and gently roused Lowell. "You need to eat for me." Lowell groaned, and Jeremy placed his hand on his forehead. He didn't feel too hot, which was good. He should have bought a thermometer while he was out but hadn't thought of it. "Can you sit up?"

Lowell groaned again, and Jeremy helped him get up. Then he grabbed some of the wad of napkins he'd taken with the food and placed them under Lowell's chin. "I can do it," Lowell said, but his hands shook, and Jeremy shushed him. He opened the carton of soup, dug a spoon out of the bag, and began feeding him. The first sips seemed tentative, but soon they got into a rhythm, and Lowell ate about half the soup before his eyes began to close again.

"Are you full or just tired?" Jeremy said, setting the soup on the bedside stand.

"Tired," Lowell said, obviously making an effort to keep his eyes open.

"Then eat a little more. You need to have your strength so you can heal." Jeremy picked up the spoon and soup and slowly fed him some more.

"It's good," Lowell said. "I feel warm and...."

"That's the soup," Jeremy told him, feeling his forehead again. "You need to be strong so you don't get any infection. The wounds looked clean, but we won't know for a while." God, he hoped Lowell was going to be okay.

"You need to eat too," Lowell said, taking the soup and spoon. He slowly ate, finishing the rest of the soup while Jeremy ate his sandwich and now cold egg roll. He loved the things, and while this one wasn't bad, he should have known better than to buy one and try to bring it back.

"How did this happen?" Jeremy asked.

"Too tired to talk now, but it seems I won a fight in a burning building. The other guy wasn't so lucky." Lowell smiled, but Jeremy knew exactly what he meant and it chilled him. "I promised to tell you and I will, but not now. I need to sleep, and tomorrow we need to get out of here."

"Lowell, you'll need to stay here a few days until you're stronger."

"Not going to leave you or let you go without me. Still may be danger." Lowell handed him the empty soup container, and Jeremy threw it away. Then Jeremy finished his sandwich and gave Lowell the bottle of juice. He drank most of it and set the bottle on the table. Jeremy pulled away the napkins, and Lowell settled under the blankets, closing his eyes. "We can get train tickets for tomorrow, and I'll take you home." That sounded like Lowell wasn't planning on staying. Jeremy wanted to ask what Lowell's plans were, but he looked peaceful, some of the pain lines smoothing out, so he kept his questions for later.

"Here, take this for the pain and you'll sleep better." Jeremy got him to take two ibuprofen tablets and then gathered up all the papers and turned out the light. Then he straightened out the bedding and stared down at Lowell as he slept. The room was still stale and none of the windows would open. Jeremy notched the temperature down slightly, and the air-conditioning kicked on. Almost instantly, the air freshened and Jeremy inhaled deeply.

"That's better," Lowell mumbled, and Jeremy settled into a comfortable chair and pulled out his Kindle from his bag and settled in to read. He'd just bought the latest Ken Follett masterpiece, and he'd been dying to start it.

As the room chilled, he shifted slightly and turned up the AC. Lowell was sound asleep, which Jeremy knew was good. He hoped Lowell slept through the night. Every hour or so, he checked for a fever and was relieved to find Lowell resting and relatively cool. Eventually he put his Kindle away and went into the bathroom to clean up. Then he settled on the other side of the bed and did his best to try to sleep.

"JEREMY," LOWELL whispered.

Jeremy jerked awake and turned to him. "Are you okay?"

"Yes. My leg aches, and I'm tired as hell, but my head isn't spinning and my mind seems to be clear. Did you sleep at all?" Lowell shifted closer and gently stroked his cheek. "I'm sorry to get you messed up in this, but there was no one else I trusted enough to help me."

"Why not call Bull?" Jeremy asked. "Not that I wouldn't have come, but he's better at these things."

"A lot of people would draw attention, and you're the one I trust above everyone, including Bull."

Jeremy swallowed hard. The admission was eye-opening for him. "Are you hungry?" he asked. "I can check the room service menu and have something delivered." He wasn't particularly interested in trying to scour the town for breakfast. He knew he'd need to go out and get food for lunch and the trip back. Although how Lowell was going to be able to do all the walking necessary to get to the train station and train was beyond him. A cab would transport them, but they would have to walk to get down to the cab station as well as out to the train.

"Order room service and stop thinking so hard. We'll figure it out."

Jeremy scowled at Lowell. "How do you know what I'm thinking?"

"It's a pretty good guess. I can do what I need to do," Lowell said with determination. Jeremy wasn't sure he believed him at the moment, but he got up, found the room service menu, and placed an order for eggs, bacon, sausage, coffee, juice, toast, and hash browns. "Was there anything on the menu you didn't order?" Lowell asked when he hung up the phone.

"I wasn't sure what you wanted, and I'm hungry," Jeremy snapped.

"I wasn't judging or picking. Just teasing," Lowell told him and held out his arms. Jeremy stepped closer to the bed, remembering he'd been running around naked. He got back under the covers, and Lowell held him close without moving. Regardless of whether Lowell could do anything, Jeremy's body was strung tight and ready for action. Jeremy silently told his wayward dick to go back to sleep, because nothing was going to happen. It didn't listen.

"Is this for me?" Lowell asked and brushed his hand over Jeremy's cock.

"Yes, you get that later, once you're better," Jeremy chided, but, damn, he wanted Lowell to touch him again. He needed that connection, that knowledge that Lowell still wanted him after he'd been such a doofus. He moved away and tried to put sex out of his mind. He lay quietly next to Lowell, closed his eyes, and listened to his soft breathing. Slowly the craving for passion subsided and was replaced by quiet peace.

"I'm going to be okay. I've been hurt worse than this before," Lowell whispered into the dimness of the room, a small amount of light coming in around the curtains.

Jeremy sighed loudly. "You seem awake and more active than you were last night." He didn't want to move away from Lowell's warmth and comfort, but there were things he had to do. "I need to check your bandage and put some clothes on before room service gets here. Then we'll see how you feel after you've eaten and rested before we make any plans about you going anywhere," he cautioned.

Lowell touched his chin and Jeremy looked toward him. "Thank you for coming here. I really needed help, and you came." Lowell kissed him gently, but there was so much in that kiss. They'd kissed passionate and hard, soft and gentle, but this was *the* kiss. "You turned my world and everything in it upside down. I'm supposed to be the strong one and protect you from me and my past, but here you are helping me when I need it most." They kissed again.

"So we're equals?"

Lowell paused and his eyes widened slightly. "We were always equals. You have so many good traits—I can never measure up. You're kind and thoughtful, strong, and loyal, but most of all you have a heart as big as anyone I've ever met. Is that part of this? That you thought I didn't see you as an equal?'

"Maybe a little. You were always trying to protect me and keep things about yourself hidden. I thought it was because you didn't think I was up to your standards," Jeremy said, his emotions rising, and he choked on the last word.

"Jeremy, you are my standard. The one I'll measure everyone by in the future. You came for me when I needed it," Lowell whispered. "To put it another way, I was lying on the floor of my own proverbial convenience store and you came and helped me. No one has done that before."

Jeremy backed away and smiled. "Then you had shitty friends and definitely need to get yourself some new ones." Lowell laughed softly but gently and nodded once. Then Jeremy shifted on the bed, pressed himself against Lowell, and kissed that laughter away.

Before he got carried away, Jeremy backed away and got up. He went to his bag and pulled on a pair of shorts and then went to the bathroom. He got one of the last towels from the bathroom and returned to the bed. He pulled back the covers and got an eyeful. "I see you are feeling better," he said randily. Lowell was wide awake now and standing at attention. "Room service is going to be here in just a few minutes." And the last thing he wanted was a knock on the door at an important moment.

"I know. But it's morning and my dick doesn't know what's important."

Jeremy pulled his eyes away from Lowell's groin, placed the towel under his leg, and removed the bandage. It caught in a few places. The wounds looked largely the same except that they'd begun to darken where Lowell's body was trying to heal. The skin was pink, and while still puffy, didn't look as angry as it had last night. Jeremy cleaned the area again and replaced the bandage. Then he covered him again and helped Lowell sit up as a knock sounded on the door. Jeremy pulled on a T-shirt and answered the door, then took the tray and came back inside the room. He set the tray on the edge of the bed and climbed on. He put the tray on his lap and handed Lowell his juice.

"I wanted coffee," Lowell groused.

"You're getting juice because you're sick and it has vitamins. You don't need caffeine. That's for me because I have to deal with you." Jeremy flashed his best smile and poured the coffee from the tiny pot into a mug. Lowell groaned, and Jeremy handed him a fork. They ate like it was a tiny breakfast buffet. If it weren't for Lowell's injury, it could have been the prelude to a fun day in bed. But it was anything but, and Jeremy was nervous.

Once they were done eating, Jeremy took the tray and placed it in the hall. Lowell's energy was already fading. His eyelids were drooping and he was hurting—Jeremy could tell by the tiny lines on his face. He got him some more ibuprofen and turned out the lights. Lowell settled right down into the bedding and was asleep within a few minutes.

Jeremy dressed and cleaned up as quietly as he could. Then he left the room and wandered through the hotel and out into Times Square. He didn't want to go far, but he wasn't going to sit in the room for hours either. He meandered through stores, but couldn't concentrate on anything other than Lowell up in the room. Lowell had said that whatever had been going on was over, but he'd also said he wanted to protect him, so Jeremy wondered what he still needed protection from.

Jeremy found a small convenience store and bought some snacks and drinks for later. Before he returned to the room, he got some sandwiches, hoping Lowell liked ham and cheese. When he got back up to the room, it was still dark and quiet. Lowell shifted and turned on the light as soon as he came in.

"Are you hungry?" Jeremy asked.

"Yes. Then we need to get out of here."

"You aren't strong enough," Jeremy chided nervously. He could tell Lowell was still tired. "And don't lie to me."

"I won't. But waiting a few hours isn't going to make a difference. I have some energy, and we need to make the most of it."

Jeremy wasn't sure about this at all, but he handed Lowell his sandwich and one of the drinks he'd purchased. Once they'd eaten, Lowell asked him to hand him his computer. Jeremy did, and Lowell got them train tickets before shutting it down again. "Okay, help me up. I need to get dressed. Our train leaves in two hours, and we need to be on it." Lowell sounded determined, so Jeremy helped him into the bathroom, and while Lowell used the facilities, Jeremy laid out his clothes for him.

When he hobbled out of the bathroom, Lowell got dressed with plenty of muttered swearing, and the lines around his eyes deepened. Jeremy helped him get his shoes on. "We'd better go." Jeremy couldn't figure out how Lowell was going to make it, but he gathered their things together.

"Rinse out everything and make sure there's no sign of blood anywhere," Lowell told him. Jeremy had been pretty careful. He checked the bathroom and found a washcloth that he needed to rinse before adding it to the soggy pile on the floor. His mother would have killed him for making such a mess, and he tried to figure out how to straighten up. He thought of hanging everything up, but there wasn't time, so he left it.

Lowell was at the door, and Jeremy got both their bags and followed him, letting the door close once they left. Thankfully, the elevators weren't too far away, and they made it with a minimum of swearing. "If you're already hurting, it's only going to get worse," Jeremy whispered.

"Once we're on the train, you can give me something and I'll sit and sleep for the entire trip," Lowell told him. "Now let's get the hell out of here."

They stopped in the lobby, and Jeremy could almost believe Lowell was feeling great. He smiled and kidded with the lady when he checked out like nothing was wrong, but as soon as the elevator door closed, he leaned against the wall for the short ride to the ground floor. There wasn't a line at the cabstand outside the hotel, so they got one right away.

Their ride to the station was silent. Jeremy could feel the pain rolling off Lowell, and the ride down the escalator and the walk through the shopping area in the station was obviously excruciating for Lowell. Jeremy could read it in the deepening lines around his eyes, though nothing else betrayed the pain Lowell was in.

Jeremy got him settled in the waiting area. There was still forty-five minutes before the train was scheduled to leave. They sat quietly. Jeremy read because he needed something to do, even though he read the same paragraph at least four times without understanding a word. A little before their train was due, Jeremy helped Lowell up and across the waiting area to the track. They were near the front of the line when boarding was announced.

Lowell seemed unsteady and leaned against him as they showed their electronic tickets on Jeremy's cell phone to the conductor. Then they rode the escalator down, and Lowell nearly tumbled to the floor at the end. He recovered, though, and somehow they made it onto the train and into seats. Lowell sighed and settled into his seat. "I never thought we'd get here," he whispered. "I'm a little cold."

Jeremy looked around and then felt Lowell's forehead, trying not to draw too much attention. He wasn't feverish, thank God. Jeremy chalked it up to him being tired. He didn't have anything with them to warm him, so he moved closer. People continued boarding around them, and Jeremy noticed how Lowell watched each person who passed. No one paid attention to them, though, and soon the flood of people became a trickle. Then everyone seemed to settle, and the train began to move. Jeremy got some ibuprofen and some water from his bag and gave them to Lowell. He wanted to check the bandages. He was sure the wounds had probably opened again. "Do you think you're bleeding?" he whispered.

"The bandages are in place, and we can't check until we get someplace safe," Lowell whispered. Jeremy brought down the footrest so

Lowell could raise his leg and get as comfortable as possible. It was going to be a long ride.

Lowell closed his eyes and after the first stop seemed to be asleep. The conductor came through to verify tickets, and then they simply rode. There was nothing else to do. Jeremy tried to read, but gave up and simply sat and worried. He looked at Lowell every few seconds to make sure he was okay, but he didn't stir much. They slowed, stopped, and sped up multiple times along their journey. Jeremy didn't pay attention to their stops; all he did was check his watch and worry. Finally, as they were getting close, Jeremy pulled out his phone and called Tristan, who agreed to meet them at the station. He should have called earlier, but it hadn't crossed his mind.

They pulled into the station a half hour later. He and Lowell got off the train, and Lowell groaned at the sight of the staircase up to the station. "We can wait for the elevator," Jeremy suggested. He pointed to the line of people already waiting. Lowell shook his head. Jeremy carried the bags, and Lowell held the railing, using it both for balance and to help pull himself up.

Somehow they made it up and out to the main station doors. Tristan was waiting, but as they approached the car, Lowell pointed. "Get in the car and hurry," he whispered to both of them. "We need to get out of here." Lowell got in the back and lay down on the seat. Jeremy got in front, and poor Tris simply appeared confused, but he drove them to their apartment.

"What was all that about?" Tristan asked as he found a place to park.

Jeremy looked to Lowell, who shook his head. "We'll tell you later, I promise. Right now, we have to get him up into our apartment and into my room." Jeremy wanted to get them alone so Lowell could explain. In fact, Lowell had a great deal of explaining to do, and Jeremy figured that now was probably a good time, once he was comfortably in bed. They got out of the car, and Lowell hobbled up the stairs, leaning on Jeremy. The pain was definitely back, and Jeremy wanted to get a look at the wounds as soon as Lowell was settled.

It took a while to do just that, but finally Lowell was settled and Jeremy had fussed over him. The wounds were open and seeping. Jeremy cleaned the wounds again and changed the bandages. "I shouldn't be here," Lowell told him as Jeremy pulled up the covers. "The man at the station was one of the ones after me. They didn't recognize me, but it's only a matter of time before they pick up my trail, especially after what happened yesterday morning. They caught up with me once already here in town."

"Maybe, but they won't expect you to come back." Jeremy finished fussing and sat on the edge of the bed. "I know you probably aren't ready to tell me everything, but why don't you start with what's been going on."

"Well, it seems my handler was the one who's been playing me. She wasn't happy I was leaving. Though I'd already made a lot of money for her, I was still a big part of her retirement plans. The long and short of it is that we had it out and things escalated to the point where she shot me. She's gone now—it was self-defense, but I'm sure the men after me don't know that." Lowell shook his head. "I can't believe I screwed up so much and got you involved in all this."

Jeremy wasn't sure what to think at this point. "What do you need to do?"

"Right now I need to rest, and then I need to go."

Jeremy shook his head. "No. We need to get our friends together and figure this out. No more doing shit alone," Jeremy told him harshly. "Look what happened—your handler's gone... and men are still after you. This has to end, and I want it to stop right now."

"How do you propose we do that?" Lowell countered. "These guys aren't going to stop."

"Will they get paid?" Jeremy asked. "You said your handler was dead. If she hired them, how will they get paid?" He leaned closer. "I think you're way too tired to be working this through right now. Get some rest and we'll talk all this over when you wake up."

"What if something happens?"

"You'll still be here, and even with an injured leg, I feel safe with you here." Jeremy smiled, and Lowell slipped his hand around the back of his neck, pulling him in for a gentle kiss.

"What did I ever do to deserve you?" Lowell asked.

"I don't know," Jeremy kidded. "But you'll figure it out." Jeremy kissed him and then left the room, closing the door behind him.

"What's going on?" Tristan asked as soon as Jeremy walked back into the living room.

"It's complicated and a little head-spinning. But I think we need to call Bull and see if he can come over in a few hours. We're going to need his help." Jeremy looked toward the bedroom and bit his lower lip. A plan was forming and he needed to talk it over with both Bull and Lowell. He also needed a few minutes to think.

"I can't believe both you and Zach...." Tristan glanced down the hallway. "I mean, I somehow doubt that Harrisburg is a center for guns for hire, but you and Zach somehow managed to land the only two within hundreds of miles. What's the attraction?"

Jeremy smiled. "If you have to ask, then you'll never understand," he quipped and then pulled out his phone. Zach answered when he called the house, and he put Bull on the phone, but only after giving him the third degree about why and what was up. Jeremy had to agree to let Zach be a part of whatever was going on before he'd actually hand over the phone.

"I'm back with Lowell and he's been shot," Jeremy explained without preamble. "There are men still after him. He saw one of them at the train station. I doubt they saw us, but that was dumb luck. We need to put an end to this and we need to do it fast."

"Do you think we can? These things take on a life of their own," Bull told him.

"We have to try. Then maybe this whole thing can be over," Jeremy said. "I want a chance with him. I don't know if it will go anywhere or if I'll be exciting enough for him, but I want to try, and I think he does too. He's already talking about leaving again because I might be in danger."

"You seem to be his weakness," Bull commented.

"Thanks," Jeremy groused.

"I mean that in a good way. He really seems to care. If he didn't, he wouldn't be so adamant about keeping you safe and secure." Bull sighed, and Jeremy heard Zach in the background. "We'll be over in a few hours."

"Thanks, and see if Kevin can come as well."

Bull growled, but agreed and disconnected the call.

"Bull will be over in a few hours, and Zach will be here and probably Kevin. We'll put our heads together and figure this out," Jeremy told Tristan. Jeremy looked down the hallway. "These guys think they can do everything on their own. They don't understand that there's strength in numbers and in having friends you can count on." Jeremy made sure all the doors were locked and checked out the front windows. Then he flopped onto the sofa to wait.

CHAPTER
ELEVEN

LOWELL WOKE from his nap disoriented, but rested. His leg ached, but not like it had a few hours earlier. Voices drifted in from the other room, and he recognized Jeremy's immediately. He remembered that he was at Jeremy's apartment and in his bed. He needed to get out of here and go far away, so Jeremy would be safe. He'd lead the men away and then figure out how he wanted to deal with them. It was wonderful that Jeremy wanted to help, but he wouldn't allow him to get hurt. Once he'd taken care of the problem, he'd come back, if Jeremy still wanted him. But that was a chance he was willing to take if it meant Jeremy was safe from his troubles and past. He'd brought this whole fucking mess into Jeremy's life and he needed to clean it up. He sat up on the edge of the bed and closed his eyes as his leg ached dully. At least the pain wasn't nearly as sharp as it had been yesterday. Maybe the damn thing was healing.

He stood up, and his leg almost buckled from under him. Lowell felt as weak as a baby, but he had to push it aside and do what he knew must be done. He got the door open and used the walls of the hallway to steady himself as he made his way to the darkened living room.

"You're awake," Jeremy said with a smile. "Do you want something to eat? Kevin made chicken soup—his mother's recipe."

Lowell nodded and looked around the room at the small gathering.

"Lie down on the sofa and I'll get you some," Jeremy said. "Then we're all going to talk."

"About what?"

"Your little problem," Bull answered flatly. Lowell couldn't fight all of them, not in this condition, so he lowered himself onto the sofa.

"Are you all serious? You're going to risk your lives to help me?" He looked at each of them one by one. "These men are dangerous, and they won't blink at hurting any of you."

"We know that," Zach said as he walked up to him. "You are a major pain in the ass. Every time I see you, trouble follows not far behind. But I'm willing to help, and so is Bull, because Jeremy cares about you."

"Easy," Bull said, placing a hand on Zach's shoulder. He turned to Lowell. "Why don't you tell us what you know about these men, and maybe we can figure out how to... persuade them to simply turn around and go home."

Lowell told them everything he knew about Moonstone, the way she'd used these men to ramp up the pressure and then how she'd paid them to teach Lowell a lesson and set an example for anyone else who tried to get in her way. "I knew she was hard—that's what it takes to do her job—but I never saw her as evil." He paused. "Or myself, until yesterday."

Jeremy came back with a bowl of soup. He handed it to Lowell and said earnestly, "You're not evil."

"You may change your mind after I keep my promise," Lowell whispered, and then he took a sip of the soup. Either he was hungrier than he'd thought or this was the best soup ever. He dug in with enthusiasm.

"Okay," Bull said, bringing the conversation back to the topic. "Basically Moonstone has put out a contract on you. You should know how to contact her."

Lowell shook his head. "Moonstone is dead. I pieced everything together and tricked her into opening a shell file that led me to her location. She attacked me and, well, she isn't with us anymore. But her contract lives on."

"So we pretend to be her, get into her communication network, and call the whole thing off."

Lowell cleared his throat and set his now empty soup bowl on the coffee table. "I thought of that too. But the entire place went up in flames, including all her equipment and half the mercenary communication infrastructure. She was a very enterprising woman."

"So what you're saying is that there's a loose contract and you have no way of calling it off other than getting to the men she contracted with," Bull asked as he crossed his arms over his chest, a glare firmly on his face. "You should have thought of that before you torched everything." Bull continued glaring at him. Lowell got defensive, puffing out his chest. While Bull had a point, his pride would not allow him to just back down, at least not completely.

"I didn't do it to cover my tracks. More like stay out of the line of fire, which didn't work so well either. I had something she wanted very badly, and I figured she'd call everything off to get it back. Then things escalated out of control. I'm sure not each of your operations went as planned. It was supposed to have been a little quid pro quo, nothing more." Lowell realized how whiny he sounded. It was a good thing he was getting out. He'd been sloppy, and that could cost him everything.

"That's enough, both of you," Jeremy said. "This is not a pissing match, and if it were, I'd win because I can outwhine both of you any day. I called you because we need to figure out a way to bring this to an end. We've had weeks of drug dealers, hit men, chases, gunfights, and God knows what else. This needs to be over so for his sake and mine." Jeremy focused his glare on each of them, and damn if Bull didn't back away. Lowell did the same. He needed all their help. "Maybe we can pay these guys more to go away."

Bull nodded, and Lowell did the same. "Have you got money for that?"

Lowell grinned. "Actually, that was the bait. I've got all of Moonstone's ill-gotten gains. That was the bait I was using. I was able to follow her money trail. She was brilliant about some things, but others not so much. She went ballistic and wouldn't see reason. All she needed to do was call everything off and agree to leave me alone. I would have given her the money back," he muttered under his breath.

"She had quite the reputation," Bull told him, and Lowell nodded. "But I wouldn't have expected her to be so aggressive."

"I think she was fine being anonymous and faceless, but the direct confrontation was more than she could take. There was a lot of ego there and it got the best of her."

Jeremy stepped between them again. "Okay, so the bitch was nuts. What are we going to do? We can't call the police."

"Where did you see the men today? At the train station?" Bull asked.

"Yeah. They were outside."

"Then let's start there. No one, not even they, are going to try something in public in broad daylight with witnesses," Bull said. Lowell stifled a scoff. He wasn't so sure about that, but Bull was probably right. "You're going to have to give me a description of the men so I can call them out."

"The guy I believe to be the leader has a wicked scar on his cheek. I can give you descriptions of the rest. They're like bulls in a china shop. If you watch, they'll stand out to you—you know the type."

"Okay. I'll go down to the train station and have a look around," Bull volunteered, and Zach walked over to him. "You are staying here," Bull told Zach.

"The hell I am. If you're going, then I'm going, and you can swallow that argument right now." The way Zach snapped fearlessly and lovingly at Bull made Lowell smile. He hoped someday he and Jeremy could have as good a relationship as those two. Bull was definitely not happy, but he didn't argue with Zach.

"What about us?" Tristan asked.

"The rest of you need to stay here and keep the doors locked. Don't let anyone in, especially a deliveryman or anything like that. No one at all until I get back. I don't care if it's the guy you see walking his dog every day. No one gets in here until we get back. That's how we get past people—by posing as someone harmless or that you see every day." Bull glared at all of them, and they nodded. Even Lowell found himself nodding. The man was a force to be reckoned with.

Lowell gave Bull the descriptions of the men. "The one I saw today was wearing jeans and a black T-shirt. He was trying to blend in, but stuck out anyway. I believe there are four of them total. They're all big guys. Like I said, the leader has a scar on his left cheek and clipped black hair. These guys were definite military and remain in the mindset. If you can, snap a picture and text it here." Lowell reached for the coffee table, and Jeremy jumped up and brought a small pad and pen. "I'll try to confirm for you." Lowell wished he could go and take care of this himself. "I appreciate this."

"We're doing this for Jeremy," Zach snapped.

"Quit being such a pit bull," Bull told Zach.

"But he brought more of this crap on us," Zach argued back.

"They asked for our help. It's what we do for our friends."

Lowell was floored. It had been a very long time since he'd had anyone he could call a friend or who called him one. He'd led a very solitary existence for a long time. "Like I said, I appreciate it, and I'd go if I could."

"It's going to get dark soon," Zach said.

"Yeah. We have to go because we aren't going to stay out after dark." They left, and Jeremy locked the door behind them and went to the window.

"It won't take them long to get over there," Jeremy said as he watched. "Is the phone turned on?"

"Yes," Lowell answered.

Tristan went into the kitchen and began cooking. Kevin camped out on the floor, with Jeremy in front of the television, and Lowell stretched out on the sofa. His leg still hurt.

"I forgot," Jeremy said and jumped up, grabbing a small bag off the counter. "Bull brought some antibiotics. He said not to ask where they came from, but that they would help prevent infection as long as you aren't allergic to anything."

Lowell took the bottle along with the instructions on computer paper. There were no markings of any kind on the bottle. Normally he wouldn't take anything anyone gave him, but these came from Bull, and he trusted him... and Jeremy. Lowell took a pill and lay back on the sofa, watching television. He was tired and knew he should sleep some more, but he was too keyed up.

His phone buzzed after another ten minutes, and he pulled it out. There were pictures of the area around the station. The message said that they saw no one but asked if anything looked familiar. Lowell texted that he didn't see anyone. A minute later he got another text, this one with a picture attached. *Him?*

Yes, Lowell texted back, and then he showed the picture to Jeremy. "This is the guy I saw this afternoon."

"I saw him too," Jeremy confirmed. Then they waited. Jeremy got up and began pacing like a caged cat, stopping to look out the window every few minutes. "They're back," he said and raced toward the door.

"Stay here," Lowell snapped with more force than he intended. "They might have been followed or there might be someone with them. We need to wait for Bull to give the all clear." Lowell was anxious as well. Finally, Bull's heavy footsteps sounded on the stairs, and Lowell got a text to let them in. He nodded to Jeremy, who opened the door. Bull came in, with Zach right behind him. "What happened?" Lowell asked.

"We had a little talk. I told them their employer was dead and therefore so was the contract. There would be no money because there was no one to pay them." Bull smiled. "That went over well, so I offered to pay them to cancel it. Ten grand each. That really got his attention. He was going to contact his friends, so I gave him a burn phone number. Now we wait."

"More waiting," Jeremy groused.

"Yeah. He wasn't the leader, but I think they'll take the money and run," Bull said. "All we need to do is get our hands on a lot of cash and I think you're home free."

Lowell nodded. Getting his hands on cash would not be an issue. That, he could do, and he was going to use Moonstone's money. He'd need to find a use for the rest of it, because he didn't intend to keep what wasn't his. Now that the excitement was over, he yawned and closed his eyes.

Jeremy sat next to him and held his hand. "You can go back to bed if you want."

Lowell wasn't in the mood to move at all. His leg was only aching slightly, he was comfortable, and Jeremy was right with him. That was heaven as far as he was concerned. "I'm fine."

"Dinner will be ready in a few minutes. I made mac and cheese casserole," Tristan announced. There was additional activity as drawers were opened and closed. Plates clanged and glasses tinked. Lowell listened, but let it all happen around him.

"I'll bring you some over when it's ready. Just rest." Jeremy squeezed his hand. "Do you really think this is finally over?" he asked. Lowell smiled and gently coaxed Jeremy closer for a kiss. It was over, or it would be soon. He felt free, and his heart soared when Jeremy gave him the tiniest of moans. Though he was tired, parts of him were very much awake and raring to go. Jeremy must have noticed, because he adjusted the blanket and giggled softly against his lips. "You need to keep that under control or all the other boys will be jealous." Jeremy giggled again, and Lowell cut him off with a deeper kiss before lying back with a smile on his face.

Lowell floated happily for a few minutes. Then everyone got quiet. Lowell opened his eyes in time to see Jeremy approaching with a plate. Lowell sat up and ate slowly. The cheesy mixture was rich and really good. Everyone else was busy eating and telling Tristan how good it was. Lowell caught his eye and nodded, mouthing a thank-you before going back to his dinner.

"Is something wrong?" Jeremy asked.

"No. It's just strange to eat like this. Not arranged or planned, just sharing a meal because everyone is here. I can't remember doing that since my mom died. It's nice, just different." He handed Jeremy the mostly empty plate, lay back, and closed his eyes. He was relaxed and happy—truly happy. It was a new feeling, and one he hoped would continue.

At some point he fell asleep, and when he woke the room was quiet. Zach, Bull, and Kevin were gone. Jeremy and Tristan sat in front of the television, watching a movie on low volume.

"You're awake," Jeremy said.

"Yeah. I guess I was comfortable and dropped off." He'd learned to sleep just about anywhere when he'd been in the service, but he never simply fell asleep without meaning to. Sometimes he'd stayed awake for days because that was what the job required. "I guess I was more tired than I realized."

"No worries. Everyone said to tell you good-bye, and we've just been sitting here quietly. Bull said he got a message and the guys after you accepted his terms. You're supposed to meet one of them at Bull's club in two days to pay them, and that will be it. Bull said to call tomorrow and he'll give you all the info. Apparently he worked with one of them in the past, so they trust him and there won't be any trouble."

"Cool." Now he simply needed to get the cash. Lowell yawned, and Jeremy tugged down the thin blanket he had over him and helped him up.

"Be careful of your leg and just lean on me. We'll get you to the bathroom and then into bed." Lowell nodded and let Jeremy guide him. It was nice to be taken care of.

"Thank you," Lowell whispered.

"For what?" Jeremy asked as he pushed open the bathroom door.

"Taking care of me. No one has cared for me since...." Lowell sighed and hobbled into the bathroom, holding the sink to steady himself.

"That's what boyfriends do," Jeremy said and then closed the door.

Lowell turned and looked at himself in the mirror. He didn't look any different, but he sure felt different. He still felt like one of the bad guys, but if Jeremy saw good in him and cared for him, then he couldn't be all bad. "I'm his boyfriend," he said out loud.

"We're boyfriends," Jeremy clarified through the door. "Now stop talking to yourself and take care of business. Otherwise I'm going to start to think that injury affected your brain." Jeremy's giggle drifted through the door.

Lowell turned and made his way to the toilet and did as Jeremy instructed. Once he'd flushed, Jeremy opened the door and helped him back to the sink. He washed up, and then Jeremy guided him to his bedroom.

"I'm glad you have a double bed," Lowell whispered and then sat on the edge. Jeremy helped him get undressed, and when he settled back onto the bed, Jeremy actually tucked him in.

"I'll be in soon." He leaned over the bed and kissed him. "You need to take your pills. I'll be right back." Jeremy hurried away and then came back with some pills and a glass of water. After taking them, Lowell closed his eyes. He heard the door close and nothing more until Jeremy joined him in bed.

LOWELL WOKE in the cool of the early morning, the sun just starting to light the window, to find Jeremy pressed right against him, his little butt against his hip. Lowell rolled onto his side, and Jeremy scooted back, pressing to his groin, which took instant notice. Jeremy shifted slightly and didn't move anymore. Lowell wasn't sure if he was being teased or not. Jeremy still seemed to be asleep. "Sweetheart," Lowell said softly.

"Do you need something?" Jeremy asked sleepily and rolled over. "I can get you something for pain."

"No. It's okay," Lowell whispered, sliding his arm around Jeremy's waist and tugging them together. Jeremy hummed softly and wriggled against him. "How long have you been awake?"

"Long enough," Jeremy answered with another wriggle.

Lowell closed his eyes as erotic sensation raced through him. Damn, that felt good. He began making small circles on Jeremy's belly, and when he dipped his hand lower, he found Jeremy in the same state he was. Lowell kissed the base of Jeremy's neck as he wrapped his fingers around his cock and slowly began to stroke. Jeremy gasped softly and then whimpered, shifting his hips slightly, thrusting slowly in his hand.

The movement drove Lowell crazy. It was just enough to make his cock jump. He wanted to thrust as well, but knew he needed to keep his leg still. Instead, he pressed Jeremy back against him and sighed softly into his ear before sucking the lobe between his lips.

Jeremy hummed his happiness and continued moving. "I want you."

"What do you want?" Lowell asked. "Whatever it is, you can have it."

Jeremy stopped and pulled away, then reached between them and gripped Lowell's cock tight. "I want you," he whispered again.

"Do you have stuff? I won't hurt you." He was instantly out of his mind with excitement and could hardly see straight. The residual pain in his leg was gone, his heart raced, and his mouth went dry, all in an instant. Jeremy slipped his hand away from him and opened the drawer next to the bed. Lowell saw him set a small bottle and some packets on the nightstand.

"Are you sure you don't want to wait?" Lowell asked. "There's no rush. I'm not going anywhere."

Jeremy stilled. "Are you sure? You're going to stay?"

Lowell chuckled. "Of course I'm going to stay. I love you. I know I haven't said it before, but I want you to know that I love you very much. I did hear what you told me the other day."

"I wasn't sure," Jeremy said.

Lowell pulled him tighter. "Well, I heard it, and I am sure. I love you, Jeremy. You're the reason I want to get up in the morning, and if this wake-up is any example, then I want to wake up next to you for the rest of my life, if you'll have me. I have a lot of things to tell you, but I'm afraid you won't want me afterward." Lowell moved away, and Jeremy shifted right with him.

"You telling me everything isn't because I'm nosy. I need to know, and you need to tell me. It's time you let go of all that baggage and let yourself be the person you really are." Jeremy kissed him hard. "But we have plenty of time for that." Jeremy stroked his cock. "I'd say this needs my immediate attention." Lowell groaned softly. "How do we do this?"

Lowell gently motioned Jeremy onto his side and then his belly. He lightly stroked up and down his smooth skin, relishing the silky warmth.

He shifted on the bed until his leg was comfortable and then spread light kisses all over Jeremy. He needed to take his time. The position was a little awkward, but he made it work and it didn't seem to matter. Jeremy vibrated beneath him.

After a few minutes, Jeremy rolled over and crawled into his arms, still shaking. He kissed Lowell hard, and Lowell held him tight, stroking his back and butt. When he slid a finger down Jeremy's crease, Jeremy hummed and kissed him harder. "Yes," Jeremy moaned between kisses. Lowell brought his fingers to his lips, wetting them before once again pressing to Jeremy's tight little opening, tapping it and caressing the skin.

Jeremy went wild, shaking with excitement and filling the room with tiny whimpers. He reached for the lube and thrust it into Lowell's hand to tell him he was ready. Lowell slicked his fingers and teased Jeremy's opening with his index finger before sliding the tip inside him. Jeremy jumped slightly, stilled, and then sighed softly before pressing back against his finger. Slowly Lowell sank in deeper before curling it slightly. "Jesus," Jeremy whispered breathlessly. "Do that again."

"Oh, I will, sweetheart," Lowell whispered, rubbing the spot and sending Jeremy into shivers of pleasure. It was perfect. He took his time, adding a second finger, scissoring them inside him until Jeremy's moans became slightly hoarse and rough.

"I'm ready," Jeremy murmured.

"Are you sure?" Lowell asked.

Jeremy stilled and placed both hands on Lowell's cheeks, staring into his eyes. "Yes. I want to be yours." Then it was Lowell's turn to shake with excitement and at the intense love he saw in Jeremy's eyes.

Lowell rolled onto his back and motioned for Jeremy to straddle him. It was the best position and would allow Jeremy to remain in control. He reached for a condom and rolled it down his shaft, then applied lots of lube and watched as Jeremy straddled him. Never in his life had he seen a more beautiful sight than his Jeremy, trim and lean, above him. Jeremy positioned Lowell at his entrance and slowly lowered himself. At the first sensation, Lowell placed his hands on Jeremy's hips and helped guide him down. "Take your time."

Jeremy nodded and gasped, his mouth hanging open. Lowell saw the moment of pain on Jeremy's face, and then he saw when it passed and morphed into pleasure. Jeremy's eyes lit up, and then his entire body rocked slightly. Lowell sighed softly when he felt Jeremy's butt press to his hips.

His cock throbbed and jumped inside Jeremy's tight heat. He felt alive and awake, like huge scales had just fallen away from his eyes and a ring that had been squeezing his heart had burst. "Jeremy," Lowell whispered. "Please move." He could barely form words, he was so overwhelmed.

Jeremy reached forward and rested his hands on Lowell's chest, flicking his nipples as he fanned his fingers over them. Lowell thrust his hips upward tentatively and found that as long as he used the good leg, he was fine. He desperately craved sensation, and then, slowly, Jeremy began to move. He was silky smooth around him, and Lowell swallowed hard, watching Jeremy move on top of him.

When Jeremy leaned back and began stroking himself while he raised and lowered his hips, Lowell nearly lost it. Jeremy's eyes were closed, and he made soft, mewling sounds. Every now and then he'd jump a little. Lowell guessed it was his own pleasure surprising him.

"Dang," Jeremy breathed more than once, but he didn't talk otherwise. Lowell didn't either. Words were completely inadequate to describe what he felt, and it seemed the same for Jeremy.

Lowell cupped Jeremy's butt in his hands and guided his speed, thrusting upward to meet him until both they and the bed were rocking like crazy. Jeremy began moaning loader, and Lowell did his best to keep in control. His body seemed to have a mind of its own, and he moved faster, trying desperately to keep up with Jeremy. Soon it didn't matter. Lowell's focus was solely on him. Every move Jeremy made, each clench of his muscles, sent a ripple of exquisite passion running through him. Lowell wanted this to last forever; he wanted this connection he felt with Jeremy to always be there. But maybe that was too much to hope for.

Jeremy clenched around him, and Lowell came off the mattress in a flurry of heat and pressure. He wrapped his arms around Jeremy and held him tight. He continued moving his hips slightly, and Jeremy settled him back on the mattress and picked up the pace.

Lowell went along for the ride… or the being ridden. It didn't matter. Jeremy moved like a pro, with no shame or reservation. Lowell met each movement, and soon they were in a world of their own, gazes locked. It was beautiful and as wonderful as his Jeremy, though the happiness and passion couldn't last; they were too powerful to contain.

"I can't wait," Jeremy whispered.

"Don't. I want to see you," Lowell rasped.

Jeremy groaned and stilled, then throbbed around him as he came, openmouthed, eyes wide, painting his passion in white ropes on Lowell's chest and belly. Jeremy's release triggered Lowell's own, and it nearly overwhelmed him in its intensity. He clamped his eyes closed even as he wanted to see Jeremy. He couldn't help it. He cried out, gripping Jeremy's hips as he came.

Lowell gasped and relaxed as he felt Jeremy shift above him. He opened his eyes, and his gaze was met by Jeremy's bright smile. He tugged Jeremy down to him, kissing him deeply. "I never wanted that to end." He held Jeremy tight. Their bodies separated, and Lowell waited for the connection to break, but it didn't. They were joined at the heart now, and he felt warmer and more content than he could remember in his whole life. "I feel different," Lowell whispered into Jeremy's ear.

"You should." Jeremy chuckled. "This seems like a weird time to bring her up, but my mom told me once that when I met the person meant for me, I'd feel whole—that small piece that was missing would be there. And it is." Jeremy hugged him and rested his head on his shoulder.

Lowell had felt that piece falling into place, but he hadn't realized what it was. But then, as he thought about it, that piece had been there for a while, he just hadn't realized it. It was Jeremy, without a doubt.

A phone dinged somewhere in the room. Jeremy groaned and moved away. He found his phone, and Lowell watched him retrieve the message, while he took care of things and disposed of the condom in the waste can near the bed. Jeremy then made a call and let out a little whoop before hanging up. "My office is closed because there's no water." He stepped to the end of the bed and just looked at him. It was strange being watched, and Lowell squirmed. "I love you, Lowell."

Lowell swallowed hard and wiped his eyes. Jeremy grinned and thankfully said nothing. Lowell had a lie on his lips about something being in his eyes, but truthfully that something was his Jeremy, and it was damn near overwhelming.

"I'll be right back," Jeremy whispered. He tugged on a pair of shorts and left the room, then returned with a towel that he used to clean Lowell up. Then Jeremy stripped back down and joined him in bed. "Don't think of going anywhere. You're mine now." Jeremy leaned over him. They shared a kiss that quickly deepened. Lowell tugged Jeremy closer and held him tight.

They had lots of talking to do, and Lowell knew there would be difficult moments, but he was going to hold onto the piece of his heart that was Jeremy. He'd fight for him, care for him, and love him forever. "I wish I'd have found you a long time ago," Lowell whispered.

Jeremy shook his head slowly. "People find each other when the time's right."

Lowell couldn't argue with that. Finding Jeremy had turned his life upside down and most likely saved him. He'd discovered his heart and he wasn't letting go.

EPILOGUE

JEREMY SAT nervously in Lowell's car, trying not to fidget, looking out the window. Back home, the autumn leaves were in full color, but as they'd traveled south, the color had slowly disappeared. "Where are you taking me?" he asked Lowell for the twelfth time.

"You wanted an answer to your question. I'm going to give it to you."

He and Lowell had talked a lot. Some of the things Lowell told him had made the blood leave his face, and a few times he'd asked Lowell to stop and not tell him any more. The places he'd visited made Jeremy jealous until Lowell told him why he was there, and then he was glad he hadn't been along. But Lowell had told Jeremy everything he had wanted to know, except the answer to one question. *Why?* Jeremy had asked that question over and over. The most difficult thing for him was not what Lowell had done, but rather to reconcile the kind, affectionate man he knew with the one who had done all these things.

Jeremy knew that in the back of Lowell's mind he had expected Jeremy to bail. But no matter how hard the stories were to hear, he had reminded himself that all of it was in the past. Jeremy watched as a huge sign over the freeway announced that they were entering Virginia. "How much farther is it?"

"Just another half hour," Lowell told him with a smile. Jeremy nodded. "I donated the last of Moonstone's money yesterday." Lowell had decided to take all that remained of the money he'd drained from

Moonstone's accounts and donate it to charity. So the schools and libraries in the area had all received sizable donations, as had the Red Cross and various children's organizations. It had taken a while, because Lowell hadn't wanted to leave any sort of trail that could lead to him.

"Who did you send it to?"

"A group that helps orphaned children find good homes," Lowell answered, reaching over to squeeze Jeremy's hand. "I think it's important that we help the children." Regret sounded clearly in his voice. One of the things Lowell had said he regretted most were the children he'd indirectly hurt or left without a parent.

"You could have kept the money and no one would have been the wiser, including me. Instead, you used it to help a lot of people." Jeremy lifted Lowell's hand to his lips and kissed it. Actions like that helped confirm that the Lowell he loved was the real one. He squeezed his hand again and smiled. "I do love you."

"I know it was hard for you to hear about all the things I've done," Lowell said reticently.

"That's in the past," Jeremy said. It was the only answer he had. He had to somehow reconcile the man he knew with the one Lowell told stories about. He was trying really hard, but up till now the answer had eluded him.

"We're almost there," Lowell whispered and turned off the highway. They headed down roads lined with trees where nature's paintbrush had just begun to make its presence known. After traveling a few miles, they stopped at a sign and then made a turn down a country road. The trees closed over them, and then suddenly opened up around a low stone building that appeared to be part of the land.

"What is this?" Jeremy asked.

"This is Westbrook," Lowell answered. He pulled up to the building and parked the dark blue Mercedes sedan. Lowell got out, and Jeremy did as well. Lowell walked around the car and took his hand. "I've never brought anyone here, ever." He led him toward the doors, which opened automatically into what looked almost like a resort hotel lobby.

"Is this one of those fancy rehab centers or something?"

"No," Lowell answered and walked up to a door and knocked. It opened, and a woman smiled at him.

"Hello, sir," she said brightly. "Can I help you?" She seemed genuinely pleased to see Lowell once he explained who he was. "You can go on back to the activity room. Donny is in there, like he is most afternoons. I know he's going to be so happy to see you."

"Thanks," Lowell said and took Jeremy's hand. As soon as they left the large central room, they entered a bright hall with bulletin boards and lots of color. It looked like a school hallway.

"What is this place?" Jeremy asked.

"This is Donny's home," Lowell said, stopping. "Donny has special needs. He's… he'll always have the mentality of a child of five or six. This is his school, and his home is on the other side of the facility. He has his own room and people who care for him. He's happy here." Lowell motioned him down the hall and pushed open one of the doors. Inside was what looked like an elementary school art room, with pictures on the walls, large tables, construction paper, coloring books, crayons, glue— every child's dream. It was clean and messy at the same time. At the farthest table, a woman sat with two men, both of them with their heads down, coloring.

"Donny," Lowell said quietly. The man closest to the side of the table looked up and smiled. Jeremy would have known anywhere that he was Lowell's brother. They looked just the same. Donny got up, hurried over, and engulfed Lowell in a hug.

"You're here," Donny said. "It's been so long." He was taller and thinner than Lowell, and he stood over him with the earnestness of a child.

"It won't be as long next time, I promise," Lowell said, and Jeremy heard his voice break. "I've found a new place to live and it's much closer than I was before." He took Donny by the hand and led him over to where Jeremy stood waiting. "This is my friend Jeremy. He came here with me."

Jeremy wasn't sure what to say, but Donny held out his hand and Jeremy shook it. "It's nice to meet you," Donny said formally, and then he broke into a smile as he looked at Lowell. "Is he your boyfriend?" Donny released Jeremy's hand and giggled, putting his hand over his mouth.

"Yes, is that okay?" Lowell asked. Donny nodded and then looked back at the table. "Go on and color if you want. Or you can go for a walk with us and show Jeremy everything."

"Even the horses?" Donny asked, and Lowell smiled and nodded.

"Okay," he agreed and looked back at his teacher, who nodded her approval.

Lowell took Donny's hand and let him lead them out of the room and down the hall to a door that led outside. Everything was green and beautifully looked after.

"The horses are over there," Donny said excitedly, pointing toward a barn.

"What is this place?" Jeremy asked.

"It's a combination school and home for people like Donny. Here he's cared for and given everything he needs by caring people," Lowell told him.

"Who looks after you when you aren't in school?" Lowell asked Donny.

"You mean at my house? Alex. He's my best friend. He reads to me at night before I go to bed and brings me breakfast." Donny walked along next to them. "There's where we run races and play games." He pointed to an open field.

Everything was perfect here, and Donny seemed very happy. "Your house?"

"Yeah. There are small, separate buildings around the campus," Lowell said. "Donny's building has four small apartments. There aren't kitchens, but it's where Donny lives. Alex cares for him and the three other residents of the building most days of the week. Donny can mostly care for himself. Can't you?" Lowell asked, squeezing Donny's hand. "I'm so proud of you." Donny grinned, and they continued walking.

Donny showed them everything, and then they walked back toward the main school building. "Can I go back and color?" Donny asked, and Lowell released his hand.

"Sure. We'll meet you there in a few minutes." Lowell paused, and Donny hurried on ahead and entered the building. "You asked me why I did all those things. This is why. I needed to find a place where Donny would be happy. After I got out of the service and Mom died, I found it hard to take care of Donny. Mom had him enrolled in a school that was terrible. He was mistreated and sometimes left alone. I found this place and it was perfect. But...."

"It cost a lot," Jeremy supplied.

"Yeah, but I wanted the best for Donny. My first assignment came in just after I visited, and they were willing to pay enough that I could pay for Donny to go here for three months. After that there was no turning back. I moved Donny here and paid for him each month. I have enough money for Donny to live here for the rest of his life. This is home for him, and he's taken care of and cared for."

"But shouldn't he be with you?" Jeremy asked. "Instead of staying with strangers?"

"These aren't strangers for him. Clara has been here since Donny came. He hugs her every time he sees her. Alex is in his midthirties, and he lives here with his wife and children. They love Donny as much as I do." Lowell paused. "Yes, I'd like to have him with me, but this is his home, and the people here are as much his family to him as I am. I thought that after I 'retired' I'd bring Donny to come live with me, but I can't take him away from the world he knows. He has everything he needs or wants here, including people who care about him. I'm living closer now than I ever have, and I can see him much more often." Lowell started walking again. "I love Donny very much, but this is where he needs to be. If that changes, then I'll consider moving him, but you saw how happy he is. I can't take that away from him. Donny has been here for years now, and to take him away would be cruel."

"I guess I can see that," Jeremy said. He looked around and then turned back to Lowell. "Let's go spend time with your brother." He began to laugh. "When was the last time you colored pictures?"

"A long time ago," Lowell answered.

"It isn't always how much time you have with someone, but how you spend it." Jeremy took Lowell's hand.

"So did you get the answer to your question?" Lowell asked as they walked.

"Yeah." He'd gotten an answer to that and a whole lot more. Jeremy leaned slightly against Lowell as they walked. "I need you to know that you're very much the man I thought you were." Jeremy swallowed hard as the last piece fell into place for him.

"What does that mean?" Lowell asked quietly.

Jeremy lightly patted the center of Lowell's chest. "It means that I love you. All of you." He glanced up at Lowell and saw that his smile went all the way to his ears.

ANDREW GREY grew up in western Michigan with a father who loved to tell stories and a mother who loved to read them. Since then he has lived all over the country and traveled throughout the world. He has a master's degree from the University of Wisconsin-Milwaukee and now works full time on his writing. Andrew's hobbies include collecting antiques, gardening, and leaving his dirty dishes anywhere but in the sink (particularly when writing). He considers himself blessed with an accepting family, fantastic friends, and the world's most supportive and loving partner. Andrew currently lives in beautiful historic Carlisle, Pennsylvania.

Visit Andrew's website at http://www.andrewgreybooks.com and blog at http://andrewgreybooks.livejournal.com/.

E-mail him at andrewgrey@comcast.net.

Andrew was the featured author at Two Lips Reviews in Feb. 2010.

Love Means… Series from ANDREW GREY

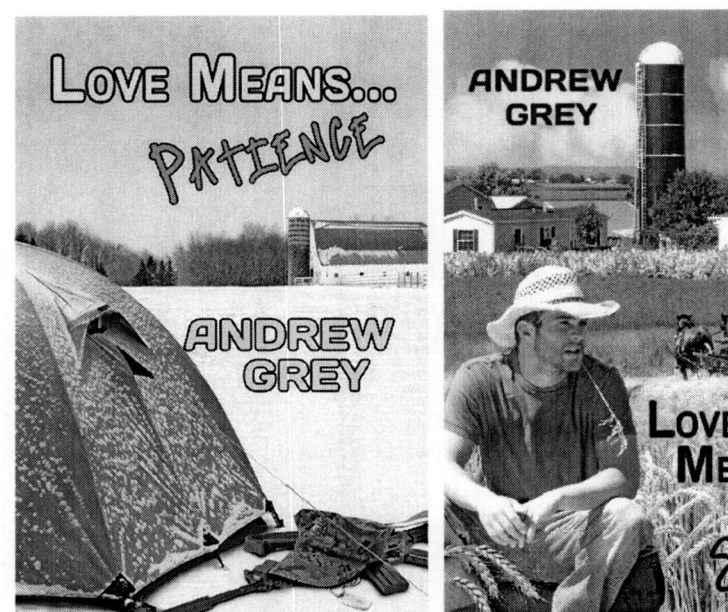

http://www.dreamspinnerpress.com

Love Means… Series from ANDREW GREY

Love Means… Series from ANDREW GREY

http://www.dreamspinnerpress.com

The Bullriders from ANDREW GREY

http://www.dreamspinnerpress.com

The Art Series from ANDREW GREY

The Bottled Up Series from ANDREW GREY

Taste of Love Stories from ANDREW GREY

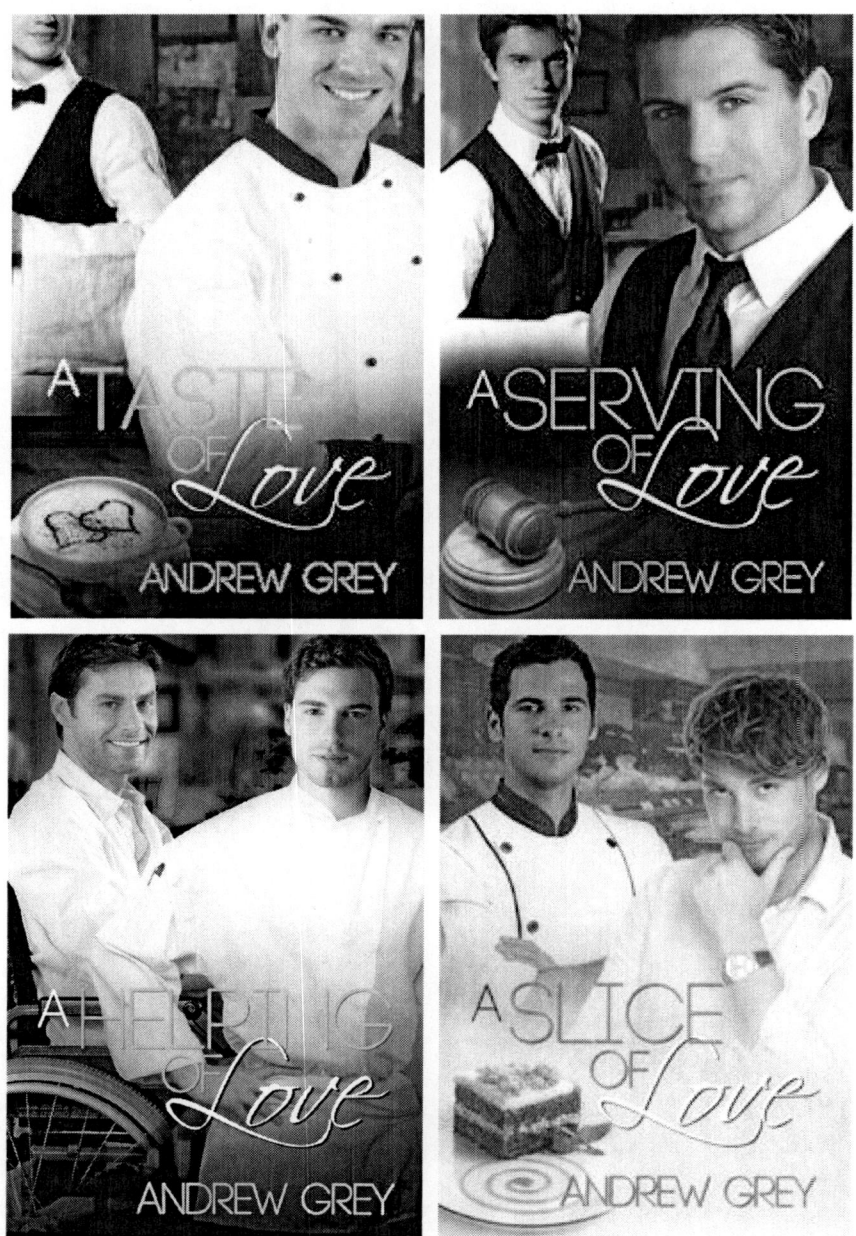

http://www.dreamspinnerpress.com

Good Fight Stories from ANDREW GREY

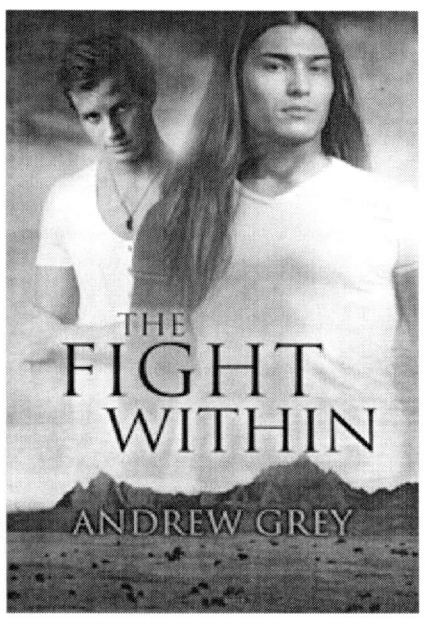

http://www.dreamspinnerpress.com

Stories from the Range from ANDREW GREY

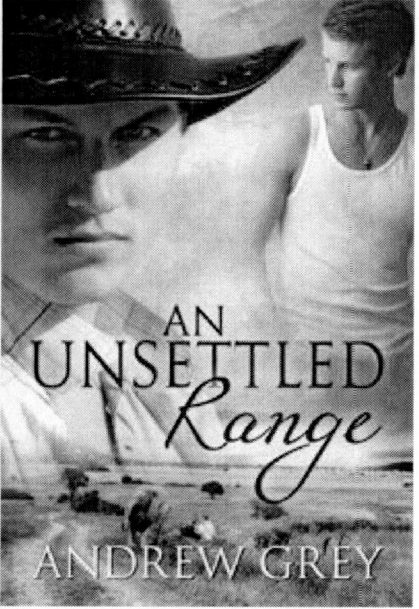

http://www.dreamspinnerpress.com

Stories from the Range from ANDREW GREY

http://www.dreamspinnerpress.com

Senses Stories from ANDREW GREY

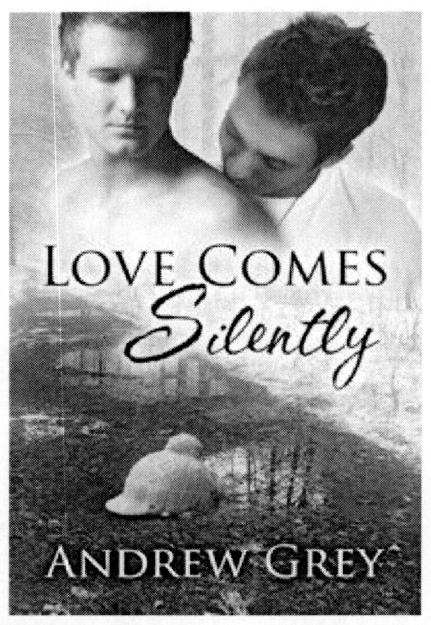

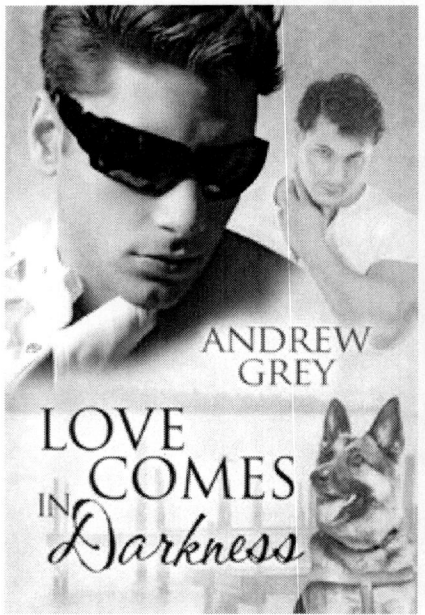

http://www.dreamspinnerpress.com

Seven Days Stories from ANDREW GREY

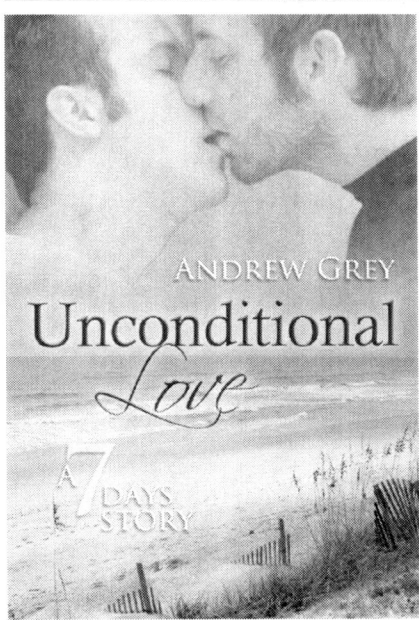

http://www.dreamspinnerpress.com

The Fire Series from ANDREW GREY

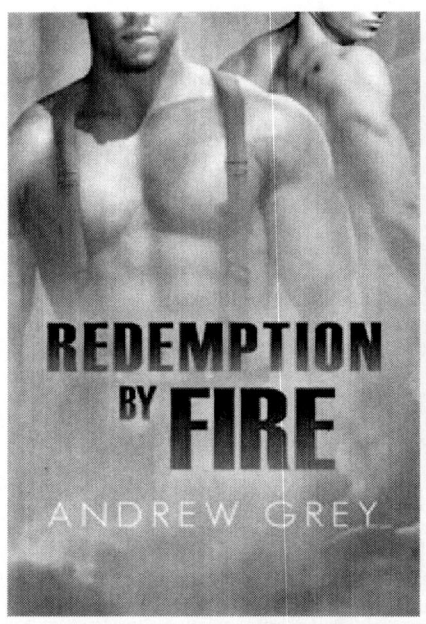

http://www.dreamspinnerpress.com

Work Out Series from ANDREW GREY

http://www.dreamspinnerpress.com

Work Out Series from ANDREW GREY

http://www.dreamspinnerpress.com

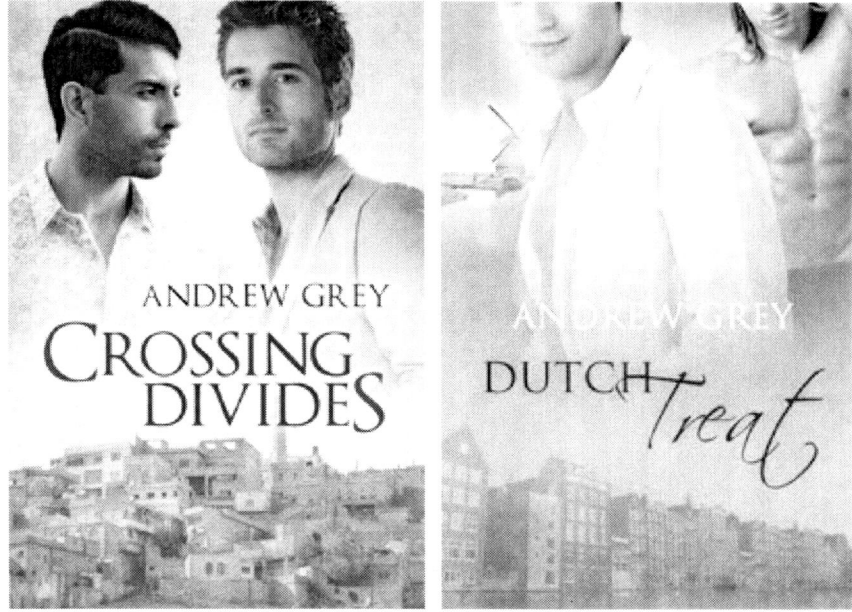

http://www.dreamspinnerpress.com

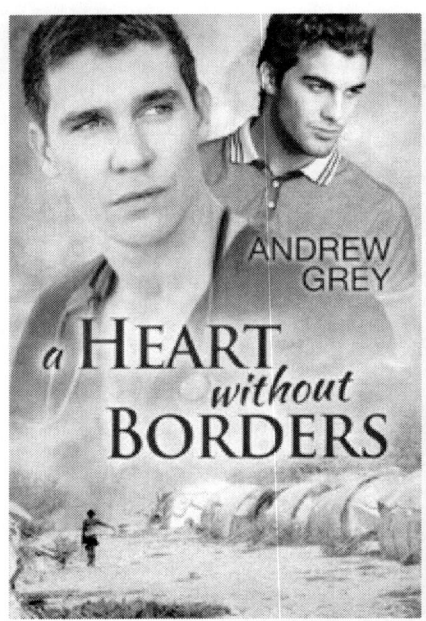
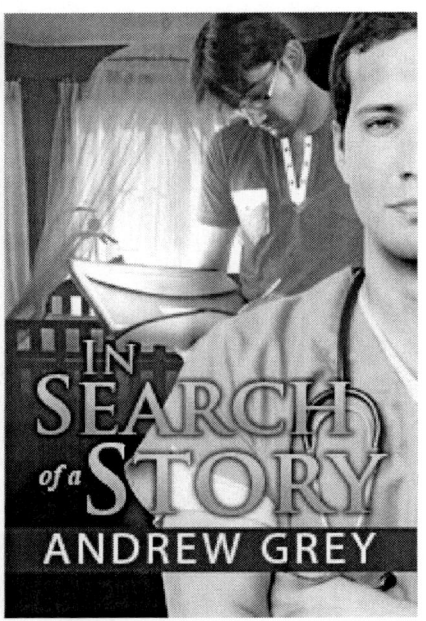

http://www.dreamspinnerpress.com

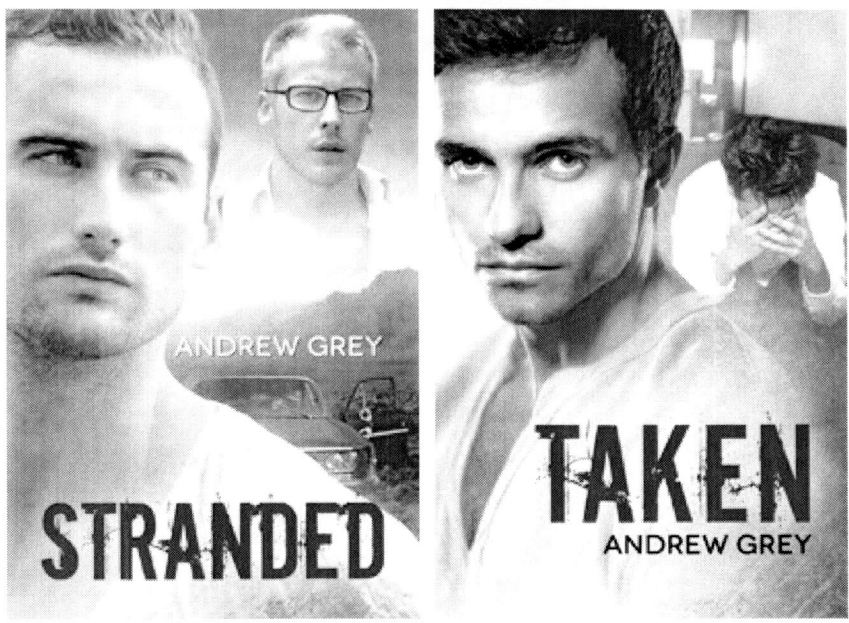

http://www.dreamspinnerpress.com

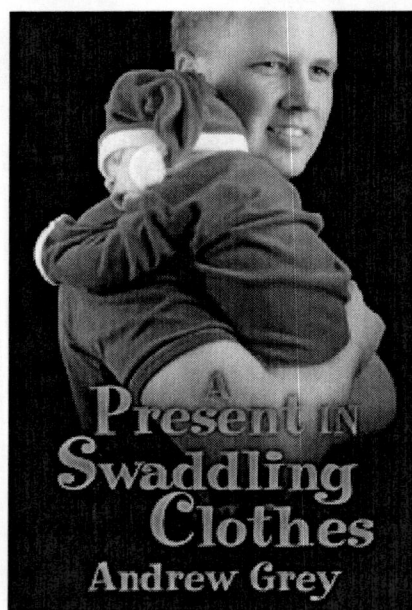

http://www.dreamspinnerpress.com

http://www.dreamspinnerpress.com

CPSIA information can be obtained at www.ICGtesting.com
Printed in the USA
BVOW05s1327160715

408903BV00011B/206/P